Dogs,
Dreams,
and Men

Dogs, Dreams, and Men

Joan Kaufman

F
Kauf

W. W. Norton & Company · New York · London

Lyrics from "The Warthog" by Michael Flanders and
Donald Swann copyright © 1955 by Chappell Music
Ltd. All rights in the U.S. administered by Chappell
& Co., Inc. International copyright secured. All
rights reserved. Used by permission.

The text of this book is composed in Electra, with
display type set in Zapf Chancery Italic. Composition
by PennSet, Inc.

Book design by Charlotte Staub.
Calligraphy by Lanie Johnson.

First Edition

7/88 NEM BF 16.95

Library of Congress Cataloging-in-Publication Data

Kaufman, Joan
  Dogs, dreams, and men/Joan Kaufman.
    p. cm.
  I. Title.
PS3561.A857D6   1988
813'.54—dc19   87-33770

ISBN 0-393-02581-0

W. W. Norton & Company, Inc.
500 Fifth Avenue, New York, N.Y. 10110
W. W. Norton & Company Ltd.
37 Great Russell Street, London WC1B 3NU

1 2 3 4 5 6 7 8 9 0

For
  Frances Jagoda Kaufman

Yet it is strange that all our life is accompanied by Dreams on one side, and by the Animals on the other, as monuments of our ignorance, or Hints to set us on the right road of inquiry.

EMERSON, *Journals* (1835)

Dogs,
Dreams,
and Men

One

*T*HE dogs in my dreams are lulled to sleep by the tolling of tape-recorded bells from a nearby church with loud-speakers in its steeple. This public call to worship has become my personal alarm.

> "Here is the church
> Here is the steeple
> Open the door
> And see all the people,"

I say, while beyond my open window, bells rouse the city's slumbering flock from their lovers' freckled arms to Christ's figurative embrace.

But I am a Jew who sleeps with a dog.

"My little sheep," I say.

All night long, my own dogs, dogs I have known, and dogs I've never met leap through my fifth-story window and land on my bed. Some of them are pets. Others are scavengers; they feed off me, the perfect host. Asleep, I shelter four-footed guests who guide me to a deeper sleep. They come and go as they please, with no regard for me. Do I want them to come? Do I want them to stay? I close the windows, lock the door, and try to stay awake. Light from a neighboring terrace filters through the weave of my bamboo shades. Sirens and horns howl; my vigilance fails; I fall asleep.

In the middle of the night, my small white dog awakens me. Without opening my eyes, I know she is keeping watch. She is my guard dog, keeping me safe, my seeing-eye dog, who leads me through the traffic of my dreams. I listen as she patrols from my side of the bed toward the windows and back. When she jumps up against the bed with her two front paws, I lift her around the middle and, reaching across my own body, set her down in a hollow among the blankets, like a nest. For the moment, she is the only dog in the room, the only dog in my life, the dreamed dogs dispersed. She gets up to circle and paw at the covers, instinctively creating her own bed. She may look like a bright-eyed, toystore dog, but she is wary, the descendant of wolves, preparing her lair. When she is ready, she settles down for the rest of the night. She will be there in the morning, stretched out by my side, or at the foot of my bed, curled up in dreamless sleep.

"It's not time to go out yet."

"Be patient, honey, it's still too early."

"Why can't you let me sleep?"

At dawn, all the voices are mine, since the dog is only an animal and cannot speak.

Today is Valentine's Day, although the church must think it's still Christmas: *In fields where they lay keeping their sheep on a cold winter's night.* . . . "Happy Valentine's Day," I say. Half asleep, Emma stumbles toward me across mounds of tangled blankets, then collapses close by me, snuggled in the crook of my arm, her small head resting between my neck and bare shoulder. I ask her if she remembered to buy me a box of chocolates. She sleeps. I tell her that not since the beginning of all time has anyone loved a dog more than I love her. "Greater love," I whisper, "hath no other dog owner for any other dog." I tell her that the sun rises and sets in her eyes, that I worship the ground she walks on, that I would follow her to the ends of the earth.

Emma sleeps through my clichés but wakens to my touch. I ask would she prefer to run in the park or spend the entire day lollygagging in bed. She rolls over onto her back, paws in the air. "Snug as a bug in a rug," I say—my mother's expression. I stroke her ears and finger the matted hair on her belly. She dozes; I hum "Noel" along with the bells. The wind billows my white lace curtains, then snags them and pulls them through the screenless windows and pins them to the brick outside.

Time to get going. "Rise and shine," I tell Emma—more of my mother's voice. At one time I tried on my mother's expressions like a child playing dress-up, but now I wear them as my own. "You going to sleep your life away?" I ask Emma. She yawns and stretches, shifts to make herself more comfortable, cozy as a cat. Even though today is Sunday, I promised my boss at the Odyssey Press I would use the weekend to move a week ahead of schedule. "Valentine's Day," I told him, "is a bogus holiday trumped up by the candy/flower/greeting card industries." This statement, powerful as an incantation, would safeguard me against a wish I considered subversive, subterranean: to receive fancy chocolates ribboned with velvet. I left the office carrying manuscripts as shields, sharpened pencils as spears, to ward off the thorny roses hawked on almost every street corner. Do not mess with me. I am a serious person. These are important manuscripts that require my attention. I do not yearn for bouquets of fragrant, budding roses, gold heart-shaped lockets, small red plush dogs collared with messages: "Be Mine." The manuscripts, clutched so near to my heart, protect me on the street; will they keep me from making dangerous, long-distance calls at home?

You two going to sleep your lives away? My mother's voice downstairs at the door to our attic bedroom, where my sister and I were in bed, naming the animals we saw in the grain of the raw plywood ceiling and walls, the various animal shapes as mobile as clouds. If I saw a dog's shaggy ears turn into wings that could fly, she saw them turn into jaws that could bite. All animals can bite, I said, but not all animals can fly. Morning transformed nighttime tigers, too scary to touch, into a litter of striped kittens with full-grown tails. While my mother was calling us, we followed their winding tails that looped around and around like mazes. Cat-tail mazes housed other cats. We teased them by trailing our fingers along the wood like long, skinny weeds.

"You going to sleep your life away?" I nudge Emma out of bed. She jumps to the floor, takes a step or two, then stretches, the stretch collapsing as she lies down, her head resting on her front cat-paws. "You want to go outside?" Her tail wags once as if in assent, but when I approach her she falls over onto her side, her feathered tail rhythmically dusting the parquet floor.

The wind blowing from New Jersey to New York across the Hudson is fierce and I keep my head down as I walk west, against the wind. Emma raises her head a little and sneezes and, when I instruct her to heel, trots briskly along at my side. At West End Avenue, I get caught by a flashing red "Don't Walk" sign just as I'm about to cross. "Let's make the light," I tell her, stepping into the street. She balks. Glancing down to scold her, I find an old woman crouched beside her, cooing, whispering, asking her her name.

"Emma."

The short distance from my apartment to the park is becoming increasingly unsafe. All along my route, lonely old women are lurking, waiting to ambush me and my dog; deft as pickpockets, they are trying to steal my peace of mind, the warmth of Emma's fur, and the devotion in her eyes. Always the same question: "What is your name?"

"Emma."

These women never offer their own names, nor ask me mine. To them, Emma is so sweet, so fluffy. so darling. They block my path to tell me about their missing children, married and with children of their own, living on the West Coast, in Boston and Washington. They tell me about their husbands who have passed away and the dogs—poodles and Yorkies and peek-a-poos (*mutts*, I think, peek-a-poos are just mutts)—who were always such a comfort. Now the dogs are gone and they want to get new dogs—but how can they, here, with such weather? A person can stay inside in bad weather but not a dog. They know I don't think that weather matters; they didn't either, at my age. Do I know what it's like to be afraid to go out? Sometimes the wind feels like it's trying to blow them away. As if the streets in New York weren't dangerous enough already, what with the muggings and the crazy traffic. How would they manage to walk a dog if they got sick or fell down? Who would take it to the vet's if it got sick? And what about the vet bills? Their old vet bills are sending their vet's children to Harvard! Still, if weather and expense were the only drawbacks, perhaps they would give in. The real reason, the only obstacle they can't ignore or get around (they lower their voices and move a little closer), is that they are no longer young. Because they are not at all young like I am ("You are still a young woman. You should find yourself a nice man. Listen: It is no good to be old and alone . . ."), they cannot bear to think about passing on and leaving their heartbroken pets behind.

"Emma," the old lady croons. "What an angel puppy! Just like my Nicky. She left me last February fifteenth. Ah, but you knew that already, didn't you? I can tell from your eyes. You can sense unhappiness, can't you, just like my Nicky."

"I'm sorry," I murmur, feeling intrusive, since she was talking to Emma and not to me. She keeps petting Emma, then begins talking to me without looking at my face. How very much Emma resembles her dog, she says. I do not believe her. No matter what she says, I'm certain her sensitive little dog wasn't anything like mine. You got us wrong, lady. Don't be fooled by my premature gray hair, Emma's white. You and I, madam, your dead dog and my live one, are as different as night and day.

"Such an angel," she says.

Minus the wings, I think.

The woman asks Emma if she's a good little poodle. "Mine's not a poodle." Now I remember: I know this woman. I've talked to her before. She's already told me about her dog; I explained to her then that Emma is not a poodle.

"She's that other French breed . . ."

I nod.

"I remember. We've talked before, haven't we? But I've forgotten the name . . ."

"Bichon. Bichon frise." I spell it out for her and teach her the correct pronunciation: *bee-shone-free-zay*, along with the anglicized, shortened version: *bee-shon*.

"Oh, yes, now I remember. Bichon frise," she repeats clumsily, standing and closing her eyes for an instant to fix the name in her mind. "She's so sweet, exactly like my Nicky. I'm on my way to church, but I could show you a picture, if you would like to meet her. She was always with me. My husband, rest his soul, used to say he was surprised I didn't bring her with me to church." She giggles. "I don't want to give you the wrong impression. My husband was very good to me. When I had to go into the hospital for my operation, he took care of Nicky. But he never understood people like you and me who get attached to animals. He used to say . . . ," she pauses and smiles to herself, "he used to say I would cry more at Nicky's funeral than I would at his."

Did she? I wonder. Did she cry at her dog's funeral? "I'm not attached," I say, a lie so monumental I flinch. "You want a dog? Here." I pretend to offer her the leash, but she is too busy rummaging through her purse to notice.

Emma is not a poodle. Emma is only four years old. The decision to get a dog seems to have been made before I became aware I had a decision to make. I didn't know I had been longing for a dog. One day I woke up and thought: I'll get a dog and when it dies I'll survive. I went to the local library and took home a dog encyclopedia and began looking for the right breed. It would have to be a small dog, suitable for a New York City apartment, and portable so I could carry it around. The photograph in the book showed a mother bichon frise with a basket of puppies, all white with beautiful dark eyes. "During the Renaissance," the book said, "this fluffy dog was valued by Italian sailors for its barter value." Barter value? I wondered if that would be useful "The bichon frise has an exceptionally sweet disposition, is equally good with children and adults, and makes the ideal city pet, except for its white coat, which requires constant care or frequent trips to the groomer." I called a few breeders and visited two kennels. Then a friend drove me to New Jersey to meet Emma for the first time. The fact that she's exactly what I wanted seems a miracle to me. I keep telling her we'll be together for as long as we live and I hope she dies before I do. Please God let her live forever.

"Nicky had a heart attack. Twelve years old. They say poodles can live longer, but Nicky was only twelve." She shakes her head and hands me two photographs. The poodle is asleep on her lap in one, curled up in her arms in the other. If there is a halo over her angel puppy's head, the camera didn't catch it. I return the photographs, which she tries with trembling hands to slip back into her wallet. She snaps her pocketbook closed and I am free. "Jewish dogs," I warn Emma, while waiting for the light, "don't get to go to heaven."

Riverside Park extends along the western edge of Manhattan from 72nd Street to 158th Street, overlooking the Hudson River and the New Jersey Palisades. The park is divided laterally by the Henry Hudson Parkway, known as the West Side Highway within the city limits. Between 72nd and 79th streets, where I spend time, the upper half of the park, close to Riverside Drive, is heavily used. The lower half, close to the river, is partially wooded and, except in the summer, when it's crowded with all the people who can't afford summer homes, less popular with casual park strollers. The compulsive, year-around users of this section of the park—the runners and the dog-walkers—reach it using tunnels that cut under the highway at either end. The walkway west of the tunnel near 72nd Street is in an endless cycle of repair and disrepair. Work crews never seem to catch up with the widening cracks, which open to abandoned railroad yards far below.

On winter mornings, the park is quiet except for the dog-walkers and joggers, both devout as churchgoers. I am a newcomer here, a convert from Central Park. Central Park was safer for Emma before she was obedience trained—Riverside Park too close to traffic on the Drive and the West Side Highway. Near the Sheep Meadow in Central Park, I taught Emma to sit, stay, come, and heel. She was learning what I wanted but not yet perfectly obedient when I moved our walks closer to home. The lessons continued. My rule: You listen to me come hell or high water (so I can keep you safe). Emma's rule: Okeydokey (unless a squirrel crosses my path).

In Riverside Park, I am quickly accepted into the fold. Dog owners introduce themselves and their dogs. The human names slide by, but we all know the names of all the dogs: Reggie, Roy, Roux, Alice, Abby, Ernie, Garbo, Gracie, Floyd (his first name is Sigmund, his owner tells me), Mr. Smith (a female), Mrs. Peel, Boo, Bagel, Bonzo, Bamboo. I know Nick and Slick, Nonny and Bonnie, Pamina and Papagena, Samson and Delilah, Skipper and Slipper, Doughnut and Pancake, Panda, Mouse, Fox, and Bear. I know five dogs named Sasha, five named Sam. I'm introduced to a beagle named Peg; I call her Peg O' My Heart. We stand in small groups and watch the dogs chase sticks, tennis balls, squirrels, each other. We stroll by the river, our conversations about our dogs, our jobs, punctuated with "Reuben, come," "Harry, get your ball," "Lorna, get out of the garbage," whistles, applause, "What a good dog you are to come!"

We are called by our dogs' names. I am called Emma's owner. Jason's owners just had their first baby; Rosy's owner is engaged to Allie's owner. Bulletin: Nick's owners are getting divorced. Nick, a black Labrador retriever, disappears along with the husband, who is rumored to have moved to the East Side. The new ex-wife returns with a yellow Lab puppy, a female named Nellie. She announces that all men are spoiled babies, shows off her new pup, and corners me to ask: As a single woman, am I afraid of venereal disease?

Near the 79th Street entrance to the park, Emma trots over to greet a Maltese wearing a woolly red-plaid coat. The tiny white dog is an inferior version of Emma, smaller, much slighter (Emma is leonine beside it), and objectively speaking, of course, not nearly as charming. I know without looking that there will be an old woman attached to the handle of its leash. Only old women bundle up their little dogs in fleece-lined coats on mild winter days.

"Yours is a woman?" she asks.

"Yes." I can tell from the change in Emma's behavior— she's practically skipping—that hers is a male.

"Interesting, is it not, how with animals the woman goes up to the man, but with people they do not."

"Some women do."

"No, with us the man must first express an interest. This is the way it has been and the way it will be always. You say in America this is different, but this is the way it has been in my country and throughout the world."

"That's the way it used to be here, too, but not now. Now women can approach men."

"A woman asks a man to bed?"

"Sometimes."

"A man waits for a woman to call to invite him to bed?"

"Sometimes."

The old woman shakes her head as if I am mistaken. "Do you have a husband?"

"No."

"Then you have a friend, a special friend?"

"No."

"I, too, have no husband now. You are still a young woman. If you want to find a man, you must not be aggressive. This is womanhood." She pronounces the word slowly, not sure of her English. When I nod she continues. "This is womanhood, you see? Perhaps you are right, but I think in these things that I am right. With animals this is much, much different." She glances at our two small dogs. Emma, already bored by the Maltese, is ready to move on. "A man must ask a woman. It *was* so, it *is* so, it *will be* so."

I retreat to the safety of my apartment, away from the warnings of old women. Perhaps I should lease a professional guard dog, a Doberman pinscher, trained to protect people who are easy to talk to and their small, pacifist dogs. The next time an old woman tries to approach us on the street or in the park, the Doberman will intervene. When she asks me if he bites, I will lie: "All animals can bite."

I feed Emma breakfast and we both go back to bed. "Lazy dog," I say, stroking her fur, soft as down, then curl my body around her like a shell.

The ringing of church bells grows louder until it seems to be coming from my phone. I reach across the bed and lift the receiver and from habit think: This will not be a man I want.

"Hi, Ann? This is Rick. Remember me? I'm calling to wish you Happy New Year."

"Of course I remember you." My memory is especially adept at recalling men I would like to forget. This is Rick the Prick— a welder turned sculptor. He answered an ad I ran in the *Village Voice* to rent my extra bedroom. On the phone he was quite a charmer, with a disc jockey's voice—all bravura and manic good cheer. "Today's Valentine's Day, Rick."

"I know . . . but since it's been about a year since we've talked . . ."

"More like two years."

"Well, then let me wish you well for both years."

His voice hasn't changed. I have to laugh at his good-ol'-boy style. I half expect him to reach out and sock me playfully on the shoulder. What chums we were! What good times we had! His memory, I note, is more imaginative than mine. "The last time I saw you, if I remember correctly, you were storming out of my bedroom in the middle of the night."

"Speaking of bed . . ." Rick wants to set the record straight on this one issue: he would love to make love to me again. And he's sorry he was so upset about my dog that night and how is the little guy, anyway?

"She's fine."

He assures me he doesn't expect a reply right away, but he wants me to know just how much he wants me. He's been getting himself in shape. No more junk food and plenty of exercise. He predicts in a month or two he should have his Army body back.

"Your *Army* body?" I don't want his Army body; the military scares me.

"Yeah—I was shooting for my high school body, but I tell you—that baby's *gone.*" He whistles like a jet taking off. "Then I tried for my college body—Lord, how I tried. That leaves my Army body, and I've almost got it. I just need a few more weeks."

I have no idea if Rick's renovated body, soon to be only twenty-two years old, would be turned on by my thirty-three-year-old model, no big deal ten years ago, and minimally maintained ever since. But I do know I would much prefer never to see Rick or any of his incarnations again.

"I'm not ready to hang out with a younger man," I tell him.

After a string of insincere pleasantries about staying in touch, we say goodbye. He calls right back: "You were so hot in bed."

I remember, although apparently he does not, that he would insist on taking a copy of the sports section to bed. Only after he'd finished reading about the Rams or the Raiders would he turn off the light and wearily reach for me.

We hang up, still cordial, but when the phone rings back, I pick it up without saying hello.

"This is the man with the golden cock."

Not according to my memory, I think, but say nothing as I hang up the phone, then take it off the hook.

For once, my recalcitrant memory remembered mostly the truth. Usually, it recreates the past to suit its own fancy: Oh, Rick, a wonderful guy, a lot of fun, why don't the two of you kids get together? I wish memory worked like it's supposed to—the way it does in the movies—as if it were a pool of remembrances, requiring the owner to do little more than cup her hands and dip in. *Owner.* Who am I kidding? I own Emma. I do not own my memory. I cannot train it. It can give or withhold, like a priest doling penance. I once knew a man who owned a Great Dane. "I do not own Missy," he informed me. "I do not believe in owning animals. Missy and I just live together."

My memory and I just live together.

All right, everyone, settle down, I have an announcement
to make. If everyone would quiet down, I would like to make
an announcement. Thank you. Next Monday is Valentine's
Day. I would like you all to bring in some goodies—cookies
or cupcakes or cinnamon hearts. On Friday, we'll be making
valentines for you to exchange with your classmates.

I don't want to bring in any goodies. I don't want to exchange
valentines with everyone. Valentine's Day has nothing to do
with a bunch of kids who hate each other's guts. If we have
to make valentines, why can't we just give them out to our
friends? I will make a special one for Angela, my best friend,
who is a Catholic. I will make one for my other best friend,
Joanne, who is a Piscopalian. I won't make one for Lorraine,
who is not my friend. She tried to kill me playing dodge ball.
I won't give a valentine to her.

I know you're only kidding, Ann. You are a very funny girl.

No, I'm not. I'm not fooling around. No one knows I'm
not fooling around.

Lorraine keeps trying to kill me whenever we play dodge
ball. I'm not exaggerating. My mother says if she's told me
once, she's told me a million times it's childish to exaggerate.
Then she laughs. Lorraine never laughs. She has cats' eyes.
She holds the ball under her arm as if she owns it. Then she
plays with it by herself—tossing it up in the air, catching it,
pretending she's forgotten our game, but I know she's just
getting ready. She swings back her arm and shoots it forward
and with a snap of her wrist releases the ball, aiming it directly
at my face. I duck behind Angela, and the ball barely misses
me, bounces off her shoulder and rolls downhill from the field
where we're lined up, through the playground, past the monkey bars where the little kids play.

Keep the ball low, girls.

I have to retrieve it—my punishment for hiding behind

Angie on the field of battle, definitely against the rules. It takes a long, long time to walk down a hill when you don't really want to get to the bottom. Every few steps, I glance over my shoulder to make sure Lorraine isn't about to throw another one, which is a dumb thing to do, I know, since I'm the one fetching the ball. I stop to retie my sneakers, although they are already tied. When I look up, the little kids have taken over our ball. They are playing with Lorraine's deadly weapon as if it were a toy. A boy I don't know puts it down on the ground, turns his back, kicks it away from me, then races after it and flings himself on top of it. "Hand it over," I yell, in slow pursuit. He hugs it. "The ball," I say. Again he kicks it away from me, but this time he doesn't chase it. I do. Holding the ball as far from my body as I can, I make my way back up the hill, past the monkey bars, where he's now hanging upside down from his knees.

"Four-eyes," he whispers.

"Marsupial." It's the first word that comes to mind, even though I can't remember what it means.

Valentine's Day is half over. No valentines for me. Because today is Sunday, no mail at all. No gifts on my doorstep—no pink satin pillows, no lacy negligees, not a single chocolate-covered cherry or cinnamon heart. No one is serenading me from my fire escape. The bells have stopped caroling. Neither Cupid nor Santa Claus has dropped by. My only holiday surprise: a mildy pornographic New Year's phone call from Rick. No card or call from Buck, of course. I dial his number. With any luck, he won't be home.

"You're home. Of course you're home. If I really wanted to talk to you, you'd be somewhere else, but since I could care less, you're sitting right there."

"Are you on drugs?"

"Is tea a drug?"

"Not the kind you drink."

"Then I'm not on drugs," I say. "Happy Valentine's Day."
"Do Jews celebrate holidays named after saints?"
"I'm not Orthodox."
"I'm glad you called, Ann."
"Why?"
"Because no one I know here talks like you."
"Was that an insult?"
"You know it's a compliment. Tell me about New York."

Tell me about New York. He always asks me the same thing. I know what he wants—local political news, threats of sanitation and transit strikes, an update on the status of American urban life. But he knows I am ignorant of all that. I only know about the old Jewish ladies who limp along West End Avenue, slowed by the weight of their memories.

When I was a girl, they tell me, there was this cat lived in the neighborhood, on the East Side, on Lexington and 52nd Street. Nobody knew the cat's name, if it had one, or maybe it's only that I can't remember it. *Ganef*, they called it. Do you know Yiddish? Thief—in Yiddish, *ganef* means thief. This cat would sneak into the bakery that old man Rosenblum ran, jump on the counter, and steal a whole row of sugar buns, you know, the sticky kind, with pecans. That thief would run away fast as it could go, leaving a trail of those buns, and the dogs would come out and eat them. There was this firehouse dog ("Dalmation," I offer) that would chase that cat like a bat out of . . . chase that cat all the way to Third Avenue. Never caught it. Never even came close. This was fifty years ago, before you were born. Such a pity you already have gray hair, at your age. You could dye it, you know. You could be blonde.

"Buck, you know I never have much to report. A church in my neighborhood played Christmas carols all morning. That's it for exciting news from here. Why don't you come visit and see for yourself? You're always welcome to stay with me."

"Tracy and I were just talking about a trip east."

"On second thought, the two of you could stay at the Y."

"Ann . . ."

"Just fooling, Buck. How are things going between you two?"

"All right."

"But not great?"

"She's pretty much told me I can have her as long as I want her."

"She must not know you like more of a challenge."

"I guess not."

"I know what you want. You want an intelligent, independent woman who seems like she couldn't care less about you, yet underneath her cool exterior she's faithful as a German shepherd and willing to drop everything the instant you call."

"You got it. A dime a dozen, right?"

"Wrong. If you'd try lowering your requirements a little, I might be able to sneak under the wire."

"I *have* lowered them. You'll never be low enough to meet them. I keep telling you, Ann, you scare me."

"Relationships based on love are sinking fast these days. Maybe we should try one based on fear."

"I'm not ready to settle down."

"You're thirty-five."

"Thirty-four and a half."

"You'll never be ready."

"I will, too." We both laugh at his mock-child voice. Then we begin to part, as usual, with the mutual promise that we'll keep in touch. I will be the one to keep our promise and Buck will be the one who has been thinking about me and—whether I believe him or not—was just about to call. But I'm not yet ready to let him go. He will come visit, he swears, in the spring or next fall—his favorite seasons in New York. He'll stock up on books at the Gotham and Strand. He'll visit a few old friends. He'll finally get to the museums he ignored the two years he lived here. He'll check out all the landmark buildings he always intended to see, neighborhoods in Manhattan from Inwood to Battery Park he'd somehow missed. Meanwhile, he says, the planes between Austin and New York fly in both directions. I have an open invitation to visit him.

"Buck? We used to have fun together, remember?"

"Of course I remember. I keep telling you how much I miss New York."

No—you don't remember me. I don't show up on your picture-postcard aerial shots of the World Trade Center and the Empire State Building and the Statue of Liberty. I'm down here with the pedestrian and vehicular traffic. I'm on my way to work, riding my bike past the horse-drawn hansom cabs in Central Park, across Fifth Avenue and Madison, turning south on Park Avenue, pedaling as fast as I can. Here I am, Buck, weaving my way through gridlock.

You don't remember me. You're too far away, moving too fast. Your rule: Never look back. My rule: Never give up. Look over your shoulder and you'll find me.

Longing keeps me going, keeps me on a path, keeps me moving from the comfort of my apartment in the city to the wilderness, where men like Buck roam. Their restlessness mirrors my longing in its dogged search for relief, comfort, and, eventually, sleep. I can no longer say what I want. When you begin a chase, you think only about the prize: *Buck—I have to find Buck.* But if the chase goes on too long, you risk sacrificing the quarry to the pleasures of pursuit. *Is it Buck I want?* To want him again, you have to stop dead, sit down on the ground, struggle to your feet, and set off for home. It's easy to keep going in the same direction, even if he's out of sight. You must turn your back and go home.

I look out toward the man I follow and make myself stop. I hang up the phone. But only for a moment. Then I call my dog, cradle her in my arms, and go hunting.

Riverside Park, like Central Park, is the creation of the distinguished landscape architect Frederick Law Olmstead. Working in the English tradition, Olmstead envisioned the park as a "natural" and picturesque environment enhanced by fountains, wading pools, baseball diamonds, and areas for racquet sports. Construction was begun in 1873. By the time it was completed in 1910, one hundred and thirty-two acres had been added to the park by filling in and smoothing out the ragged shoreline of the Hudson. In my section of the park, there is a promenade directly beside and fifteen feet above the water's edge. The lower Hudson River is an arm of the bay, the place where the freshwater current meets the saltwater tide.

I go back to the park for my usual winter evening dogwalk—once around the path that circles the small cinder running track, from the entrance to the track past the baseball field to the promenade. Tonight there are no runners in sight. Overhead, trees loom black against a sea-blue sky that fades gradually through shades of violet to pollution-pink at the horizon. Seagulls silhouetted against the cloudless sky are black as bats. Behind me, the ebb and flow of traffic on the highway falls into the redundant, rhythmic beat of the sea.

The wind is fierce, the river at high tide, blue-black and choppy. Emma springs ahead, weaving among the benches that separate the concrete walk from the grass. I yell at her to come, not because I want her, but for the comfort of my own voice. It sounds unfamiliar and muffled in the wind. On the ground, a small, blue sphere rolls toward me. When it vanishes, Emma is at my feet. "Hi, sugar," I shout, "you're a good girl to come." I mouth words of praise against the wind.

Emma takes off. "Where are you going?" I ask aloud, as if she could hear. I'm wading through shadows deep as a river. The weight of my soaked pants legs slows me down. A stranger—

neither runner nor dog owner—is ahead, walking toward me along the promenade. He pauses to lean against the railing and stare out at the river. His hands disappear into the wooden ledge on top of the railing. His start-and-stop movements, and the increasing darkness, remind me of primitive motion pictures with their halting frames of black and white. I will not pass that man. Where's Emma? We have to go back the same way we came.

"Emma, come," I shout, my mouth full of wind. I see her now, but she can't hear me. I watch her approach the man with no dog, no running shoes. I will have to go get her. But I'm unable to move, hobbled by water, blocked by wind. I'm still watching her circle his ankles, sniffing, when the man with no hands picks her up like a rag and hurls her into the river. The wind, the water, muffle my screams: *I can't swim I can't swim.*

Emma appears from behind a bench and races to me. I resist the impulse to pick her up in my arms. "Now you're safe," I say, ridiculously, since she can have no inkling of the images in my mind. I'm aware that I've been clutching her wadded-up leash in my pocket; its metal clasp is imprinted on the palm of my hand. I fasten the leash to her collar. "We're attached," I say, stating the obvious. Now what should we do—keep going or turn back? Keep going, I think. The man without a dog is standing motionless, his clothes ballooned by the wind. A sheet of newspaper blows across the promenade and flattens against the back of his legs. He twists around to peel it off and, gripping two corners diagonally, turns toward the river and lets the wind pin the paper to his chest like a bib. He manages to fold it lengthwise, then makes another fold, then another, then quickly several more. He raises his arm and takes aim at the sunset. The airplane arcs upward into a streak of deep coral that vanishes as swiftly as the plane plunges, spirals, and dives, then caught in a momentary lull, wafts like a falling leaf toward the water. The wind seizes it and pitches it into total darkness where I can no longer see it, yet I watch it land upside down and be consumed by the waves.

I complete my circle of the track and head toward the graffiti-scarred tunnel leading to the upper section of the park. As usual, the lights in the tunnel are out, but I know what one wall says: "He fell in love with her and didn't show it—now it's too late, he thinks he lost her," in black scrawl. The free-form letter shapes, barely discernible as writing at all, remind me of the animals in the wood grain of my childhood walls. The tunnel floor, which glistens with broken glass from the smashed lights, is littered with assorted debris left by the home-less, who retreat there on rainy days as if it were a cave. I hesitate for a moment, hoping for a runner, a dogwalker, a knight in shining armor. No one. I pick up Emma and hurry toward the sweep of lights, welcome as the beacon of a light-house, of Riverside Drive.

Outside the tunnel, I release her. Excited by the wind, she bounces by my side. She won't leave me now that it's com-pletely dark. I decide to cut across the field. As I climb up a small rise, she whips around my ankles, pausing from time to time to jump up on my legs, spring ahead a few strides, and dash back. I laugh at her and applaud.

The sound of applause, not mine, comes back to me. On the top of the rise, the shape of another man; it solidifies and moves toward me. I stop and reach for Emma; then I notice a dog by his side. As he approaches, I see that he's a very young man, perhaps a teenager, with a lanky, long-eared dog.

"Quite a night!" he shouts as we pass, then smiles at me in a way that makes me smile back.

I keep going toward the playground, circling it from the West Side Highway to Riverside Drive. Every few strides I turn to get out of the wind and take a few easy breaths. "Quite a night," I shout to Emma, still prancing. A flick of her tail and the turn of her head tell me she's listening. I'm yelling, but the wind and the roar of city traffic reduce my shouts to the volume of normal speech. "Happy Valentine's Day," I yell. On my way home, I spot the boy and his dog again, captured for an instant under one of the old-fashioned street-lights marking the bench-lined walks closest to Riverside Drive. He waves to me; I smile back. By the time I realize he can't see my smile and I raise my arm to wave, he has turned away from me and stepped ahead into darkness.

Two

*T*HE Odyssey Press publishes fine bindings of already published works, which it sells by mail order as collector's items in "limited edition" series. I write the introductions: one-paragraph biographies of illustrious authors, three-hundred-word summaries of classic world literature. Thanks to me, all across America and in nine countries abroad, discriminating subscribers to the leather and gold-embossed volumes comprising "One Hundred Immortal Works of Literature" will never have to read their books. I am the moral equivalent of "Monarch Notes."

Today I'm greeted in the office by a round of good mornings and a glance or two at the receptionist's clock, friendly reminders that I'm forty minutes late. My boss's office is still dark. Where is he? I don't ask anyone if Malin has called in, just in case he hasn't. I know if he's running late, if he overslept or has a hangover, he'll call me so I can cover.

I check the schedule for the day's work and find a pair of nineteenth-century *M*'s. "*Moby Dick,*" I begin, "written in 1851, blasted by the press of the day as a work of little merit, and badly received by Melville's formerly devoted readership, is now considered by many to be the outstanding American novel of the nineteenth century." Forty-one words so far. (The date counts as only one word.) I dole out words the way grocers weigh out dried fruit or hunks of cheese. Occasionally, I write the piece straight through without counting a single word—a half-pound of cheddar in one neat slab. Then I begin to re-write. On my second time through, "*Moby Dick* . . . now considered by many to be" becomes "*Moby Dick* . . . frequently considered. . . ." Savings: four words. On my third time through, "American novel of the nineteenth century" becomes "nineteenth-century American novel." Savings: two more. I write and revise and write and revise and finish one final draft that I refuse to revise and then give in and revise.

I quit *Moby Dick* and take up *Madame Bovary*. (Where the hell is Malin? It's almost noon.) This one will be harder. I have to concentrate and not get distracted by the plight of poor Emma—surrounded by such disappointers—Charles, Léon, Rodolphe. I know she'll make a play for my sympathy. Such a terrible fate, to be trapped in the provinces. Can't I see she's wasting away? Will I help her find a way out?

Pardonnez-moi, Madame, but I cannot be of assistance. Besides, you appear to be doing pretty well on your own. I may seem like a success story to you. It is true that I moved from the provinces (we call them the suburbs) to an apartment in the big city. But I live alone; you're only pretending. Every evening, Charles kneels on one knee before your cold fireplace, carefully building you a fire. He dozes, and fails to see how quickly it burns out. While he sleeps on the hearth, faithful as a dog, you sit beside him, his master. He must sleep to dream. He hasn't needed a daydream since the day you con-sented to be his wife. How can he see you daydreaming your way through chandeliered ballrooms, across marble porticoes, down lush garden paths, toward elegant, ignorant men?

Do not envy me. My apartment contains no fireplace, no hearth, no man to instruct in the proper method of building a fire. Only my dog is as faithful as a dog. The last ball I attended, even in my dreams, was Cinderella's.

But Charles is such a dolt, you say.

You know what my mother would tell you? She would say, "The grass is always greener." She would say, "Be thankful for what you have."

I agree with my mother, not because of Charles, who is steady as a rock and just as interesting, but because of your own baby Berthe, asleep upstairs in the nursery, where she is being rocked in her cradle by your maid. Count your lucky stars, Madame, for the baby girl you can carry in your arms.

But I wanted a boy, you say.

Isn't one boy enough? I ask, turning to her devoted spouse. Wake up, Charles Bovine (do you know that's what everyone calls you?), put down your beer, turn off the TV, take Emma in your arms, take her dancing. Heed my advice: If you cherish your bride, don't let her ride horseback through the woods.

My apologies to you, Monsieur Flaubert. I am about to reduce your four hundred pages of meticulously wrought French prose to three hundred lifeless English words. I leaf through the novel, reading, re-reading, skipping from place to place. The word *dog* catches my attention: "She confided many a secret to her dog, after all!" *Ah, mon cher Gustave,* I have yet to reveal my worst disservice of all: I named my little dog after your heroine—Emma Bovary, *le bichon frise.* She is so easy to please.

Malin arrives just at one-thirty. I recognize his footsteps behind me as he scurries into his office and closes the door. My telephone rings.

"Ann." His telephone greeting is always the same, a statement, sure of itself, half observation, half announcement. Yes, I want to say, congratulations—you picked me out of the crowd. Malin is a boy-sized man with a bass voice. Size-wise, I tell my friends, Malin is to men what Emma is to dogs. He's five-feet-four, an inch shorter than I am, but he moves at twice the speed.

He and I constitute an entire department. With the exception of punctuality, an office-wide requirement, we are the most independent department at the press. If anyone notices or objects to our spending our time in Malin's office, our laughter clearly audible through the closed door, they don't comment to either of us.

"Malin," I say, imitating his greeting to me. "Better late than never."

"How's your work going?"

"Fine."

"Anyone looking for me?"

"Me."

"Anyone important?"

"No."

"Have you had lunch?"

"I didn't want to leave until you got here."

"Let's go eat."

"You mean together?" Although Malin and I have become good office friends, we have never gone out to lunch.

"My treat."

We rendezvous at the elevator. Malin smiles and hurries to help me on with my coat. "Thanks. Men aren't supposed to do that sort of thing anymore."

"We southern boys can't help ourselves." He transforms his Arkansas accent into a Deep South drawl. "Did you enjoy your weekend?"

"It was fine—quiet. I spent most of it checking the names in the *Brothers K*. I worked like a dog. Not like *my* dog, who spent the weekend taking naps and eating bonbons. How was your weekend?"

"Insane."

"Anything wrong?"

"I'll tell you about it over lunch."

Malin and I occupy the last available table. We talk shop for a while. I know he's stalling; eventually, he'll get around to letting me know why we're here. Finally, he asks if I've ever met someone who seemed like the man of my dreams.

"The dog of my dreams, yes, the man of my dreams, no."

"Someone I used to know a long time ago showed up out of the blue this weekend. Someone I used to—well, it doesn't matter who she was. She just showed up at my apartment on Sunday afternoon and announced she wanted to party. We walked around the Village, had dinner, went uptown carousing, and ended up dancing half the night. When I offered to take her back to her hotel, she invited herself over. . . . Do you want a cup of tea or something?" He flags down the waiter, orders us tea, chit-chats to fill the gap until it arrives.

I know he has something he wants to disclose. I sip the tea to give him a chance. Revelation in a packed Second Avenue coffee shop requires an imaginative leap—the illusion of infinite time and space. The waiter is pacing nearby to hurry us along. Take your time, Malin. I finish the cup, call the waiter, order another.

"At my place, we drank a few beers, more like a few hundred, did a little—what's the expression you always use?—'messing around.' I went into the bathroom and when I came out she was in my bed with practically no clothes on. But when I got into bed with her, she wouldn't let me touch her."

"Then what was she doing in your bed?"

"That's what I wanted to know." He laughs, but when I don't, he looks as if he might cry. "I ended up sleeping on a sleeping bag on the floor. Only I didn't sleep."

"And you didn't throw her out because you're a gentleman."

"I should have. It was a horrible night. I drank too much. I'll never drink again." He smiles at the thought. "I felt like such a goddamn fool."

"I'm sorry," I say, offering him the blanket apology that his true love should have given him. If I had a real blanket instead of words, Malin, I would wrap you in it. But would I tuck you inside it and hold you on my lap? Or would I get under it with you and prove her wrong? We sip our hot tea, the silence between us expressing his hope, and my confirmation, that he is no fool. Sometimes I drink tea for the solace of a warm cup. Malin holds the body of his cup with two hands, like a child would, the same way I do. "Are you all right?"

"I'm just hung over. You don't drink, do you?"

"No."

"So you've never been hung over."

"Never," I smile. "But it looks like fun."

"How did you get to be so pure?"

"God knows I never wanted to be this way."

"One of these days we'll have to go out and get you drunk."

"Didn't you just say you will never drink again?"

"I lied. But I will say this: I am never going out with a woman again."

But he can go out for a drink with me, I think, because in his eyes I'm a friend and not a woman. Just once, I want to tell him, just once I would like to be both. "I've always thought celibacy was overrated."

"So is sex."

"What happened when she left?"

"She got up early and let herself out."

"Did she say anything?"

"She said . . ." He's pretending he didn't trail off intentionally by asking our waiter for the check.

"I didn't mean to pry, Malin."

"You're not prying. Suddenly, I'm self-conscious. Maybe I shouldn't be admitting what a jerk I am."

"You're not a jerk. Or to put it another way: this conversation doesn't make you any more of a jerk in my opinion than you already were." He laughs. "Did you say anything to her?"

"No. When she closed the door, I threw a beer can at it. Luckily, it was empty." We both smile at that, the silliness and futility and satisfaction of it. "Then I reset my alarm and went to sleep in my bed. When the alarm went off this morning, I considered calling you at home to tell you I wouldn't be in because I was trapped by this sex-crazed woman, but I couldn't find the telephone, which says a lot about the state of my apartment—just a studio—not to mention the state of my mind. I didn't wake up again until noon. I would have been here sooner, but I was trying to find an old picture I wanted to show you. Mother just sent it to me."

"As long as it isn't a picture of your dead poodle . . ."

"Should I know what you're talking about?"

"Not at all. Where's the picture?"

"I left it in my briefcase."

"Then let's go see it."

He gets up to pay the tab. I try to contribute my half, but he won't let me. I've earned lunch, he says, for holding down the fort at work. I've earned more than lunch for listening to him. He says if he can return the favor, I have only to let him know.

We go back to the office and close his door against interruptions. His desk is covered with manuscripts, duplicate sets of galleys, newspapers, copies of the monthly production schedule and yearly budget. He searches for his pack of cigarettes by patting the surface of the paper like a blind man.

"You are hopeless," I tell him.

"Found the little buggers." He lights a cigarette, takes a swig of Coke, and offers the warm can to me. I fetch two cups of ice from the supply room and clear off enough space among the clutter on his desk to set them down.

"I'm not sure if you need a maid or a mother."

"Both."

"Where's the picture you wanted to show me?"

"It's no big deal, Ann. I don't even know why I brought it."

In the black-and-white photograph, a boy about fifteen,

wearing blue jeans and cowboy boots but no shirt, has his arm draped around a pretty girl of the same age, in jeans and a light-colored checked blouse, her hair held away from her face by a hairband. I recognize Malin because of his small size and something about his eyes—not how they look to me, but the way they are looking at the camera, as if he were staring out of some private place, peering out into daylight from a cave. In the background, a corral, desert, a feeling of space.

"Who's the girl?"

"She was my girlfriend. But that's not what I wanted you to see."

Then I see what he wanted me to see: a horse in a corral, its nose deep into a pile of hay, its white face partially hidden. "Cat. Is that Cat?" He doesn't bother to answer. Of course that's Cat. I recognize him from Malin's stories. He's one of the main characters, along with Malin's dog Bad Boy, his mother Lilly, who lets him call her by her first name, and Lilly's father, Warren. Cat was ugly—even for an App. We've agreed that Appaloosas aren't our favorite breed. I learned about breeds of horses in the *World Book Encyclopedia*, the same way I learned about breeds of dogs. My sister and I called Apps "dalmations."

"I told you he was ugly. You can't see the shape of his head here. I used to call him 'Jughead.' He had a disposition that matched his looks, but he was my first horse and I loved him."

"Beauty is in the eye of the beholder," I say. "How old were you when you got him?"

"Nine. We were still living in Rainbow. We moved from Arkansas to New Mexico the next year. Cat was such a weird horse—he could freak out over anything, a bucket turned upside down, a rake in the wrong place. My grandad said we made quite some pair: a jittery boy on a skittery horse. I must have told you about the first time I rode him."

"I'm not sure." I am sure. He told me the story of his first

ride during our office Christmas party. The next day he remembered spending time with me, but he couldn't remember
what he had said. Apparently, he also doesn't remember what
he did: he slid his arm around my waist and, leaning close to
me, brushed his face against my hair. Malin hasn't seen Cat
in fifteen years, yet I can tell from his stories that the touch
of Cat's mane is as vivid to him as the touch of Emma's fur
is to me. Malin told me at the party that Cat's real name was
Freckles, but everyone called him "Cat"—short for "Fraidy-
Cat." Don't be such a fraidy-cat, Malin. I should admit that
I already heard this story and that I want to hear it again.
Which one of us is the fraidy-cat? "Malin, why don't you tell
it again?"

He begins, as always, with no introduction. Unlike Cat,
who had to be prodded and cajoled into gear, Malin's stories
spring from the gate. Like Cat, once they take off, they're not
easy to stop.

"Cat was only fifteen hands, but he looked like Bucephalus
to me. My grandad saddled him up for me. He lowered the
stirrup so I could get on—practically had to lower it to the
damn ground. He said all a horse like this needed was a little
confidence. He said if I showed him I knew what I was doing,
the horse would settle down, but if I flopped up there like a
goddamn fish, he'd spook himself back to the barn. After all
this time, I can still remember how it felt putting the toe of
my boot in that stirrup, grabbing hold of the horn, pushing
off the ground, swinging myself up, and landing in the saddle,
sitting up there proud as a peacock, my grandad holding the
reins. It was always so dark in the barn, even with the lights
on, but I could see out the barn door (it wasn't closed tight)
over to a piece of our house, and a slice of blue sky above it,
but I felt like I could see everything, and for some reason (this
is weird, I think, because I know it must have been daytime),
I remember seeing a starry sky lit up behind that big white

house, and the glider on the front porch was gold from a yellow bug-light (I used to sit out there at twilight, swinging) and the rosebushes in bloom in front and along the driveway, my grandmother's white Honor roses, were shining with a light of their own the way the moon seems to when you're a kid and you can't believe that it doesn't. Mother opened the barn door wide and my grandad let Cat outside and handed me the reins. My dad and my grandmother were watching me from the porch. Horse smell and the smells of the saddle and the barn were all mixed in with my grandmother's honeysuckle and white roses.

"I started off at a walk and got maybe fifty feet from the barn when Cat took one look at a ladder leaning against the shed and stopped dead in his tracks like somebody had turned off his motor. It was like he had died on me and forgot to lie down. I remember my grandad asked me if I was intending to just sit there counting Cat's spots or if I was intending to ride him, when Cat whirled around and took off for the barn and skidded up to the closed door. I should have fallen off, but I didn't. My grandad said I had a choice: either I could pay proper attention on my own or the horse would give me lessons. I was scared to death but I wouldn't get off him. I remember feeling like I was literally sitting on top of the world. 'Are you scared?' Mother asked me, and Grandad shooed her away like a cat, told her to go over to the porch with everyone else. I thought that was where she went until I finally got him heading in the right direction and walked him back past the shed to the field. Grandad said a fraidy-cat horse could be worked with but not by a fraidy-cat boy. Cat wheeled around again but this time I was ready and I wouldn't let him run. Lilly whooped from the hayloft and swung herself partway out the door and flapped like a flag on a flagpost."

Malin's office on the thirtieth floor of a Third Avenue building, its sweeping southern view of the breadth of Manhattan below 48th Street dominated by the Chrysler Building, whose silvery art deco arches in daylight seem to blaze with a light of their own the way the moon does, offers Malin a less impressive view than the one he had from the height of his fifteen-hand horse. What are you doing in New York? I want to ask him. I already know the facts: how he got married and came to Columbia to go to graduate school and liked it here and thought he would enjoy a career in publishing and got divorced. He is as happy in New York as he would be anywhere else—except Tahiti, he says. He knows I think he's misplaced—but I'm wrong.

I want to hear another story. "Maybe I better get back to work."

"Maybe I better start, or I'll be here all night."

At five o'clock, on my way out the door, I hand him my two manuscripts and their respective photographs and picture captions. Each Odyssey Press volume opens with a rendering of the author and one or two related pictures or drawings. I wrote the *Moby Dick* captions to cheer him up; the real ones are on my desk. "The white whale," I wrote, "was almost as popular a pet in Melville's time as the bichon frise." I've taped Emma's picture below an engraving of the whale. "Above, the frontispiece to the first edition of Melville's masterpiece, depicting the two white animals that obsessed the writer—Moby D. and Emma B."

No bike today. I walk north and west to Fifth Avenue and 57th Street to wait for the bus, which arrives, as usual, just as I'm about to give up and walk home. Surrounded by stylish, attractive women, I wish I had decided to walk. My corduroy jeans, fine for the Odyssey Press, are too casual, too crumpled, to compete with midtown city chic. I do have a brand-new skirt in my closet, but I can't wear a skirt because Emma chewed the zipper out of one of my good leather boots, my only winter shoes. I've been keeping the boot closed with safety

pins. "You are a rotten little dog," I yelled, as she retreated
and cowered under the coffee table. When she sneaked over
to jump up on my knees, certain of instant absolution, I heard
myself think, but did not say, *After everything I've done for
you?*

The bus seems to be parked. A middle-aged woman across
the aisle frowns and begins to make clicking and whistling
sounds, like a parakeet on a swing. At this I begin to take
heart; she's worse off than I am. Perhaps I am not the worst-
dressed woman on the bus, perhaps not the least attractive.
But when I glance around, everyone else looks fine. Meanwhile, the parakeet has learned a new trick. Repeatedly opening and closing her purse, wagging her head, she boasts in a
child's sing-song voice, "I know something you don't know."
Then I notice the ad framed above her head.

Miss Marie, Advisor/Astrologer, will fix anything bad—luck,
habits, health; she'd tackle bad karma, I think, even though
it's not on the sign. Does she treat birds? Does she fix boots?
Will she help me? Only one thing's for certain: I'm beginning
to believe in signs.

I twist around to discover the message over my own head
and find a chubby, half-nude couple, their tortoiseshell glasses
askew, their mouths poised for a kiss but inches apart and
gaping. Turn frogs into princes, ducks into swans, with Insta-
vision's magic contact lenses. I've worn glasses for almost twenty-
five years. In third grade I wore pink pearl ones like all four-
eyed little girls; in sixth grade they were navy and white striped.
Can you turn this lump of coal into gold? I change my seat
in hope of a better sign, but I don't turn around to read it.

Sixth Avenue and 57th. The engine roars, but we've only
gone half a block. Pedestrians streak by, their long scarves
trailing in the wind. Above the dim shops on the street level,
hair salons glimmer like fishbowls. Hairdressers, their brushes
and combs held like magic wands, glide through iridescent
light among spiderplants green as seaweed. Poster-size black-

and-white photographs of women—their lips parted and pouting, their stares glassy as fish—hang outside the doors downstairs. The bus smells of gas, perfume, and roach spray. No windows are open. Maybe I should get off and take a subway. Or another bus. I could walk home, easily, from here. I stand up and sit back down. Maybe I should get off. No, I have to convince myself I can sit on this bus and survive.

Finally, it begins to inch forward. Then it stops, bucks, stops. What am I doing in the middle of 57th Street on a horse I don't know how to ride? All I need is some confidence, I think. If I act like I know what I'm doing, I'll be all right. If I keep flopping around up here, I'll spook Cat back to the barn. I steady myself by holding on to the aluminum bar beside my seat. I'm too old to hold on to the horn of a saddle, but I can't help myself. Kamakazi delivery boys fly through the snarled traffic on ten-speed bikes. I should have taken Fred, my bicycle. To hell with the ice, the cold. I know how to ride Fred. I try to read the posters outside Carnegie Hall. I picture the inside of the hall, the whiteness of the proscenium, the rows and rows and rows of red velvet seats, the long climb to the balcony, where I usually sit. The poster is for tonight's performance. Van Karajan and the Berlin Philharmonic. I close my eyes and hear the opening of Brahms' First. Only one block more till Eighth Avenue. I open my eyes and see the "Sold Out" banner flying above Van Karajan's baton; the poster's a tease—the concert's completely sold out. The bus won't budge; I've got to get off.

Be patient.

I can't.

Be patient and you'll get a prize.

What prize?

When you get home, Buck will be there.

Buck's in Texas.

Why don't you ever have any faith?

My first act of faith is to ask a question: What sign did I

receive by virtue of having changed my seat? As soon as I see
it (what was I doing, tempting fate?)—the shape of an animal
upside down, the world for an instant topsy-turvy—I know I
should never have looked. There is a message beside the black-
and-white photograph of a horse—I already know it's a horse,
in spite of my determination not to see. I focus on the words:
"When people are abused, they can fight back. Horses can't.
This horse was killed in a traffic accident." Nice type, I think,
trying to remember the name of the typeface, trying to judge
its size in points (type is measured in points the way horses
are measured in hands, I explain, as if someone were listening
to my thoughts), but when I look at the lines and not at the
individual letters and words, I see that the lines have been
badly laid out (*laid out,* is that what you say? Laid out like a
corpse?), with apparent disregard for sense or rhythm:

> When people are
> abused, they can
> fight back. Horses
> can't.

Words can't be set down willy-nilly. Words are organized
into phrases, and phrases have cadences and meaning. What
kind of designer would arrange words like this? Their place-
ment must have to do with the photograph, the photograph I
saw for an instant but did not apprehend, something about
the way the horse was sprawled on its side in a tangle of traffic,
dying a raucous public death, its own shadow (I think it was
only a shadow) spilling out in all directions, something about
an upturned feed bucket and a severed carriage wheel, something about the horns and sirens and the disarray of bright
lights—streetlights and headlights—exactly like the noise and
lights outside my bus window, where a hansom cab drawn by
a dappled gray storybook horse with ears too big for its head
is traveling home down Seventh Avenue, cars, taxis, more
buses surrounding it, bearing down on it as if it were one of

them, just another machine. Doesn't anyone know the difference? This sign, a "public service message," is for those drivers, not for the passengers inside this bus. This is not my sign. Do you hear me? Stand up, horse! Don't be dead. *I will not accept this as my sign.*

I leap off the bus and my elevator doors close behind me. Buck is standing in the doorway to my apartment. I gallop toward him and leap into his open arms. He kisses me. I step back to see his face. He's grinning.

"You're grinning," he says.

"I'm happy to see you."

"I said I would come visit. You should have more faith."

He reaches inside my coat, tucks his hands under my arms, and picks me up easily, holding me high above his head. I order him to put me down, but he refuses. I become small and light in his arms. I laugh as he threatens to throw me higher, then lowers me to his chest and wraps his long arms around me.

"I've missed you," he says.

"Have you?" I stretch to match his height so that I can press the entire length of his body against mine. I hang on to him; he holds me, and together, uprooted by our pleasure, we begin to rise. As we rise higher, my legs lengthen and grow stronger and entwine his. We embrace each other, our feet paddling, keeping each other aloft.

The bus is at my stop and I'm off. Luck is with me; white "Walk" signs mark my path. Across Broadway, down my street, up two stairs, key in the outside door, the elevator's broken, up four flights of stairs, key in the apartment door, flinging it open to find Buck.

Emma is there, dancing at my feet. I can barely breathe. She dashes off and comes back with two gifts—a ball and a wad of socks—my rewards for coming home. I take off my clothes and tumble among the blankets on my bed. She scoots across the room and under the bed, then jumps up beside me. She crouches down, ready to spring.

"I'm happy to see you, too," I tell her, as she leaps across my body and for an instant seems suspended in midair.

When I finally find my old friend Buck, he's asleep in my childhood bed. He sleeps, unaware of the animals prowling in the unpainted wood right over his head, unaware of me, on the prowl, beside him. I've been informed he spent the night with someone named Linda. Who the hell is Linda? I ask him. He swears it was no big deal—just a matter of convenience. It was just that she was there.

"Like Mount Everest," I say. I remind him I was downstairs. If it was merely a question of proximity, why didn't he choose me? "It's because I'm ugly, isn't it?" His silence seems to confirm that I'm on the right track. "You won't sleep with me because I'm ugly."

"You're not ugly . . ."

I sense he isn't finished. There is something else he is reluctant to say. If I don't stop him, he will tell me precisely what I don't want to know. Beside me in my childhood bed, Buck, who is too tall to fit in such a bed, fits easily. I'm lying on top of him. I try to shield my breasts with my arms so that he can't see me—the woman he doesn't want. He assumes incorrectly that I seek the truth. *Lie to me, Buck. Tell me a lie.* He touches my breast with a fingertip and trails his finger along its curve the same way I used to follow the cats' tails in my walls. The animals are mutable but I am not. Does Buck know that? *Tell me a lie.*

". . . You are very, very plain."

Now have you heard enough? Now will you wake up? My dog Lucky appears and leaps up beside me and licks my face. His chain collar jingles as I hug him and wipe my tear-soaked hands on his fur.

I wake to the sound of my own sobbing. Linda is the name I use in my dreams for women who are pretty, blonde, graceful— everything I will never be. Buck lives a thousand miles from here. Lucky has been dead for eighteen years. I struggle to get up and write down the dream in the travelogue I've been keeping to document my time from sleep to rising. In the morning, in my bedroom with its blank, white plaster walls, I read: "Buck slept with Linda in my own head." Underneath I write: "Moral: Never ask a question unless you're prepared to hear the answer." I hear a quaver in my voice as if I've spoken the words aloud, as if I've spoken them underwater.

The day of Jefferson School's annual pet show, my mother drove my sister and me to school with our entry, a boxer with a rubbery black mask and a pushed-in face, pacing in the back seat of our '53 Chevy. We tied Lucky's leash to the playground fence because that was the rule—no loose pets—even though we knew Lucky would never wander away from us. There were four categories: Largest, Smallest, Most Unusual, and Most Beautiful. We knew without discussing it that Lucky was the most beautiful dog there, and probably the most beautiful pet. Our teachers smiled and our friends laughed and asked how we could call such an ugly, mean-looking dog beautiful. They called him Godzilla. I asked Lucky to sit and give me his paw. The trick impressed them—they all agreed he was smart—but they still thought he was the ugliest dog they had ever seen.

They suggested we enter him in the "Largest Pet" category, but we knew they were just ignorant. Boxers weren't large dogs, even if Lucky was almost the largest dog there. We knew that German shepherds and Great Danes and even collies were all bigger than boxers. We knew from the pictures in the *World Book Encyclopedia* about massive dogs, St. Bernards, mastiffs, and Newfoundlands, twice Lucky's height and weight. We knew there were Russian wolfhounds and Irish wolfhounds, that the Russian kind were called borzois, and they were all three times taller than our beautiful brown and white dog.

Nevertheless, we acquiesced. When they announced our names as winners of the green ribbon for the third largest dog, neither my sister nor I, sitting on opposite sides of the auditorium, would stand to receive it. They al. thought we were shy. My friends whispered in my ear, "You won . . . ," as if I hadn't heard. They nudged my elbows, bumped my legs with their knees. "That's you," they said. I shook my head and they gave up. My sister and I would not budge. We had capitulated to their vision and were ashamed.

"Beauty is in the eye of the beholder," my mother explained to us after assembly. She opened the back door of the Chevy and Lucky bounded in. As she started the car, she glanced at him in the rearview mirror and laughed, reaching around to give him a pat. "A face only a mother could love," she said. She told Lucky that all the time.

I'm in bed with a handsome man. I know he sleeps with pretty women exclusively; he's making an exception for me. We're lying on our sides facing each other, waiting. Slowly, simultaneously, we lean forward like timid lovers on tiptoe. Then I take charge. Slipping my left hand behind his neck and up to the back of his head, I draw him toward me. The weight of his skull sinks into my palm; his silky hair spreads through my splayed fingers. I press my right hand against his cheek, his jaw, his throat. His throat rumbles like the body of a cat. *No pets allowed.* I narrow my focus until the purring stops. He nuzzles me and tries to lick my face. Is your name Mittens or Whiskers? *Buck,* I think. *Let's call you Buck.* Welcome back to New York. I am no longer likeable, no longer easy to talk to. Buck gasps for air and words. He wants nightclub chat. Come here often? I ask with my eloquent right hand. Speak! I say, as if he were a dog, but when he tries to bark, I lock his mouth with mine. Did you hear me say there are no pets here? My hands are weary of pets, my mouth sick and tired of talking. This choke-hold on conversation is our first, lingering kiss. Kissing him, I eliminate all distraction until I am aware of nothing but my lips against his, my mouth fixed on his, our mouths jammed with our tongues, and then I forget about his and concentrate only on mine, my cavernous mouth chock-full, teeming. He senses that my eyes are open and opens his. You can't tell a book by its cover, I tell him. I breathe deeply and rest. I will prove to him what an unattractive woman can do.

I'm awakened in the middle of the night by a soft, pleading sound, a two-pitch call, high to low: *"Pup-py."* Through a double web of branches—the leafy, white lace trees in my curtains and the bare trees of heaven outside my open window—I watch a man and a woman on their terrace. She's in a yellow or white sweater and blue jeans, her blondish hair tied back with a ribbon. He's balding and has a cropped gray beard. He rattles a dish of food, then sets it down and pulls his dark robe tighter around his waist. She stands with her hands on slim hips: *"Pup-py."* She climbs down the fire escape and swings one leg over the railing, then the other, and drops softly into the garden, out of view.

She reappears with a huge white cat and, holding it high above her head, hands it to the man. They must have been calling "Fluffy." A fat, white, long-haired cat, with a tail graceful as a plume. The woman vaults back over the railing and clambers up the fire escape. The man is holding the cat in his arms and she wraps her right arm around his waist. They pull their terrace door closed and disappear. When they turn off the terrace light, my bedroom brightens and I see Emma, her white fur a ring of pale feathers, curled up asleep in the center of my bed.

Three

"*E* MMA, come. This way. Wrong direction. No—
wrong—wait—halt. . . . Where do you think you're
going? Will you please stop? Do you see me over
here? Over here? No fair quitting in the middle of a game!"

Emma is tired of playing fetch. I've been crisscrossing the
baseball field, throwing a small red ball, no bigger than a golf
ball, behind me. When she brings it back, I tell her she is the
best dog in Riverside Park, on the Upper West Side, on the
isle of Manhattan. Listening to my compliments, she keeps
her eye on me instead of the ball and anticipates my throw
incorrectly, taking off at top speed in the wrong direction.
When she doesn't find it she stops, then swivels her head as
she scampers about, searching. The much acclaimed canine
sense of smell seems to be absent in the bichon frise. "Cold,"
I shout as she turns too far to the right. "Colder!" The dog
sits, staring at me, confident that if she waits long enough I
will relent and find it.

This time, I know the game is over and go looking for it
myself. No ball. I'm about to give up and head home without
it when I hear someone shout, "Hey, here it is." "Here it is,

pup," he calls again, grabbing his own dog's collar as he tosses the ball to Emma. I thank him. When he smiles back, I realize I've seen him before.

"Your name is Ann, isn't it?"

I nod. "You look familiar . . ."

"My name's Drew. I saw you here one night—you remember—the night in the wind."

He smiles again and I see that he is indeed the same kid, only older in daylight. Twenty or twenty-one.

"This is Rover."

"You named your dog Rover?"

He laughs, then shrugs. "And you're Emma, right?"

"Right," I answer. "The dog doesn't talk."

"Pleased to meet you, young lady." He bends down to pet her, but she ducks behind my legs out of his reach.

Rover's a lean, brown, short-haired, floppy-eared mutt, mostly hound, I guess. His markings, a patch of white under his chin and a white left forepaw, remind me of a cat's. He's five times Emma's size. He leaps on top of her, sniffing. She rolls over onto her back, compliant, then jumps up and takes off. He springs forward and speeds after her, reaching her easily in a few strides. The dogs both dash back to us. Emma keeps making smaller and smaller circles with abrupt starts and stops while Rover, panting, whirls around her.

"Looks like they're already friends," Drew tells me.

Rover takes Emma's blue coat in his mouth, picks her up and carries her off. The two of us laugh, but when I see that Emma is frightened I chase Rover and order him to put her down. He drops her and looks contrite. "You're forgiven." The dog, suddenly pleased with himself, lopes over to his owner, tail wagging.

"There's nothing worse than a smug dog," I say. Emma shakes herself as if she were wet and jumps up against my legs. I tell her not to worry, and take off the coat. She spots a squirrel and streaks toward it, Rover in pursuit. When she trots back, I praise her: "You almost got that one, honey." She wasn't even close.

We stand side by side, watching our dogs, sharing the usual park chat: who's your vet, how long did housebreaking take, what do you feed her, does he know how to behave? After a while, I notice we're standing so close our shoulders graze. Is the closeness his doing or mine? I glance at his face for a clue but find none. I think he must be responsible, but I notice I make no move to step away. When I finally decide to head home, he waves and calls out, "Bye, ladies," to me and my dog.

The weather turns warm, a tease of spring. The next time I see Rover's owner, he's teaching the dog to play Frisbee. He lets the Frisbee fly, then jumps up and down like a cheerleader, waving his arms, shouting, "Go get it, thatta boy, don't let it hit the ground!" The Frisbee lands and Rover retrieves it by pawing at the fluorescent green plastic disc until it tips up so he can grab it. He gallops back to his owner and drops it, staring down at it intently, as focused as a foxhound on a fox, the tip of his nose smudged with dirt. The Frisbee doesn't move. Apparently, Rover's owner doesn't know that houndlike mixed breeds aren't classified among "Sporting Dogs," the official American Kennel Club designation for the group of dogs most people call "hunting" dogs—retrievers, spaniels, and setters. Besides, "Sporting Dogs" traditionally have been used in the sport of hunting—not the sport of Frisbee. The bichon frise, not surprisingly, given the way Emma plays fetch, is categorized by the AKC as a "Non-Sporting" dog.

"I think he's getting the hang of it," the young man says.

I laugh.

"No, really. He just needs a little more practice."

"Practice makes perfect."

"Unless you started off perfect in the first place." He winks at me.

"Like Adam and Eve?"

"Exactly," he smiles.

"Like Adam and Eve and Lassie," I say, making him laugh.

"I'm glad you brought Ann out for a walk," he says to Emma.

I wish I could remember this guy's name. Listening to the dogs' names but not the owners' has become a bad habit.

"You're not usually around in the afternoon," he says.

"I'm playing hooky today. What about you?"

"I guess this is when we always do our morning walk."

I make a show of looking at my watch. "It's quarter to two. Don't you work?"

"Not exactly."

"Sell drugs?"

"Sometimes."

"Or are you a kept man?"

He smiles a rooster-in-a-henhouse smile. "I'm trying to become a rich, famous little rock star. What about you?"

"I'm an editor. I'm not trying to become anything."

He laughs again—a good audience. "I perform and record my own songs. I'm Drew Gold."

Drew Gold. Now I know I'll remember his name. "Is 'Drew' a noun or a verb?" I ask him.

"I guess this means you've never heard of me."

"I'm sorry. But I don't know anything at all about post-Beatles rock music. I'm basically a classical music fan."

"Don't apologize. My training was in classical music. My mother used to be an opera singer, so I grew up with opera. Besides, my stuff isn't really rock. Mostly, I write ballads, soft rock, some silly songs. I'll play you my albums sometime, if you're interested."

Play me his albums? "Any time," I say. We leave the park

together and he shows me where he lives. His apartment is on the first floor. I walk by his window four times every day on my way to and from the park.

We begin running into each other on weekends, the only time our schedules coincide. After a while, I look for him whenever I go by his apartment. Sometimes he's at the piano. Rover jumps up beside him and licks his ear, then sticks his nose through the wrought iron gate to greet me.

"Just what I need—an editor," Drew says. "Do you make housecalls? What rhymes with *strong* that isn't *long* or *wrong?*"

"You don't need an editor. You need a poet. *Oblong,*" I say. "Does it matter that *long* is in it?"

He seems inordinately pleased. *Oblong* isn't in his rhyming dictionary. He holds up the open book. "Can you see? There's *sarong, oolong . . .*"

He invites me to come in, but when he comes out to open the locked front door, he says hi as if he's surprised to find me there.

"How about this: Oblong to you and you belong to me."

"That was awful," I say, pretending to leave. He grabs my arm.

"I couldn't help myself. Come on in."

He's wearing a T-shirt and blue jeans, socks but no shoes. His hair is crumpled, as if he just got up from a nap. He leads me to his half-open apartment door. Rover tries to sneak out, but Drew snags him by the collar and blocks his exit.

"I guess the place is a mess," he says, pushing the door wide open. "Don't pay any attention."

I pay no attention to the ripped couch in the living room, the foam from its cushions littering the parquet floor. I don't notice the broom, dustpan, and half-filled plastic garbage bag piled in the center of the room. I don't see the variety of chewed items scattered across the furniture, the floor: paperbacks and cassette tapes, dog toys, the sleeve from a sweater, running shoes, a pink plastic hair roller. Drew asks me if I'd like to hear his records and leads me across the room. He kicks aside torn and broken things, clearing a trail through the undergrowth as he goes. The chewed hair curler spins then rolls under a table and out of sight, hits the wall, and ricochets back across my path.

The bedroom is filled with the paraphernalia of his dream: a turntable, receiver, speakers, tapedecks, microphones, amplifiers, his Baldwin grand, a synthesizer, one bass and two acoustic guitars. Records and tapes are piled everywhere and strewn across the floor. There is a dirty ashtray on the piano with an open pack of rolling papers.

Drew notices me notice. "You want some?"

"No, thanks."

"Mind if I do?"

"Not at all."

I sit down at the piano and Rover tries to crawl into my lap. "Off!" I tell him. The dog has no idea what I'm talking about. I push him away, then when he's on the floor, pat him and tell him he's a good dog. Emma has found a piece of dog biscuit and is chewing it under the piano bench, where Rover can't get to her.

"Something tells me Rover doesn't know too much," I say.

"He knows how to open the refrigerator. He stole a container of cottage cheese."

I ask Rover if that's true. "I only meant that he doesn't know he shouldn't jump up on people unless he's invited."

"You're right. I guess I don't want to restrict him. That's why I never use a leash."

"Not even on the street?"

"I don't even own one."

"A leash can keep him safe."

"He'll be all right. He's street-smart."

How can you be so damn sure of yourself? I want to ask

him. So cocksure, I think but do not say. "Is he your first dog?"

"After my parents split up, my mother got us a dog—Puccini. Poochie was a crazy, spoiled dog. She ate whatever we ate. Actually, it was a miracle she wasn't hit by a car. She used to chase them. But my mother wouldn't tie her up, not even for her own good." He takes a drag on the joint. "I guess I take after my mother."

"Play me your albums."

He says first he'll play a hit song from his second album. Actually, it wasn't a hit here, just in England, and in popular music, America's the only place that counts. Nevertheless, he points out the gold record for sales in England, which hangs on the wall near his bed. I remind him I don't know anything about current pop music and—although I would very much like to hear it—I'm worried I won't have anything to say.

"I'm a little nervous, too," he says, relighting his joint. "I value your opinion. I knew that when we first met. You worry too much. This is called 'Zoe.' I'm singing and playing the piano."

Drew's voice, much fuller, higher, and younger than I expect it to be, fills the room, although the song begins quietly, his left hand playing a steady waterfall of soft arpeggios. *Zoe lives across the courtyard with her houseplants and her cat.* . . . The music builds steadily to the chorus, a plea for understanding, which sounds to me like a warning: *If this is all I have to give, how can I promise more?*

I tell him I like it very much and ask whether there is a Zoe in his life. There was, sort of, in England. The woman he called Zoe is really named Susan. He borrowed the name from her overweight roommate who never went out with men very much. I wonder if someday the real Zoe will rate a song of her own. He could call it "Susan." I ask him to play it again. *Zoe says I can come and go as I please, and I believe her.* . . .

He presents me with the album. The record jacket is a tight close-up of his face. I take it home and listen to "Zoe" while getting ready for bed. *I sleep with a woman who thinks I'm a child, well maybe I am. . . .*

Drew leaves for England on a three-week tour the last week in March. Although a friend of his is staying with Rover, I've agreed to take the dog to the park with me on the weekends. I ring his apartment and a woman wearing skimpy running shorts and a man's white T-shirt answers the door. As usual, I'm bundled in my park clothes—jeans, turtleneck, two sweaters. I introduce myself and Emma.

"I'm Terry." She manages a smile. "I don't know why Drew imposed on you. I told him I would take care of Rover."

Rover tackles me, then Emma, who ducks under a chair. "Maybe he thought it would be a good idea to spread his favors around." I'm embarrassed by my choice of language, but Terry doesn't seem to notice.

Drew's apartment is unrecognizably neat—swept, dusted, organized. I suspect he didn't clean it for her. She appears to be settling in. His idea or hers? At first we chat about the weather. She's from Virginia, she says, where it's warmer. But she's in the process of moving to New York. She begins to describe the difficulties "women her age" face in finding apartments and jobs. She's twenty-two. I'm thirty-three. Drew is twenty-four. Staying with Drew isn't the answer, she tells me, even though she is welcome to stay as long as she wants. She and Drew go way, way back. But at twenty-two, it's time for her to be on her own.

"I better get going." I call the dogs. Rover, unaware of his speed, barrels toward me as if we were already outside, reaching me in three strides. He's so rambunctious that I pick up Emma to keep her from being trampled. Terry kneels down to hug him goodbye—a silly thing to do, I think, given his behavior, size, and weight. He almost knocks her over. She pats his head to steady herself. "Poor Rover, he ignores you, too, doesn't he?" she asks, regaining her balance. "He has no business having dogs or girlfriends."

Apparently, she is giving Emma and me notice that there are no more vacancies in this particular hotel. I could tell her that I already have an apartment more impressive than Drew's, except for its grand piano. Her territoriality is misplaced. If you want to protect your interests, I could tell her, forget about Rover and keep a leash on Drew, especially in Riverside Park.

Terry complains that whenever Drew comes back from Europe, Rover sleeps between them in bed. "Drew's a real scrambled egg," she says.

She is devoted to Drew, although I suspect she would never admit it. She thinks she can take him or leave him, no big deal. But while he is away, she cleans his apartment, does his laundry, walks his dog. She'll keep a lantern burning in the window, a steaming pot of soup on the stove, a fire in the fireplace, his slippers warming on the hearth. She'll be there with arms outstretched when he walks in the door. All I know is that he didn't bother to mention her name.

Two weeks after the end of his tour, Drew is leaving the park just as I arrive. My usual timing, not quite too late, not quite on time. He apologizes for not having called me to thank me for walking Rover, but maybe he could make it up to me by taking me to dinner.

"Is Terry your girlfriend?"

"One of them," he laughs.

"How many are there?"

"I have lots of women friends, but no one special. Not right now."

I can't tell if he's biding his time or shopping around. "She called you a scrambled egg."

"She was jealous of you."
"Why should she be jealous of me?"
"You're an older woman."
"So what?"
"That's all. You're just older."
I wonder, but do not ask, if he told Terry that he and I are just park friends. I suspect he didn't, and laugh.
"I like your laugh," he tells me.

Drew is starting a new album and wanders about the park in a drug-induced daze. He looks exhausted, older. If he keeps going at this rate, I tell him, he'll be as old as I am. He's spending days in the recording studio, nights writing, revising, arranging his new songs. Five down, four to go. I tell him again that he looks like hell and he should get some rest. But he swears he's fine. The songwriting will be fine. Six days to write four songs is plenty of time. He likes to work under pressure. He's more worried about the recording sessions. The guys in the band are all experienced musicians who know a lot more than he does, but he's the one who has artistic control. He has to learn how to listen to them and to himself at the same time. "It's all a matter of trust," he says. "I've got to trust that whatever I'm doing is right."

I don't give him any advice because he doesn't seem to want it. He talks steadily for a while, then settles down and looks a little sheepish, as if he's said too much.

"I'm fine. Everything's OK, really." He knows I don't believe him and touches my shoulder. "I'll play you the songs I'm working on."

His apartment, like a reclaimed wilderness, is returning to its former primitive state with alarming speed. I note with some satisfaction that Terry's domesticity did not take hold. He motions to me to sit beside him at the piano. He opens a spiral notebook and follows the pencil-scrawled hieroglyphs indicating lyrics and chords. The sudden crash of the piano and the volume of his voice stun me for a moment. *"I found you at the ASPCA,"* he sings. It's a love song. The lyrics seem to be talking about a dog, but the music says he found passion plus a pet at the pound. Drew's eyes are green. I wonder why I never noticed that before, even in the photograph on his album. But now they're badly bloodshot from the drugs and lack of sleep. His hands attack the keyboard like a jackhammer.

He finishes it and plays me the music to the next one. He's still waiting for the lyrics. They will come, tonight, tomorrow night. He has confidence. They must come to him, I think, the way my dreamed dogs come to me.

He nudges me from the piano bench to his bed, a mattress on the floor, and kisses me—a little off target. I adjust my head to match my mouth to his. The weight of his hand against my shoulder suggests I lie down. He half kneels by my side, lifts my sweater, and brushes my stomach along the top of my jeans with his fingertips. I keep my hands out of trouble at the back of his head. We're still kissing when he slides on top of me, holds me, rolls us over once, twice, so that he's back on top, and when I laugh, repeats the trick, once, twice.

"Wait," he whispers.

When he shifts his body slightly, I sense he wants to get up and I let him go. He jumps up and switches off the lamp. He begins pulling off his shirt as he comes toward me, singing his new song with no words.

"I'm sorry, Drew, I can't stay. I'm meeting a friend for dinner."

"Just for a little while?"

I can't stay. He shouldn't have turned off the light. The darkness made it too easy to go.

At the doorway to his apartment, we're transformed back into innocent park friends. "Don't look so serious," he whispers. He puts his arm around me and tells me to have a good evening.

"Likewise. Good luck finishing those songs."

61

He caresses my cheek. "Everything's fine. Take my word for it, all right?"

We both know he's not talking simply about the songs. All I can think about is Drew's pounce, quick as a cat's. Park bulletin: Emma's owner seduced by boy rock-star owner of Rover. Drew is a tabby, orange-striped cat. I am large, powerful, human. I flip him over, his knobby hocks furry against my hands. I finger the downy, long hair on the inside of his haunches.

Is this too good to be true? Is it? Is this too much to hope for? I am thirty-three years old and have yet to learn the proper measurement of hope.

In Riverside Park, I've been keeping watch for budding forsythia, for crocuses poking up their little phallic heads and the emergence of spring grass, translucent as cellophane. The groundhog has long since seen or not seen her shadow; it doesn't matter to me, since I can never remember which one predicts an early spring.

How could I have forgotten the most obvious cliché?—the onset of April showers. I wake up to the drone of the rain outside my window, the crackle of raindrops on my air conditioner. "Short walk today," I tell Emma. "It's raining cats and dogs." She hates getting wet. But this is no ordinary downpour: on the street, the fragrance of spring that rises from the wet pavement reminds me of sodden earth and dripping daffodils. "Short dogwalk for a short dog," I say, carrying Emma.

In the park, worms have bailed out of the flooding grass and are strewn along the wet macadam like sunbathers. This morning, the smell of spring rain overwhelms the night's exhaust fumes and the reek of factory waste. *April is the cruelest month* or *April showers bring May flowers*—which one? The mist-covered river blurs into the overcast sky. In the 79th Street Boat Basin, cabin cruisers and houseboats are moored on clouds, while seagulls glide through deep water like fish. Gradually, the dogwalkers converge and comment on the changes that the dogs all sense by sniffing the air. I sniff the air, too, searching for Drew.

Following several weeks of previews for which no one knows how to dress, spring formally returns to the park with its original cast and brand-new costumes and set. In this season's revival, there are two stars: The Man Who Catches Birds and The Lady Who Kisses Trees. The bird-catching man has the best prop: a gold pagoda birdcage, its empty birdswings swinging. He circles every tree along the edge of the park. When two trees are very close, he does figure eights around the pair. I make the mistake of half smiling at him. He thinks I want to know what he's doing. He says, as if I've asked, that he's the man who's famous for catching birds. He's been interviewed in newspapers, on radio talk shows. He's searching among the park's boring wild birds, robins and starlings, who live in these trees and are not lost, for a bird who belongs in a pagoda. He's after Carlotta, a runaway parakeet that took off from an apartment on Columbus Avenue and headed west, toward Riverside Park. I can tell he's dedicated to his task, relentless as a bounty hunter.

"I'm the only man in the city for this job," he crows.

"Good luck," I say, intending to leave, but he keeps chattering like a magpie. Apparently, he's a composite of birds.

"Luck! This has nothing to do with what you call luck! Would you like to know how I do it? Sure, you would. You think anybody can catch a bird, don't you? Do you think *luck* can catch a bird?" He puffs out his chest like a preening parrot. This is the man who is famous for catching birds. He's been interviewed in newspapers, on radio talk shows.

He even talks like a parrot, I think. Who taught him to talk? He repeats everything as if he has been trained by rote. When I was a little girl, my mother's best friend had a parakeet named

Gabby who perched on her shoulder while she did housework. "Take a bath you big big bum," Gabby used to say. Obviously, that parakeet had a sense of humor, an asset The Man Who Catches Birds lacks. I've got to get out of here before he traps me like a bird and makes me his captive audience. "I have to get going," I say, cutting him off. I walk away from him, but he sticks close, too close, the empty birdcage jangling with every step, until I reach the edge of the park and step off the curb, which stops him dead, the park caging him, the street shielding me like a wall.

The Lady Who Kisses Trees has neither lines nor props; nevertheless, she has the best costume—a black cape. She embraces each tree: the osage orange, which I call the rat tree, because of the rats I used to see near it on rainy days, the flowering crab beside it, too small to hug, the linden, my favorite. One tree, a pin oak that stands apart from the others, appears to be special. She embraces it reverently, her black cape flapping in the wind. She bows her head, then gazes upward through its budding branches. According to Sunshine's owner, The Lady Who Kisses Trees used to have a little brown dog whose name began with a *b*—Billy or Brownie—Buster— *Buddy*, that was his name. He wasn't much bigger than Emma. The dog must have died, because she started coming to the park alone. But no one ever asked her. Even when she still had the dog, she was the kind of owner who kept to herself. Then she started kissing the trees. Did she bury Buddy under her favorite tree? I wonder. Is she praying at the grave of her dog? Are you looking at the sky and the ground, I want to ask her, or at heaven and earth?

Now that the weather is getting warm, I run into Drew more frequently. But I begin to see him with other women. If I acknowledge him with a nod or a smile, he stops to introduce us; if I keep walking, so does he. Some of them are his girl-

friends; others are women, like me, whom he meets in the
park. I can't tell the difference. He always includes Emma in
the introduction. I barely notice the women and never listen
to their names. When I walk away, he calls out, "Bye, ladies,"
to Emma and me.

He invites himself over to my apartment for coffee after one
of our Sunday afternoon impromptu walks I'm standing at
the stove, boiling a kettle of water, when he sneaks up behind
me and winds his arms around my waist. He holds me just
below my breasts as if he were about to lift me, as if I were
small enough to lift. I lean my head back and sway toward
him a little. I expect him to slide his hands higher. He doesn't.
I place mine over his. Even though I'm not leaning against
him, I sense his kneecaps at the backs of my knees, his lips at
the back of my neck. When he unclasps his arms, I step away
and he asks, "Would you like to mess around?"

I lead him through my living room into my bedroom. He
sprawls on my bed. I lower the bamboo shades and close the
curtains and lie down in his arms. He's wearing a New York
City subway-map T-shirt. He takes off my glasses and gently
places them beside the bed. We're lying close enough so I can
see his face, but the red, blue, brown, green, pink, purple,
orange, yellow subway lines merge and blur. My bedroom is
a stop on one of these trains on one of these lines: BMT, IRT,
IND. Uptown, crosstown, downtown. How can I get anywhere
from here? BMT, IRT, IND. The roar of the subway silences
me, the sparks from the friction of wheels against tracks threaten
to set my white lace curtains on fire.

"I have to make a decision," I tell him.

"What decision?"

"The local or the express." He laughs and tries to kiss me.
When I turn away, he asks me what's wrong. I'm distracted
by the curls just visible at the top of his shirt. Should I tell
him what's wrong? Manhattan is an island. If I choose the

wrong train, it will take me too far. It will take me across the East River, where I won't be safe. I could end up like a tourist, lost in Coney Island.

"I feel like I have to decide pro or con and not pretend I'm being swept away in the passion of the moment." I would love to be swept away in the passion of the moment. Or at least I think I would. The fact is, all the trains are long gone, now, and I simply let them go.

"OK," he says, leaning back against the pillow, folding his arms behind his head. "You want to know what this will do to our friendship."

I nod. He's quiet for a while, then says he wants me very much, but he doesn't think we'd make it as boyfriend and girlfriend. I agree with his observation; nevertheless, I feel silly, unwanted, too old.

"Your hair is like spun pewter," he says, touching it.

"I know as well as you that we're not suited as serious lovers. We're in completely different worlds." My summarizing state-ment, my office habit, the universe of a novel reduced to a single page.

Drew refuses to accommodate two-dimensional space. "If we didn't share a lot of essential stuff, we wouldn't be as close as we are. And besides—I really do want you."

His warm body settles over mine. We're almost the same height and weight and our bodies fit together comfortably. He lifts his head and looks at me, smiling, and I kiss his smile while I raise my hips and keep pressing against him, breaking his rhythm, then re-establish it only to break it again. I re-member thinking he was a cat. I wish I were a cat. Cats can get what they want.

I relax and touch the small of his back to ask him to be still. He listens. Being with him is like playing with matches. I want to undress him. I stroke his face and keep looking at those curls at the top of his shirt. I could pull the shirt off

right over his head. *Hands to heaven*, Drew. What am I doing?
I have no common sense, no sense of direction. He's wearing
a map, but even a map won't help. Having escaped from my
gold pagoda, I'm still lost in Riverside Park. Is this the man
who is famous for catching birds? Let me take off that map,
Drew. *Hands to heaven.* My own hand opens and closes by
my side.

Drew says I'm not acting my age. He says I remind him of
what it was like going out with girls when he was sixteen.

"You're wrong. I'm acting my age. That's exactly what I
am doing." He waits for me to go on, but there is nothing
else I'm willing to say. I will not tell him that I refuse to be
compared with a dozen of his attractive young female friends.

He gets up and draws a joint from the front pocket of his
tight jeans, lights it, and comes back to bed. I take only two
tokes. He finishes the joint and holds me close. I feel myself
falling asleep in his arms. I should get up, make him a cup
of coffee, apologize. I'm sure he doesn't want to lie here like
this, holding me, an implacable, intractable thirty-three-year-
old teenager, unwilling to be seduced. He adjusts the position
of his left arm across my hip. He seems heavier, more solid,
but his breathing is lighter and more regular. He's asleep. I
let myself drift and join him.

When we wake up, we're still entwined. Drew says he better
get going; I offer to walk him home. But neither of us moves.
Finally, he props himself up on one elbow and gently strokes
the arc of my eyebrow with his thumb, then lowers himself
and lets his cheek rest between my breasts.

"Maybe I should have been more persistent before."

"Maybe. I wonder if I was trying to keep you from always
getting what you want."

"Or what *you* want." Now that we're awake, Emma joins
us in bed. "Don't worry," he says. "Who's that over there?"
He's pointing at a photograph on my desk.

"My father and Lucky, my childhood dog."

"Nice picture. I like your apartment. It's comfortable—like you are."

"You mean it's a wreck."

"No, I mean it's easy to spend time in. My apartment— remember my apartment?—that's a genuine wreck."

"Which one of us do you think I'm thwarting?"

"Look, it doesn't matter. You have to be comfortable with whatever you do." He kisses me. "There's no use pretending you're someone else."

I nod my head and smile, although I'm not certain I agree. Of course. There is no use pretending I'm someone else.

"Ladies and gentlemen, welcome to the Yellow Rose! Tonight the Yellow Rose is pleased and proud to present Drew Gold!" Applause, whistles, catcalls as Drew, bathed in yellow light, leaps onto the stage, guitar in hand. He ducks under the guitar strap and adjusts the mike while the spotlights play havoc with his hair.

"Hi, everybody," he says, his voice small and sweet—a kid on his best behavior. A volley of hi's echoes across the dark room. "I'm happy to be back here tonight." The lights turn blue and Drew seems to float off into the distance, to some other sphere, his voice beamed across blue light-years of space. He finishes tuning his guitar, sets it down against one of the speakers behind him, goes over to the piano, and sits down. A quick glance around the room. "Anybody here have a phone book?" Empathetic laughter on all sides. A waitress hands him a phone book and earns a barrage of applause. Drew sits down on all of Manhattan and lets his fingers skitter across the keyboard, accompanying bar and restaurant racket, the nonstop chatter, the clatter of glasses and plates being set down, picked up, emptied, filled.

The spots turn to red and then to yellow. Drew, center

stage, guitar in hand. "What do you call a bird that flies over the sea?" No answer. No one can hear. Will you repeat the question, please? "What do you call a bird that flies over the sea?"

"A seagull," a man yells from the bar. His buddies applaud and clap him on the back.

"And what do you call a bird that flies over the bay? . . . A *bagel*," Drew replies, as if he had just figured it out. The audience moans and hisses, but Drew keeps smiling as if he hears only applause. "Kind of cute, isn't it? My little cousin told it to me." More hisses and boos. "Aw, c'mon, she's only three," he says, his voice still sweet, his smile impervious to the disapproval. "The seagull—wasn't he the star of that play *The Seagull*? I bet you didn't know I read stuff like that, did you? It's by Chekhov. I *think* it's by Chekhov," he says, glancing over at me. "I always get Chekhov and Ibsen confused." He slings the guitar across his chest and basks in the changing lights, quietly strumming a few chords. The chords become the melody of "My Bonnie Lies Over the Ocean," which only those of us sitting up front and paying attention can hear. Then he tosses his head and stamps his foot and hurls his body forward, a spring uncurled, ready to bound right over the crowd.

Behind Drew, a wall-sized mirror painted with a single yellow rose in full flower. Across from him, behind the table where Malin and I sit, the bar, and behind the bar, the identical mirror. Everyone can see everything at once, a paranoiac's wish fulfilled: everyone can watch everyone watching. The audience gets to see what Drew sees: the waitresses, wearing lemon-colored Yellow Rose T-shirts, balancing trays of barbecued chicken and ribs, the crush at the bar—disembodied arms extending like poles to snag beer and bourbon, the exchange of money and banter and matches, the pick-ups, the continuous milling around from downstairs to upstairs, from the bar to the bathrooms, from left to right and right to left—all the while Drew, center stage, is talking, telling bad jokes, singing his songs as if he were playing Carnegie Hall.

Drew gets to see what the audience sees, what I see: an attractive young singer with brown, shaggy hair, undistinguished as a mutt's, his face nice-looking with a body to match. When he's singing ballads, his mouth is full and pouty. But when he relaxes and smiles, his smile promises hope to the hopeless, good cheer to the cheerless, and a good time for anyone willing to give it a shot, or so you think. It makes you feel special. After all, no matter how many other people fill the room and listen to his songs, laugh at his jokes, or don't, he is smiling that smile only for you.

"Thanks very much," Drew says to a smattering of applause. "Stick around for the second show." He jumps off the stage and squeezes by my table on his way upstairs to the greenroom. "Hello," he says, kissing me on the cheek.

"Hi." I introduce him to Malin.

"I'm enjoying your singing very much," Malin says warmly.

"Thanks," Drew says, with a wink at me. "See you later."

"What was the wink for?" Malin asks.

"I think it was half flirtatiousness, half his wondering who you are."

"I think he's a pretty talented guy—especially with a guitar. It's just that the whole act could use some polish."

"I wish he'd stop the lousy jokes."

"He can't."

"I know, but I don't understand why not."

"He thinks they're funny."

"I wonder if you'll make him jealous . . ."

No comment. Malin flags down the waitress and we both order ribs, fries, cornbread, Cokes. Malin's on the wagon; he's been out drinking with his friends three nights this week.

"I think you should have ordered a drink," he tells me.

"What for?"

"So you can get drunk."

"What good would that do?"

He grins at me. The Yellow Rose blasts the room with canned soft rock and country-western music. We can't hear each other now, even if we shout.

A group of people I recognize from the park wander in: Nana's owner, a teacher who works with emotionally disturbed teenagers in Harlem and who owns a fierce cat in addition to Nana, an epileptic St. Bernard; Nellie's owner, who must have gotten over her fear of venereal disease, since she abandons the others and cruises the bar; and Sir L's owner, an actor who used to be married to an actress. They have joint custody of Sir L (Olivier, not Lancelot), an Old English sheepdog who shuttles crosstown in a cab. I see Drew's younger brother Frank, who doesn't own a dog, and other familiar faces, mostly women I've noticed with Drew. A few people in their fifties linger near the front door, waiting to pay the cover charge and have their hands stamped, like teenagers. Frank greets them and directs them to a reserved table up front. Could one of them be their mother?

I fill Malin in on what I know about Drew's family history— his mother's sporadic breakdowns, his parents' divorce when Drew was fourteen. Drew left home as soon as he could, at sixteen, when he finished high school. He moved to Washington from their home in suburban Maryland, found an apartment in the District that he shared with some older musicians, went to college for a semester, quit, traveled, came back, and intermittently attended college until he finally moved to New York and earned his degree in music at age twenty-two. Frank followed him. When Faith saw they were both staying—for a year she had hoped they might come back—she rented a two-bedroom garden apartment in Ho-Ho-Kus, New Jersey. According to Drew, the spare bedroom was her way of telling him and Frank that if they ever needed a place to run to, they could run to her.

Drew, center stage, revving himself up. The loudspeaker: "Thank you all for coming to the midnight show at the Yellow Rose. Once again we're pleased to welcome Drew Gold!" A roar from all his friends, applause, smiles of greeting rebounding from mirror to mirror. A nod of acknowledgment from Drew, a slight backward roll of his hip away from the adulation, then a step forward to the mike.

"You're just trying to keep me from singing."

A chorus of denial followed by more applause. Finally, a cascade of spotlights in rainbow colors soothes the crowd like a hypnotist's prism. The house lights dim, leaving Drew awash in a waterfall of yellow light.

"I'm not going to tell any jokes this time," he says, to a burst of applause. "I'd like to dedicate this first song to Faith." The lights turn red, then blue. He is serious now, alone in an empty room, although the mirror behind him reflects a crowded bar. He begins to sing "Home, Again," from his first album, the song he wrote for his mother, *about* her, too, he's admitted to me. The final lines: *"Are you home again? Are you home to stay? Which one of us is crazy? Tell me—am I driving you away?"*

"OK, so this is the deal: for my next song, I'll need the help of two beautiful girls." He peers out at the audience. Only two, Drew honey? Why not ten? Abracadabra, two pretty blondes materialize near the stage. You can get what you want. They're wearing tight, faded jeans. A hoot resounds from the bar.

"I'd like to introduce you to these young ladies," he says, turning toward the one wearing a Yellow Rose T-shirt. He slides his arm around her. "Hello. I'm Drew."

"I'm Andy."

"I thought Andy was a boy's name."

"Not always." More applause and whistles from the bar.

"I'd like you to be The Maid, OK?"

"I don't do windows."

Drew grins at her. "Not *that* kind of maid." He turns to his left and winks at the girl wearing a pink halter.

"I'm Cindy," she says.

"And you'll be My Date." Another smile, teasing. "Fine, not too loud, now . . ." He pivots halfway around, his right hand vibrating against the strings, and leans toward The Maid, whispers the lyric into her ear, then yanks the mike toward her.

"*No parking!*" she snaps. He nods his approval while the crowd claps and whistles. Obviously, the place is packed with fans. They all know the lyrics to "The Meter Maid," Drew's worst and silliest song.

"*Well, where would you like me to park?*" he sings. Every time he pauses to cue in one of the blondes, the rhythm is fractured, but he keeps on playing, repeating phrases or whole lines, filling in gaps, smoothing over breaks, prancing toward one woman and reeling toward the other. The one in pink stretches out her arms and steps in front of him, a Las Vegas showgirl let loose. He's still singing when he nudges her out of the way with the neck of his guitar, then turns to face her. She curls her arm around his waist. With the other hand, she pushes her long hair back from her face. He leans so close his lips graze her ear. "*We could keep driving all night, or we could stop somewhere . . . ,*" he sings, wide-eyed, cuddly. The Date, seduced and suddenly shy, withdraws from him, then recovers and meets his gaze with a challenge of her own. He rests his hand on her hip.

"Keep your hands on the wheel," she says, ad libbing. The place explodes with laughter and applause as Drew, pounding his guitar, gets ready for the big finish, but the crowd is out of control and no one can hear him. He swings the guitar up and off, bows, and swivels to kiss both blondes. They jump from the stage, flushed and smiling. Drew, winding down, murmurs a few soft thank you's. The applause weakens and dies. He sits at the piano. The lights fade to blue. Meanderings on the keyboard lead into one of the new songs, "Strays," the song he played for me at home. I remember how he looked when I sat beside him at the piano, how he threw back his head, how he looked at me.

Drew has disappeared from the park. "Anyone seen Drew lately?"

"Who's Drew?"

"Rover's owner."

No one has. I keep checking out his apartment when I pass by—the lights are out, the window closed, the window-gate locked. He must be out of town. I wonder where he is, when he'll be back, whether he's alone, whether he's with Terry. Maybe he's on another tour. I'm beginning to miss him. I find myself staring at his window, but with no lights on inside, I see nothing but my reflection. I look for any sign of him, listen for his piano. I've been playing his albums almost every day. Sometimes I follow the lyrics on the record jacket and try to sing along. I have to keep my bedroom door and window closed so the neighbors won't hear me and call the cops. Emma is my only audience. She doesn't applaud, but she doesn't seem unhappy, either. Actually, she just sleeps.

I receive a note from Buck:

Dear Ann,

You tell me you're always home, but you're never there when I call. I just wanted to let you know that my visit this spring will have to be postponed. My pickup and my barbecue kicked, and with the mortgage on my new house, I just can't afford a trip east.

Tracy and I broke up last month. The usual ultimatum—marriage or else. Not surprisingly, I chose or else.

Yeah, yeah, I know all about it—you think I'm afraid of commitment. You think I'm afraid to grow up. You think I'm a sniveling little coward. You're absolutely right.

I miss New York and you. What are you doing July 4th? Do they still have fireworks over the Hudson? I WILL CALL YOU.

Love,
Buck

Dear Cupcake (I write),

For the sake of our continuing although faltering friendship, I think it would be better if you didn't suggest that you can't come visit because your barbecue broke down. I don't want to appear unsympathetic, but I don't even understand how a barbecue *can* break down. Can't you just get yourself some charcoal and a match?

Sorry to hear about you and Tracy. I assume when we next talk we'll discuss things at length. Meanwhile, the question is: Are we still planning to marry each other if neither of us is married by the time we're fifty? Should we up the age? I am looking forward to, but not holding my breath waiting for, your call. (Excuse the crummy syntax.)

They moved the fireworks to the East River.

Your friend,
Ann

P.S. Have I told you I met a golden retriever named Buck? He sort of looks like you.

In the park, Buck's owner complains that Buck won't come back when she calls. She fastens a thirty-foot nylon lead to his collar and lets it drag along the ground while they play fetch.

"Shouldn't you hold on to the leash?"

"It seems to work just as well when I don't," she says. "I think it's symbolic of our connection."

J'VE gotten into the habit of singing "Drink to Me Only with Thine Eyes" to Emma. Holding her on my lap, I prop her front paws against my chest and gaze appropriately into her eyes. She keeps looking away. *"The thirst that from the soul doth rise doth ask a drink divine . . ."* She struggles to get down. Is it my lousy singing you hate, or my repertoire? She squirms in my arms like a fish.

I don't carry on long conversations with Emma. Except for telling her in declarative statements the many ways in which I love her, most of what I say is interrogative: How are you? Where are you? Are you hungry, tired, thirsty, sick? Are you happy? Are you a good dog? My devotion to her is reciprocated fully. If she loses sight of me in the park, she panics, as I do when I lose sight of her. At home, when friends visit, she much prefers their laps to mine, yet no matter where she sits, she stares at me. My friends try to distract her, to get her to face in their direction, but she keeps turning toward me like a compass pointing north. When we're alone, she feigns disinterest. She follows me from room to room as if she were merely resettling in a new place where I happen to be. I leave her asleep on my bed and go into the living room to read; within a few minutes, she climbs up on the opposite end of the couch. I go into the kitchen, and glimpse her feathered tail as she disappears under the table. I'm back on the couch again when I hear the scrape of her paws against the cushion and the soft thud as she lands. She appears to be instantly sound asleep, her tail just touching her nose, as if she had never moved.

Time for our daily dog lesson. "You want a lesson?" Emma turns away from me and heads back to bed. "That was a rhetorical question," I tell her. She flips over onto her back, paws in the air, tail thumping—her non-rhetorical answer. I stand her on her feet. "Listen to this," I begin. She collapses into a lifeless ball of fur. "Will you wake up and listen?" Emma sits and yawns as I read to her:

> The Bichon arrived in France in the sixteenth century via Italy from its home on Teneriffe Island (hence its original name, Bichon Teneriffe), although it was probably transported there from the Spanish mainland. Legend has it that Henry III (1574–1589) was so devoted to his Bichon that he carried him everywhere in a tray-like basket, which he supported by tying it with ribbons he wore around his neck. At court, ladies carried the perfumed and pampered dogs as ornaments, which led to the coining of the word *bichonner*, meaning to curl, to pamper, and figuratively speaking, to caress.

I stop reading. This wasn't exactly the passage I intended to read. How did I forget my audience? With a little luck, Emma wasn't listening. I glance at her, hoping she's taking a nap, but she's alert, watching me. "Ignore all that," I tell her. "I read the wrong paragraph." I scan down the page until I see the heading "The 20th Century," then begin again:

> Although he was no longer in high fashion by the turn of the century (neither, of course, was the monarchy), the Bichon

won himself a different kind of following with his quick intelligence and sprightly style. No longer a pampered pet, he had to survive on the streets by his wits. He gained a reputation as an exceptionally talented trick dog, performing at circuses and fairs. Occasionally, this jaunty little dog was even used to lead the blind.

That was the paragraph I intended to read. I reread it, changing the words *he* and *his* to *she* and *her*. Emma appears to be listening attentively, although I suspect she paid more attention to the first passage than the second. "OK, ready?" I ask her. She doesn't move. "Do you see how much harder life could be? So would you please just give me your paw?" I extend my hand, lift her little paw, and give it one shake. I repeat my action with the command, "shake!" I try again, patient, hopeful, and again, patient, less hopeful. One last time: "Shake!" The lesson is over for the day—Emma a failed pupil, me a failed teacher, but I know never to quit on a sour note. "Sit," I tell her. She sits. I use my hand signal for *down* and she collapses. Her favorite trick. I praise her and applaud.

My father has taken on the task of teaching Emma to shake hands. He doesn't understand what's wrong with me that I'm having such a hard time. Anyone who knows what they're doing can get a dog to shake hands. Maybe if I watch I'll learn something for a change, since I'm a college graduate and apparently didn't learn much of anything there.

He's holding a piece of steak. My trick dog is twirling at his feet. "Sit, Emma." More twirling. "Emma, sit." She sits. "Say 'how do.' " Emma lunges for the piece of meat. "No," he scolds, crouching on the living room floor, Emma at his knees. My seventy-year-old father tries a new approach, explaining to the dog that when she agrees to give him her paw, she will get the treat. No paw, no treat. Get the picture?

I can tell that if Emma has any picture at all, it must be a very murky one. My father picks up the dog's paw and shakes it, then gives her a scrap of meat. She watches him with a perfectly blank expression. He shakes her paw again.

"Do like this," he tells her. He gives her another scrap. She is staring at the hand holding the meat. I'm impressed by her level of concentration, but my father is not. He turns to me, angry, as if I'm responsible. "What is she, stupid?"

"Stubborn, not stupid. What do you expect? She's getting all that meat without doing a goddamn thing. My dog trainer never thought she was stupid. She was the smartest dog in class."

"She was the smartest dog? If she was the smartest dog, what were the others—retarded?"

He thinks he's being funny, but I don't laugh. I know I'm overly sensitive where Emma is concerned. I hate being teased. I try to relax and let people have a little fun. After all, she's only a dog. She doesn't understand English—certainly not very much English. Her entire vocabulary consists of words related to food: *breakfast, dinner, chicken, hungry*. Emma is a pragmatist. She is devoted to my father, who criticizes her but, more important, gives her treats. In this regard, I try to emulate her. But I cannot. Emma is the recipient of much of my maternal love and the catalyst for much of my maternal instinct. To me, my father's verbal attack on her is as life-threatening as a physical attack. I hold my ground, my dog-child at my side, and stay very still. If he makes a move to harm her, I will leap at his throat.

"How do you know she was the smartest dog?"

"My trainer told me she was."

"Maybe you should give him a call and find out if she's so smart why she can't learn how to shake hands."

When Emma was ten months old, I enrolled the two of us in a bargain-basement obedience course sponsored by the Humane Society. The classes were held crosstown on a concrete playground strewn with broken glass and junkies, near the 59th Street Bridge. The other dogs seemed more appropriate to the setting, all of them mutts assembled from used-dog parts: German shepherd markings, collie noses, retriever ears, beagle tails. Emma was the smallest dog in class.

Our turn was always last. "Let's have the little darlin' try it," the burly instructor drawled. His southern accent appeared only when talking to Emma; it vanished the moment he spoke to me or to any of the rest of the class, canine or human. His grin seemed to me like a dare.

"Heel," I commanded my fancy, flouncy little dog. Emma, the class star, heeled perfectly, looking up at me with total devotion.

"Let me try it." I gave him the leash. Next to giant-sized Burly Bill, Emma turned into a cartoon dog. "Heel," he said. Emma stared at me. He tried to tug her away from me but she panicked and planted her feet. I lectured her, explaining that a dog is not considered fully trained unless it responds to a handler as well as to an owner. But, as usual, I was secretly pleased and ashamed of the pleasure it gave me: Emma would not leave me any more than Lassie would have left Timmy. Only Lassie was acting and Emma was not. She was becoming a one-woman dog. "Quite the little princess," he said, handing me back the leash.

Emma jumped up on my legs to greet me before sitting, quite correctly, at my left ankle. "She is pretty cute, isn't she?"

Bill shrugged and walked away to begin work with the next dog, a rangy black mutt, which the owner had bought as a six-month-old puppy six months before, although to me it was obviously a small, full-grown dog, four or five years old. By the time he took the dog to the vet for the first time and found out his error, he was already too attached to give the dog up. This must be the man my parents used to tell me about when I was little, I thought. Had Emma known how to shake hands

on command, I could have introduced her: "This is the man
who bought the Brooklyn Bridge. Sit, Emma. Say 'how do.' "
   "Now for a *real* dog," Bill snapped. The real dog whirled
around and snapped back, barely missing h.s leg.
   "There is no accounting for taste," I yelled after him. Another of my mother's favorite expressions. He turned and winked
at me.
   After our last class I brought him home. Look what I found
on the playground! We sat down on my couch and turned on
my television as if we were going to watch it. I could tell Bill
wasn't a real stray, not even a temporarily lost dog, more like
a tomcat out cruising. Emma and I both like cats, and I had
even considered getting one to keep her company, but to me
a cat seems unnaturally confined in an apartment. When I
was little, friends of my parents owned two males, a white
long-haired named Snowball and a seal-point Siamese named
Celery, who roamed free at night. The family lived in the
city—in my memory, their building was a tenement, but that
may be the distortion of a suburban child. The cats came and
went through the kitchen window, which opened onto a fire
escape that led to the alley out back. What floor were we on?
I remember standing on the opposite end of the warm, well-
lit kitchen, longing to see through that window outside, where
fire escapes zigzagged like lightning bolts and laundry was
strung between windows and fire escape railings on every story.
I imagined the cats stepping off the windowsill and venturing
out into the night by walking the clotheslines as if they were
tightropes, leaping down into the dark alley, traveling a net-
work of alleys where they pursued their "lady friends" (as my
father called them), scrapping with other males, scaling trees
and fences to thwart stray dogs, and, finally, taking the same
treacherous route home. Although I kept a lookout for their
return, and imagined I saw them outside the window (their
shapes were so different—one was plump as a pillow, the other

willowy), I never really saw one come back. Somehow, one or the other of them would simply appear inside, curled up on the sill, as if it had never left. Then the second one. They washed themselves or each other—I especially liked it when one of them washed the other's ears, the way the crumpled wet ear would bounce right back—while behind them, the clean white linens were fluttering in and out of the light.

Bill said what do we need a bed for when we're doing fine where we are? Where *you* are, I thought. Without his even noticing, I went over to the fire escape window, which I never use, raised the bamboo shade, withdrew the pole that secures the iron gate, worked at the stuck window until I managed to force it open, went out onto the landing, the branches of the sycamore well within my grasp, and climbed down to the backyards that are inaccessible from the street—quite an accomplishment, since I was carrying a bichon frise in my arms. Fire escapes, I observed, work for all sorts of fires. I looked for the cats—where are all the cats? I asked Emma. Where are Celery and Snowball and Fluffy? I decided if Fluffy's owners came looking for him (he's huge; he must be a male), I would let them rescue us. My address and telephone number are on Emma's tag. Would Bill answer the phone? Maybe Fluffy's owners would offer to keep us for a while. We could pretend we are cats and lap cream from saucers. We could learn how to purr and lick our paws clean (a skill I want very much for Emma to acquire). If they were kind enough to give us a home, we would show our appreciation by sleeping between them in bed.

Bill said he had to get going because it was getting late and, to be honest, it was late and he really had to get going. I watched him get dressed and imagined myself letting him out my fire escape window. I wondered if he would fight with the other toms out back. Would he spend the night on the prowl or go home to his wife? "Are you married?" I asked.

"To tell you the truth, I live with two German shepherds."

"Are they well trained?"

"Let's just say they behave better than their owner." Because it was the middle of the night, Emma was doing her rug imitation when Bill tried to tell her goodbye. "I just want you to know I enjoyed giving you a hard time in class because this little twerp was the best dog there."

"Maybe we should take your novice class."

"About those dogs I'm living with . . . they come with a woman."

"I was only asking about the class."

"Just so you know. You're not an easy woman to lie to."

I was tempted to show him to the window, but I behaved myself and walked him to the door. Shoo! I thought, as he kissed the back of my neck. I unlocked the door. Skeedaddle! The thought of keeping him had never even crossed my mind.

"What do you need a professional trainer for?" my father asks me. "Did a professional train Lucky? I trained Lucky. He was some smart dog. This dog here's got the mind of a flea."

"And Lucky was brilliantly trained, right? Lucky never did anything wrong. Lucky never slept on the furniture because he wasn't allowed." The boxer would jump off the couch, my father's armchair, my parents' bed, the moment he heard our car in the driveway, the click of the key in the lock. Warm, dog-hair covered cushions, flattened by his weight, gave him away. Lucky was perfect and I didn't choose him. Emma is entirely mine.

"What do you need a dog for?"—my father's only comment upon hearing that I had put a fifty-dollar deposit on a bichon frise. "Dogs tie you down."

My parents were driving me to New Jersey to fetch my new puppy. Did I have any idea what it would be like to have a dog in the city with no yard and no car? my father wanted to know. Did I think about what it would be like to have a dog in an apartment where I couldn't open a door and let it out?

"You mean I can't just let her out?"

"She won't be tall enough to reach the elevator button," my mother said.

"What are you planning to do with it when you want to go away? Take the dog with you? Do you think you can take a dog with you wherever you go?"

"I'll let you two babysit."

"Not me. Maybe your mother. I'm not babysitting for any dog."

At the breeder's, my father refused to get out of the car. "Aren't you coming in?"

"What for?"

"To see the other dogs."

"What do I need to see them for?"

"How should I know?"

I slammed the door, thinking, you're the one who loves dogs. You're the one who lets them break your heart. You want to stay in the car? Be my guest.

My mother and I reappeared with a puppy that still smelled from the shampoo and talcum powder Dorothy the dog breeder had used to make her bright white. Dorothy had instructed me to bring along an old towel for the puppy to sleep on in the car. When we got home, I should use it to line the crate or box that would be her bed. I held Emma on her towel on my lap the long drive back to New York. My father pretended he wasn't interested. He'd seen dogs before—why make such a big deal about this one?

Because this one is special, I could have told him. I could have told him that this puppy is all white, except for a patch of honey-color around her left eye and on the fringes of her ears; that she watches my every move with beautiful black eyes that look just like her mother's; that her tongue is pink and the size of a cat's, but without the roughness; that she is so tiny I'm supporting her head with my thumb. You want to know what's so special about this dog? Only the fact that she's mine.

"How much was she?" my father asked.

"A hundred." A lie.

"I thought you already paid fifty."

"I did. And another hundred today."

"A hundred and fifty dollars for that piece of fluff?"

"Love isn't cheap." My mother knows the real price—three hundred dollars.

"Do you remember how much Lucky cost?"

"Of course I remember. It's not my fault if no one offered to give me Emma. Besides, she was marked down." She really was marked down, from four hundred dollars.

"What do you mean, 'marked down'?"

"She has bad teeth."

"So what?"

"I may have to find an orthodontist."

"Did you pay with cash or a check?"

"Credit card."

"Since when do you have a credit card?"

"I'm only kidding. I paid with a check." I paid cash.

"Did you get a guarantee?"

"Of course."

"In writing?"

"Yes." Another lie. Dorothy gave me her word she would take the puppy back and give me a full refund if everything didn't check out all right at the vet's. In turn, she asked me to promise if ever I decided to give up the dog, for any reason at all, even if I wanted to sell her, that she would have the right of first refusal. She stood at the threshold, carrying the puppy, not yet ready to let her go. In Dorothy's heavy arms, pressed against her huge breasts, Emma seemed even smaller than I had remembered. Dorothy asked me to keep in touch, to call if I had any questions, and to send pictures. She told the puppy to be good, handed her to me, wished me luck, and turned away quickly, tears in her eyes. "I'll call you," I said. "Don't worry."

When we got into the car, my mother praised Emma for her good taste in having chosen me as her owner, then wished us a healthy and happy life together.

I was free-lancing at home for the Odyssey Press—not working there full-time the way I am now—when I decided to buy Emma. The trick to easy housebreaking, I knew, was to get a puppy outside as often as I could, at least after every meal and whenever she woke up from a nap. During the first three weeks, Emma had to be paper-trained, since she couldn't be walked outside until she was fully immunized. "Meanwhile," Dorothy had suggested, "since you have this bizarre fear that Emma will turn into a scaredy-cat dog, you should carry her around your neighborhood, just to familiarize her with all the noise. But don't put her down on the ground or let her have contact with any other dogs."

As Dorothy had predicted, nothing bothered Emma, not the sirens from police cars or ambulances or firetrucks (there is a firehouse nearby on Amsterdam Avenue), or the barking dogs or the blasting radios or the traffic, the squealing brakes, backfires, the incessant blaring horns. I took her on her first subway ride. I watched Emma sleep on the express train between 72nd Street and Times Square—for those thirty blocks, the din often forces riders to cover their ears—and nicknamed her The Valium Queen.

As soon as she had all her shots, I began to take Emma out for real walks. She was just beginning to get the hang of housebreaking when a snowstorm countered my injunction that sidewalks were for walking and for nothing else. Snow-plows buried cars parked along both sides of the streets (alternate-side-of-the-street parking had been temporarily suspended). Car owners dug them out by shoveling the snow onto the sidewalks, which building supers cleared by shoveling it back into the gutters, where it iced over and solidified into mountains for Emma to climb, attracted by previous canine climbers. "This is the sidewalk!" I yelled at her, pulling her away from what would be the sidewalk, if she could see it, toward the street. On the avenues, the boundary between sidewalk and gutter was much more distinct than on the less traveled side streets. I tried walking Emma along West End Avenue, but old women who ventured outdoors as far as the canopied entrances to their buildings scolded me for taking her out in the cold. They didn't care that I was trying to housebreak her. They weren't impressed by her red turtleneck sweater. "You should carry her!" they said. At first, I tried to explain that carrying a dog wouldn't help housebreaking, but eventually I gave up. "It's people like her who shouldn't be allowed to have dogs!" one woman complained to her doorman, loud enough for me to overhear.

"What are you doing with her outside?" Dorothy asked me. This was the first of what would become a series of telephone consultations, although it was actually my second call; I had called a few days after I brought Emma home to reassure Dorothy that Emma had passed the vet check and seemed to be doing fine.

"Trying to housebreak her."

"How long are you staying out?"

"Until she takes care of what I'm out there for." Ordinarily, I avoid this kind of circumlocution, but I didn't know Dorothy well enough to speak more directly.

"Have you been hitching her up to a sled? Tying her up to a doghouse? Anything like that?"

"Not quite. Sometimes we're out for twenty minutes or half an hour."

"She's not a parakeet, Ann."

"But she's the same size as a parakeet."

"Does she seem all right to you?"

"She seems fine."

"Then I'm sure she *is* fine. How are you two getting along?"

"She's the cutest puppy on four feet and I can't wait for her to grow up."

"What's she been doing?"

"The last thing she did was steal an unopened box of cereal off my kitchen table. She must have jumped onto a chair and from the chair to the table, which seems impossible to me, since I've never seen her jump at all. I wouldn't have cared, except she managed to rip the box open and drag it into the living room and spread the cereal over every square inch of my living room floor. I have a very large living room."

"You see? She's a dog, not a parakeet. Do you really want my advice? Go get a pen and write this down: 'For sale, one female bichon frise.' Copy it over a few times and leave the notes scattered around the house where you think Emma will see them. Leave one near her water dish."

"Will you be serious?"

"I recommend crate training. Confine her to a crate when you go out. When you get home, you'll both be happy to see each other. You won't be such a grouch."

"I wouldn't have minded cornflakes. But all those little raisins . . ."

She laughs her earth-mother laugh. "Then I assume, except for the biddies on West End Avenue and the raisins on your rug, everything is going OK."

"And one pair of chewed shoes."

"That will teach you not to put your things away. Anything else? Don't forget to send me a picture."

"I won't forget. I apologize for disturbing you, Dorothy."

"You're not disturbing me. I told you before: Emma is your dog now, but as far as I'm concerned, she will always be my puppy. All the puppies I've ever bred stay my puppies."

"You want to know what your puppy is doing right now?"

"Of course."

"She's chewing the fringe off my fake oriental rug."

"Maybe she wants you to buy her a real one."

I'm distracted by the television. My father, behind me, still trying the steak. "Say 'how do.' " Suddenly, his voice loud, louder than the TV. "Good girl!" Again, even louder, "You're a good girl!" To me: "Look—she can do it!" I can't believe it—a Helen Keller breakthrough—Emma shaking hands on request. Now that she's learned this trick, I wonder what new ones she'll be able to learn. My father repeats the command again and again. She really has learned it.

"And you thought she was stupid," he says. "I told you I could teach her."

"That's enough, now," he tells Emma. 'No more. It's all gone." She is not convinced. She follows him to the refrigerator, sits, lifts her paw, and says "how do," training him to get her more.

I'm walking the short distance between the railroad station in my hometown and my parents' house, my childhood home. The streets are littered with rubble and broken glass. Ramshackle houses have boarded-up windows. Stoves and sinks that are supposed to be in kitchens and bathrooms stand on porches beside broken screen doors.

I find a small white dog half buried in the snow in one of the yards. I pick up the dog and stroke its fur. She's very quiet, as if she's asleep, although her eyes are open. She looks exactly like Emma, but I call her a different breed. She may be a stray, I think, knowing that's not true. She is owned by the man I can see peering out from behind the curtains of this house.

I set her down in the snow. I don't want to leave her but I have to because she's not mine. Her owner doesn't give a damn about her. He thinks a dog is a dog. Eskimos leave their dogs outside all winter, don't they? Maybe if I walk away she'll follow me. I can't be accused of stealing her if she follows me home. I take a few steps and concentrate all my strength into a single, unspoken command: Follow me. I sense I have failed and stop. The dog hasn't budged. She won't try to follow because she doesn't know what it's like to be loved. I'll take care of you, I think at her. I *swear*. But the dog doesn't move. She's afraid of the man in the house.

I wake up struggling to remember if I simply walked away from the dog. Or did I try to buy her? Perhaps I have that idea only now that I'm awake. Who's to say that wasn't Emma? I may have abandoned my own dog. And if it was only another dog that resembled mine, why couldn't I have rescued her? I find no comfort at all in the knowledge that I made her up. She lingers, abandoned, in my mind.

Occasionally, I awaken in the middle of the night and watch Emma sleep the same way I've heard that new mothers watch infants in their cribs, waiting for each new breath. Emma is fine. I sleep on the right side of my double bed, Emma beside me, the rest of the bed available and empty. Is this the way widows sleep? I wonder. Do they sleep cramped along one side of their beds, or do they languish in the middle wrapped in blankets they don't have to share? I'm saving room not for someone who is missing, but for someone I have yet to meet. I want a nightwatchman for my dreams during the hours when Emma is off duty. He will need no uniform. I will curl up against him the same way Emma curls up against me. Unlike Emma, he will be able to talk. He will whisper to me that I'm all right.

Until he arrives, I face the same nightly test: Can I save my own dog? I have to be so careful, so clever. First I have to determine who Emma is in the dream—the little white dog that resembles her, or some other dog, or cat, or child. All of them could be Emma in disguise. I do not understand the source of this extra burden. I feed Emma, walk her, groom her, play fetch with her. I love her beyond measure. Why should I have to save her while she sleeps beside me, safe? I wake up exhausted by my efforts, wretched from an inevitable sense of failure.

The streets of New York are dangerous, the ladies on West End Avenue keep warning me. Years ago, the city was a different place. People used to live in real apartments. Now they live in closets stacked on top of each other like dishes. There are no more neighbors, just strangers who live next door. Years ago, when there was such a thing as a neighborhood, people looked out for each other on the street. Now you can get mugged in broad daylight and nobody sees. If you get run over by a taxi or a bicycle, who cares? What kind of city is this, where pedestrians can't cross the street?

I'm acquainted with many of my neighbors on my street and on the neighboring blocks, especially the dog owners. Most of the time I feel safe on the street and in the park. Nevertheless, the city I don't live in—the one inhabited by the old women on West End Avenue—is the city of my dreams. Dreamed city streets are impossible to cross. They are dark and narrow as alleys and overrun with strays; wide as boulevards, so wide I can't see all the way to the other side; pitted and craggy as ravines; water-filled, overflowing—all of them heavily trafficked and with curves I can't see around, all of them testing me.

Owning a dog is a responsibility, a privilege, my father used to say. Lucky's three dishes—for food, milk, and water—were lined up near the radiator in the kitchen. My mother kept a kosher kitchen. Although the dog ate canned, non-kosher dog food, his meat and dairy dishes were always separate.

"Lucky needs water," my father howled. "Doesn't anybody ever notice that his dish is empty? What do you mean you didn't notice? What are you, blind? Why do you think you have eyes in your head?" Lucky, the traitor, had greeted my father at the back door with a forlorn glance at his dry dish. "I know, I know, I'm the only one who gives you water." The dog drank, leaving a trail of water on the pink marbled linoleum as he walked away from the dish. "If I've told you once, I've told you a thousand times, the dog has to have water."

"Enough, already," my mother said. "They heard you."

"They heard me, you say. They hear me but they never remember."

"The dog was fast asleep in the living room until he heard your car in the driveway and then he ran in here to stare at his dish. He's a faker."

"He's a faker? Does a faker drink like that? How many times do I have to tell you that a dog has to have water?"

"So he'll be a little thirsty. He'll wait for you to get home. What's the big deal?"

"What's the big deal? No one around here gives a damn about anything, that's the big deal."

My father was the one who gave Lucky water, my father was the one who taught Lucky to dance. Standing on his hind legs, Lucky was the height of my father's chest. My father used to sing "The Anniversary Waltz," his voice raspy and high and totally off-key: "*Oh, how we danced on the night that we met* . . .," then sing the melody with no words, counting time for the dog, "*one*-two-three, *one*-two-three," as they waltzed.

My mother has parked our red and white 1953 Chevy along the shoulder of a highway. She is staring at me, waiting for some signal, and when I give her none, she puts the car into gear. Even though I know (and my mother agrees) that I have done the sensible thing, I shout, "No, wait!" and open the car door to call Emma. When she doesn't appear, I go looking for her. She must be very near. "Where are you?" I shout, as if she might answer.

Still no dog. My mother taps on the window to hurry me along. At last I see Emma out on the grassy island that divides the four lanes of traffic. "There she is," I whisper aloud to no one. I call her name. Forgive me, I almost say. Emma glances up at me, alert to my call but not yet ready to come back. Her expression tells me there is nothing to forgive. I am certain she had no idea I intended to abandon her on that unfamiliar road.

I call again, louder, trying not to sound too urgent. She pricks up her ears and slowly heads toward me, nose to the ground. Cars whiz by. She begins to cross the highway just as I notice something in the distance—a speck, really—that I refuse to recognize because I know the moment I do, it will turn into a real car. I keep my eyes on Emma. But engine noise turns it into a car even though I didn't look at it—not even a glance. I swear to you, Emma, I didn't turn it into a car.

It's speeding down the left lane, the lane closest to her. Should I tell her to stay or come? "Stay!" I scream, as the car swerves into the empty right lane. Emma, almost close enough for me to reach now, only a few feet beyond my grasp, less than one lane away. "Come!" When she takes a few more steps toward me, I scoop her up into my arms and, holding her close, vow that I will always keep her safe.

When I awaken, Emma is watching me. Why didn't I go get her? I know how to cross a highway. I know how to gauge the speed of oncoming cars. I stroke her and try to find the missing key to the dream—the reason I abandoned her in the first place. But I seem to have abandoned the part of the dream that could tell me.

"I will never leave you," I tell her, as if she knew even my dreams.

I ask my mother if she knows why men bark. She says what do you mean, men bark? On the street, I tell her. Men pass me on the street and they bark at Emma. Sometimes, they lean out of open car windows and bark at her. Some of them do it in the park, although more often in Central Park, not Riverside. My mother was born and raised in Manhattan and perhaps she can answer that question, too: Why are men more likely to bark in Central Park? Do they bark in Battery Park? In other boroughs? What about Brooklyn? Do they bark in Prospect Park?

My mother says she didn't have a dog when she was young and lived in Manhattan. "Don't women bark?" she asks.

"Never." I am reluctant to tell her that these sorts of riddles—why men bark and women do not—seem symbolic to me, that I feel if only I could penetrate these secrets I could unlock the mystery of relationships between the sexes. "Baloney," she would say.

I examine my conscience and my sense of humor. I suspect that men bark at Emma to be funny—if they're in a group, they giggle as if they were sharing an off-color joke—but they don't seem funny to me. Are they speaking in code? I keep expecting them to smile at me or at the dog. Do I expect too much? Old women on West End Avenue who do not bark tell me their life stories. Young, barking men tell me nothing. I am somewhere between them, no longer young, not yet old, too mature to bark, too immature to have a story to tell.

I'm walking with my mother near my parents' house in the suburbs. My mother thinks we've left Emma home. She must

have forgotten how she tucked the dog inside her coat. I lift
Emma out of the coat like a rabbit from a hat.

I'm holding Emma's leash as she pulls me along like a
seeing-eye dog. She's going too fast for me; I'm afraid I will
fall. Maybe I should drop the leash. I sense that I'm dreaming
and tell myself to wake up. *Drop the leash.* But Emma, powerful as a horse, is still dragging me and I let myself be dragged,
inexorably, toward the sea. She pulls me down a very small
wooden staircase and out onto the beach. The ocean is bottle-
green, rough, and thick with seaweed. I can't swim. I expect
her to go toward the water, but she veers away and pulls me
back behind the stairs, toward the dunes. In a few strides, the
sand is deep, as deep as the ocean. With the next step I will
fall in. She is still dragging me deeper into the dunes. I raise
my hands over my head and in a moment of determination
and self-possession dive headlong into the sand.

Emma is scampering around my parents' front yard, happy
to be outside, exploring unfamiliar suburban smells.

"Emma, come!" I call. She is too close to the road. She
ignores me and runs straight across it.

My father, standing at the front door, watches as Emma
disobeys. He comes outside yelling, complaining to me that
she's a bad dog, that she doesn't know how to listen, that her
disobedience is my fault because if she did that to him once,
she'd never do it again.

He doesn't mean half of what he says, I know, but I want
to scream at him anyway, What are you going to do? Beat her
up? Kick her? You want to beat up my ten-pound dog? Instead,
I say nothing at all and walk away to get her.

"You say she listens. You call that listening?" he yells.

No, I don't call that listening. I call that being stone deaf,
the way I am to you.

"You're a bad dog," he yells when I finally catch her.

I could wring your neck. Emma tries to defuse my anger by frantically wagging her tail. "I do not need you to make me look like a fool in front of him." I carry her home. When I'm close enough for my father to hear me, I say, "Now we're both in the doghouse," hoping I'll make him laugh.

He doesn't laugh. Emma is oblivious to his disapproval and jumps up against his knees, hoping for a treat. He is watching television. She keeps trying to get his attention.

"Get away from me," he yells. "You get down." He dismisses her with a wave of his hand. "You don't listen. When someone calls you, you don't run into the street." He's not kidding around, the tone of his voice incongruous with my tail-wagging, jumping-jack dog.

"Come here, sweetheart," my mother calls. Emma gives up on my father and springs onto the couch, landing in my mother's lap. "You're a good girl, aren't you?" Whenever my mother stops petting her, Emma nudges her hand with her nose.

"Just ignore him," my mother says to me as soon as we're alone.

"I'm trying."

"You know he likes Emma."

"I know."

I'm walking along Amsterdam Avenue near 72nd Street when a man appears from nowhere and lunges at me to stab me with a knife, but I grab Emma and hold her in front of my body like a pillow to block the knife and it cuts through her, killing her instead of me. I am saved; nevertheless, I collapse on the sidewalk, Emma's blood drenching me, the weight of her body against me, cutting off my breath. Tell me I didn't kill her. Tell me I didn't let her die. Tell me that in a moment of terror and selfishness I didn't sacrifice this creature I love.

My sorrow rouses me from sleep, heaves me back onto land from suffocating swells of deep water. I wake up exhausted, brokenhearted, with Emma right there, as always, dream-free and in perfect health, inches away.

My father on the floor again, trying to teach Emma to roll over. She almost has it. She lies down and my father scoops her up and over, an easy movement for my porky little dog. Finally, she does it on her own. He rewards her with praise and cheese. She repeats the trick again and again. But she is so excited that she gets confused; instead of rolling over, she stands and spins around three hundred and sixty degrees, making him laugh.

"Did I say turn around?" he asks her gently, then answers for her, "No, I said *roll over*. Roll over."

Emma spins. My father, laughing, wants to know where I got such a stupid dog. Of all the dogs I could have picked, how did I manage to pick *this* one?

Lucky didn't know how to roll over, I could tell him.

As I walk past Drew's building, the lady with the Maltese emerges from the front door and greets me as if she were expecting me. Does she live here? I don't know her name, not even the name of her dog.

"What does it mean," she asks, "when a person dreams about dogs?"

Who places this woman in my path? "I have no idea."

"I dreamt that my Sasha was hurt, very badly hurt. He was dying, I knew it, and so I brought him to the hospital for dogs—you know which one I mean?—and when I got there they would not let me in. They said this was a hospital for people and not for dogs. Then they said I was mistaken and Sasha was not a dog and so they took care of him, but he looked the same as always to me."

The lady has my dreams; the Animal Medical Center, where I have never been, recurs in mine, too. What does it mean that a middle-aged Russian woman has my dreams?

"So do you think this is a good dream or a bad dream?"

I don't answer, but she stays right by my side as we cross Riverside Drive and enter the park. I tell Emma to stay and unfasten her leash. "Free dog!" I say, with a wave of my hand. Emma scoots off. I want to follow her, but I'm trapped by the woman with my dreams who never lets her dog off his leash.

"Do you think this means something good will happen or something bad?"

"I don't believe dreams tell us about the future. Sometimes I think they're trying to tell us about the past."

She doesn't seem to be listening. "I have dreamed of many dogs. I know this is good, to dream of many, many dogs." She nods and smacks her lips to emphasize her certainty.

This time, I agree with her. To dream of many, many dogs seems like a blessing to me.

Five

J'M taking Drew out to dinner tonight to celebrate the completion of his new record—at least I think I am. Unfortunately, he said, he had to accept my invitation with this one caveat: he might get stuck in the studio. I said that hot young rock stars aren't supposed to use big words like *caveat. Aspiring* hot young rock stars, he corrected me. He's been teaching himself vocabulary from the *Reader's Digest* for years. Are you telling the truth? I asked. Not exactly, he answered. He said he took three years of high school Latin and the only Latin he knew was *e pluribus unum*. Did you really study Latin? I asked him. Yes, he did. What kind of rock star are you? The Jewish kind. The Jewish kind would know Hebrew, not Latin, I said. He asked me if all editors thought in terms of stereotypes. What a scary thought, I said. I asked him what he would be doing in the studio. Working with the producer on the final mix. Then he'd be playing it for the two assholes who pretend to run his record company. They run it about as well as Rover would.

Now you sound like an aspiring rock star, I said.

I called him as soon as I got home from work, even before I said hello to Emma, who was waiting to greet me, as always, on my bed. No answer. I checked out his apartment on my way to the park. No Drew. Now that I'm on my way home, he's strolling toward me with a woman I don't recognize, his arm around her shoulders. Rover, as always, is ahead and unleashed.

"Ann, this is Randy. Randy, this is Ann."

Well named, I think. "Hi."

"Hi."

Drew releases his hold on Randy, but she slips her arm around his waist. "I just tried to call you . . . I'm going to have to pass on that dinner tonight."

"No kidding," I murmur. Drew is incapable of sarcasm and oblivious to mine.

"Do I get a rain check?"

"Do you see any rain?"

He crouches down to pet Emma and tells her to have a good evening. "You, too," he says, glancing up at me, his green eyes as irresistible and conniving as Emma's. A line from one of his songs: *Can't you see the love in my eyes? You think I'm telling you lies, but I'm so sincere. . . .* "And I'm sorry about dinner."

I go to bed early, wake up too early, but when I get to the park, Drew is already there. He's never awake before noon, never in the park until early afternoon. Is he looking for me? I pretend I don't see him. On my way to the lower half of the park, I meet a couple walking a pair of Yorkshire terriers. While the male stops to play with Emma, the impatient husband walks on ahead with Ginger, the female. As usual, I know the dogs' names, but not the owners'. Bobby and Ginger are littermates.

"Rob, be careful of big dogs," the woman yells.

"Did you name your dog after your husband?" I know I shouldn't ask strangers personal questions, but in this case I can't resist.

"It was my mother's idea," she says, smiling. "Because I'm

barren. They're both named after us: Rober, Jr., and Little
Virginia. But we call them Bobby and Ginger."

I am silenced by the word *barren*, panoramic vistas of snow
and sand sweeping through my mind.

"We can't have children of our own," she explains.

"Dogs are wonderful company," I say, stupidly, unable to
think of anything more appropriate. And what will you do
when they die? I want to ask her. Get another brother/sister
pair and give them the same names?

"Look, Bobby!" she says. "Look at Daddy and all those
bunnies!"

Her husband is surrounded by citified squirrels, who pan-
handle for peanuts without fear. I glance at Virginia to make
sure I heard her correctly. She releases Bobby and points toward her husband. "Do you see all those bunnies?"

"Emma, come." I attach the leash to her collar. She doesn't
understand why it's not fair to chase squirrels while they're
being fed, and strains in their direction. "Heel," I command
her, leading her away from the babydog-talking woman and
her namesake dogs.

Rover appears from nowhere, scattering the bunnies. "Your
dog should be on a leash," Virginia yells at Drew, who doesn't
pay any attention. I release Emma so she can play with Rover,
but I keep walking and don't stop or turn around when I hear
Drew's voice say, "So when do I get to use my rain check?"
I want to tell him about the bunnies.

He catches up to me and walks by my side. He's silent; I
talk to Emma and Rover and greet other dogwalkers. We reach
the 79th Street Boat Basin and circle the baseball field without
having exchanged a word. Emma takes off across the field.
"Where are you going?" I ask her, then see her answer: a
miniature black poodle with a red bow on each ear. The
poodle's owner must be one of the boat owners, I decide—
not a brilliant observation on my part, since he's wearing a

yachting cap. The poodle jumps onto Emma's back. "Hey, Pep!" the owner calls, "Romance her a little." From a distance, Emma thought she was interested in the poodle, but now she communicates her lack of attraction by sitting down. "Peppy, do you call that romance?" The dog won't quit. The boat owner rescues Emma by picking up his dog. "Pepper, is this what you call romance?"

I'm waiting for the dog's response when Drew says, "Guess you're mad at me."

"Evidently." I call Emma, who gallops back to my side.

Drew apologizes and explains that he always finds it awkward when he's with one woman he likes and runs into another. I am not sympathetic and do not accept the apology. I'm tempted to point out that since my park schedule is very routine, and since he obviously knows me well enough to find me here this morning, he must have known he'd see me yesterday evening, when he was out with what's-her-name instead of me.

He says he hopes he didn't hurt my feelings, but he thought we had *tentative* plans. He's very sorry, especially since I was going to take him out to celebrate his album, but I shouldn't make mountains out of molehills. He says Randy is the piano player in his band.

I tell him I'm not interested.

"We're old friends," he says.

You're not old enough to have an old friend, I think.

"She's a terrific musician."

I'm not listening.

"She's been helping me finish up the record."

I don't care.

"I've told you I love different people at different times."

"I know. When you're not near the girl you love, you love the girl you're near."

"Exactly." Drew kisses me and I feel manipulated and wanted. "I still want you to seduce me," he says.

It's clear to me who's seducing whom. "You'll have to wait until I like you again." Drew looks up with that snake-oil, altar-boy smile. Damn him, I think.

Drew is an aberration, a creature almost as cute as Emma. Wherever I go, the dog trots along at my heel and looks up at my face with adoration. Passersby notice her and smile; couples look at each other and say "cute"—I can read their lips even when I can't hear the word. Then they smile at me, an afterthought, just to be polite. Or maybe they're smiling because they think I'm the kind of person who deserves to own an adorable dog. Does Emma's charm rub off on me? Does Drew's?

The New York City Parks Department has started its semi-annual crackdown on off-leash dogs. Not only must all dogs be leashed, they must be properly leashed: no six-foot leads, no letting leashes drag along the ground, the way Buck's owner does. Violators of the law are subject to fifty-dollar fines. Dog-walkers have two choices: to try to explain to their dogs that stick-chasing is now illegal, or to throw the stick anyway and risk being hounded by park police. Many of us have developed an unofficial early-warning system to communicate information about the movements of Parks Department vehicles— when they were last sighted, where they seem to be heading next. When we're not close enough to shout, we signal each other with a wave of a leash.

If we are caught, we lie. We use pseudonyms and phony addresses. When asked, we spell our false names and report exactly where our nonexistent apartments are located. Just in case we are asked our dogs' ASPCA numbers, we have made up fake ones with the proper number of digits and are ready to rattle them off. They never double-check anything. Dog owners rarely carry identification to the park, and although many of the dogs are wearing ASPCA tags or their own ID, the park rangers never get close enough to read them. Apparently, touching any dog is off-limits, even a fluffy little dog like mine. Nevertheless, I worry that one of them will try to inspect her tag. I will tell him that all dogs bite—even Emma. I will tell him that you can't tell a dog by its cover.

No dog owner I've met has ever actually paid a fine. A few of them who have difficulty lying were ticketed but refused to pay. In the beginning, like many new owners, I didn't want to lie. I thought I could explain that dogs enjoy chasing squirrels; that my playing fetch with Emma was not hazardous to non-dog-owners, other dogs, other owners, or to society at large. I thought I could explain how much I enjoyed playing with my dog.

But they weren't willing to negotiate. The law was the law. *All* dogs—got it, lady?—*all* dogs must be leashed. Enforcement is not open to interpretation. Therefore, a roaming Doberman pinscher is as unlawful as my miserable bichon frise, five feet away from me, knee-deep in unmowed grass, grazing in the pouring rain. Ordinarily, Emma would never tolerate the rain. Her stomach is upset; I knew that as soon as we hit the street, when instead of shivering under the awning in front of my building waiting for me to pick her up (her usual rainy-day behavior), she moved forward like a dog on a mission. Her instinct is to eat grass, which is probably a bad idea, since the park grass is likely to carry parasites that will do her more harm than good. Perhaps I should bring her home and give her something medicinal. I'm too busy wavering between my inclination and Emma's to notice the approach of a three-wheeled vehicle, or its green-leaf insignia, or the ranger in a green uniform, pencil and ticket book in hand, who is walking toward me. He says my dog should be on a leash. It's raining, I say. He says, rain or shine, dogs have to be leashed. "My dog has an upset stomach."

"You shouldn't let him eat grass."

All I need, two crimes: allowing a sick dog to eat grass and a dangerous dog to run free.

"Do you see that this dog is no more than six feet from me?"

"I see that your dog is not properly leashed."

"Do you see that it's raining?" You would think that a park ranger—unlike a rock star—had been trained to recognize rain.

"Could I have your name, miss?"

"Do you see that she's about to throw up?"

"I'm not going to argue with you, miss."

"I didn't want to get my sneakers soaking wet. If the Parks Department would cut the grass once in a while, it wouldn't be a foot deep."

"Is your dog wearing an ASPCA tag?"

"Do you understand English?"

He speaks only bureaucratese. I give him my phony name and address and Emma's phony ASPCA identification number. He probably knows I'm lying but he doesn't care, since he has fulfilled his duty. Emma retches and throws up and jumps up against my legs. I carry her home under my umbrella.

Finding Drew in the park is getting to be a snap; there he is with another attractive woman. I wonder if I've been introduced to this one. I wave and keep going. Ahead, an old woman is talking to herself in a language I don't recognize and gesticulating toward a tree, her arms cutting wide, uneven arcs. Only when she stops whining do I figure out the source of her distress: far above our heads, a gray-striped kitten is clinging to the trunk of the tree. Its mews turn into squawks. A small crowd gathers. A teenaged girl is holding a small white dog in her arms that from a distance looks like Emma. I approach her to meet the dog, but she backs off a step or two. When the white ball of fur uncurls in her arms, its movement as fluid as a cat's, I realize it *is* a cat, its claws pricking her bare arm, leaving red welts. She doesn't seem to notice. Her skin will never be tough enough to support her own cat the way that tree trunk supports its kitten. When she sees that Emma won't bother the cat, she leans toward me and asks, "Do cats ever fall out of trees?"

"Never." *Rarely*, I could have said. *Almost never.* Having lied to her, I am forced to walk away.

If this were a small town, the fire department would come and rescue the cat. But this is New York City, and no one expects a hook and ladder.

Rover appears and socializes among the crowd. I grab his collar and ask him to be quiet. He struggles to escape. I'm showing off: I can control this dog—I know his owner; then think, I know this dog—I can't control his owner. The kitten is terrified and keeps moving higher, then scrambles out onto a much smaller branch. The woman bows her head; for a moment, I think she might be praying: Lord, spare your innocent creature and return it to me.

I sense Drew behind me. Rover bucks free of my grasp and jumps up against his chest. "Look," I say, pointing upward. He leaves his girlfriend—not really his girlfriend, he would probably say, just one of his girl friends—and circles the tree, then grabs the lowest branch, swings himself up, and begins to climb. The kitten crawls even higher and out of reach. He calls to it, his voice so quiet I can barely hear him. "Come on, honey. I'll help you get down." The cat won't budge. "Have a little faith. I wouldn't lie to you." The cat moves higher, out onto a skinnier limb. For a change Drew's charm isn't working. "Come on, baby," he croons. It's all a matter of trust, I think. Someone appears with an open can of tuna fish for a bribe. How much hunger will overcome fear? How much love? I decide not to stay around for the climax since, as far as I'm concerned, no happy ending is possible. Either the kitten will be forsaken, or Drew will rescue it and leap like a hero into his girlfriend's open arms. I leave them stranded in the tree. On my way home, in spite of the traffic noise, I can still hear the drama, part of a spontaneous, improvised program of free opera in the park: the old woman's lament, the rock star's promises, and the kitten's screech. The tiger-striped kitten is running the show. Should it let itself be captured, or act like a real tiger and survive on its own?

I keep wondering if I'll ever get to see Drew alone. There he is—in his usual place, toward the back of the field, close to the highway. I wave to him and he waves back. Emma and I are circling the basketball courts and the children's playground. When we complete the circle, we head in Drew's direction. But someone has taken his place; a stranger is sitting cross-legged on the grass beside Rover. Or is that Drew? Of course that's not Drew. Whoever it is, Rover jumps into his lap. I hesitate, move forward a step or two, then stop.

"What's wrong?" he yells.

His dog, his voice. I approach slowly. He's shorn off almost all his hair. He reminds me of the hairless kittens that recur in my dreams. "Nothing," I yell back. He smiles a Drew-like smile and tosses a stick for Rover. Emma takes off after him. There have been other dreams: dogs with no fur—one covered with a tough green hide the texture of cauliflower, another spiny as a cactus. It was only a puppy. I picked it up carefully and held it by threading my fingers among the spines.

"How do you like it?" Drew calls.

I *hate* it! I want to yell. If a frog can turn into a prince, a prince can also turn into a frog. Hardly a profound understanding, but one I tend to forget. I like to pretend that transformation isn't a two-way street. I'm still walking toward the man who used to be Drew, but my impulse is to shriek and run away.

"Someone once told me he cut off all his collie's hair for the summer," I say. "The dog freaked out. He couldn't get it out from under the bed." I'm astonished how easy it is for me to behave myself and talk to him politely. How well trained I am! Watch me sit and heel and shake hands.

"I kind of like it," he says.

What I don't comprehend is how Drew could do this to himself. His owner didn't cut off his hair. Drew may call it a summer haircut, but to me it's an act of self-mutilation. "Beauty is in the eye of the beholder," I say.

"Don't worry—my hair grows fast. Have a seat."

I sit beside him and hold Emma on my lap. "I just need a little time to get used to it. It's fine, Drew, really." *Drew.* Saying his name seems to help. Ann, this is Drew. Say "how do." No, actually we've already met.

I wonder what all his women friends think, whether they've seen him yet. He hasn't changed, has he? Good old Drew, young Drew, my talisman, my lucky charm. When I was little, I carried a rabbit's foot in my pocket. Did I know it was a rabbit's real paw? Emma's paws, no bigger than a white rabbit's, could be sold in a dimestore and end up in children's pockets. "My pet," I whisper, touching all four paws.

"Imagine me with no hair," I say to Drew. He flattens my hair against the top of my head and gathers up the curls from around my neck. Get your hands off me, you freak. I don't even know you. I pull away from his touch. What's wrong with me? I could fake it easily enough when we were just talking. Talk to him, Ann. Say something before he figures out that you're the one who's changed. "Or imagine Emma," I say. He smooths down her long, fluffy hair. "You should see her when I give her a bath: she's no more than a white rat without all that hair."

Soaking wet in my kitchen sink, Emma does resemble a bug-eyed, pink-skinned, long-tailed white rat. I can see that.

But I don't care. I sing "You Are My Sunshine" to her. She moans—because of the bath, I assume, although I'm sure my singing doesn't help. I lift her out of the sink and wrap her in a towel and tell her she's the prettiest dog I have.

After a while, other dogwalkers appear. A trio of sled dogs— a husky, Samoyed, and malamute—joins our group. We speculate about how they would look with no hair. I'm still sitting beside Drew. I remember, at the Yellow Rose, when he took a bow, how his shaggy hair gleamed in the spotlight. When he was playing the guitar, his hair would spin across blue, red, and gold shafts of light. "He's a Mexican hairless," one of the dog owners says. Drew laughs and turns away from me. I notice a patch of pale scalp, like a fallow field, at the center of his head. A grown man with the head of a baby, a Mr. Potato Head.

When my sister and I used to play Mr. Potato Head, we made my mother get the potatoes from the brown paper sack that she kept on the cellar stairs. The potatoes were the thick-skinned kind, still covered with dirt. It was dark on the stairway and you couldn't see inside the bag. If you reached your hand deep inside, you could grab a potato with eyes.

"They're only eyes," my mother used to say. "Because the potatoes are old. They won't hurt you."

Eyes? Is that what she said? A potato had no business having eyes. Whitish nubs that felt cool and white against your fingertips. My mother cut them off with a knife and we jabbed in real eyes—bright blue plastic bug-eyes rimmed in black— and toothy red grins.

When I stand up to go home, Drew asks me whether I'll still talk to him and I promise I will, but I can't look at his face.

An old woman with four pretty, impeccably groomed toy poodles—white, apricot, chocolate, and black—says hello to

Emma and tells her how gorgeous she is. "This is a bichon frise, is it not?" she asks me, pronouncing Emma's breed in perfect French. She asks me Emma's name and guesses correctly that I named her after Madame Bovary. *"Que tu es ravissante, n'est-ce pas?"* she asks Emma, who is from New Jersey, not France, and doesn't answer. Compared with her poodles, Emma is a mess, badly in need of a bath and a haircut. But in this lady's eyes, Emma is stunning enough to be a movie star, not a trashy, modern movie star who can do nothing but disrobe in front of a camera, but glamorous, the way actresses used to be before I was born, real artists: Marlene Dietrich, Greta Garbo—no, she is a young Ingrid Bergman—don't I see the resemblance? Her eyes, especially, are a beautiful woman's eyes.

Emma has a dog's eyes, I think, the only kind a dog can see through. "I bought her for her eyes," I say, somewhat of an exaggeration, but when Dorothy showed me Emma's mother I was impressed by the sweetness and intelligence I saw in her beautiful eyes, which Emma inherited. I walk with this woman so that, for the moment, Emma can be a queen instead of the cutest dog in the whole world, my crowning compliment. The woman asks me who my veterinarian is; my instinct, the result of too many walks in the park with too many strangers eager to tell me what I don't want to know, is to lie: "I don't really have one," I say. She is a compendium of every disastrous trip to a vet during the past twenty years: dogs who died of improperly administered anesthetic, insufficient testing, misinterpretation of test results, outright negligence or incompetence. One of her own dogs, a little boy, died from being given too much worming medicine for his size (he was no bigger than Emma), and the shock of it, seeing him die like that, so unexpectedly, almost killed her, too, right there in the vet's office. Imagine the shock, she keeps saying, but I listen and do not imagine it.

"This boy," she says, pointing downward, "my beautiful black one, is not quite as special, although you can see that he, too, is gorgeous. But he is not reliable. My vet advised me to put him to sleep because he cannot be trusted. When he was a puppy, I startled him when he was sleeping and he ripped flesh from my breast. You can imagine the pain. I almost fainted. It was horrible, but I would not put him to sleep for that, because it was not his fault that I startled him. But that is the worst thing a dog can do, I think, to rip flesh from a woman's breast."

Spring turns to summer and in the evening the park no longer belongs exclusively to runners and dogwalkers. Crowds of costumed supernumeraries converge on the park and mill about. With so many extras, last season's stars—The Man Who Catches Birds and The Lady Who Kisses Trees—have vanished. Park rangers wearing Smokey the Bear hats tool around in their miniature green trucks. Uniformed baseball players armed with bats carry coolers of cold beer. Roller skaters in their knee and elbow pads and bicycle riders wearing helmets and elf-shoes seem innocent enough, but I know they are dangerous to Emma. I keep her leashed. Other dogs run free. I worry about the small ones. Are their owners less cautious or more confident? Am I overprotective? I don't care. Emma trots along, safely, at my heel. When I stand still because of the heat, disciplined adults and undisciplined children race past me, creating a breeze.

Only in the early morning hours can the dogwalkers and runners regain center stage. But even then we're not alone. Around us, at the fringes of the park, people with no place to go are sleeping in rags or rugs or rolled up in blankets. They construct cardboard houses that disintegrate in the rain. Some of them have lost only their homes; most of them have also lost their minds. A towering black woman clothed in nothing

111

but a filthy blanket screams at me about Jesus' love and the Devil who is the howling beast called Dog, who walks around on all fours shitting and pissing and fucking like Dog. She squeals and bellows, her voice operatic in its size and range. You Devil-kissing white cunt, she screams, crossing herself, cursing me and the devil I pick up and carry in my arms.

Drew's hair is beginning to fill in, like newly seeded grass. I hope it does better than the grass they keep planting at the 72nd Street entrance to the park, which never lasts a whole season. I haven't seen him in almost two months. He's grown a beard and mustache. He kisses me a friendly hello on the mouth, his beard soft and warm as Emma's fur.

"This is my rabbinical look."

"When I was a little girl, I wanted to marry a rabbi. I thought they were cultivated."

"Cultivated for what?"

"Good question."

"You never struck me as the rabbi-marrying type. Do you believe in God?"

"Not yet. I'm probably not the rock-star type, either, am I?"

He laughs. He seems flattered, and looks at me flirtatiously, flattering me. "At least you wouldn't have to believe in God. I think you should hang around down at Juilliard and find yourself a hot little classical trombone player."

My turn to laugh. "Why the trombone?"

"Why not?" He shrugs. "Getting it on with a trombonist may be just what you need."

"That's why I wanted to marry a rabbi," I say.

"Why?"

"Because he wouldn't use an expression like 'getting it on.' "

Rover steals a Frisbee from an unsuspecting little girl. Her mother and Clark (Gable, not Kent), their small black-and-white mutt, are park regulars. "Rover, drop it," Drew orders.

The dog ignores him. The little girl clings to her mother's skirt, pointing at the Frisbee, afraid to go get it.

"That's just Rover," the woman says. "Remember? He's gotten big, like you have. He used to be a puppy. That's his master, Drew. Remember Drew? He always looks different, so he's harder to remember. Sometimes he has long hair, sometimes short. Now he has a beard. Drew always looks different, but on the inside he stays the same. You can always tell who he is, though, because he's the one with Rover."

I watch Drew's smile as the woman teaches her daughter about the mysteries of constancy and change. Drew straddles Rover and extracts the Frisbee from his jaws. Then he wipes it clean on his jeans and kneels beside the little girl.

"Rover left teeth marks on it. You want to see?"

She examines the Frisbee and smiles back at him, taking her mother's hand. "Ma-ma," I hear her say as I walk away, the two syllables distinctly separate, reminding me of the artificial speech of a talking baby doll. Only when I call Emma to me do I realize what the little girl is saying: my dog's name, "Em-ma," spoken by her for the first time.

I seem to be able to find Drew whenever I want to now. Instead of asking Emma if she'd like to go to the park, I ask her if she'd like to see Rover. Drew is there when I expect him to be, absent when I don't care. But I have limited control. Once he's in the park, I have to find him. I expect him to be playing with Rover in his usual place—the field in the upper section of the park—but he and Rover are down below, sitting on one of the benches near the river on the far side of the track. I circle the track clockwise, hoping that if he and Rover move they will walk counterclockwise. Wrong again. Since all four of us are moving in the same direction, if I don't call out to him, I will never catch up. But I'm unwilling to claim that much public attention. I encourage Emma to run ahead and catch Rover. I am too old and too out of shape to run after Drew.

I still see him with other women. I assume they're all young and pretty, although I rarely look at them. Drew's hair has grown in and it's been bleached by the summer sun. His beard is full and neatly trimmed. When he's with a woman, he never stops to talk to me, but that is my fault, not his. He would be happy to introduce us. He would like me to meet all his friends.

When we're alone, he walks with his arm around me, tells me how much he loves talking to me, and says I can get what I want, just like he does. He has confidence and I don't. That's the only difference between us.

"The *only* difference?"

"Will you behave?"

He swears you can get what you want.

"That depends on how much you're willing to forgo," I tell him. "How low you're willing to let your standards drop."

I laugh, but he doesn't. I'm wrong, he says. I don't have enough confidence. I'm an attractive, intelligent woman. I can get what I want.

"I couldn't get you," I say.

"You didn't even want me when you had the chance. First you have to figure out what you really want."

"How do you do that?"

He shrugs. "How should I know? I'm just a kid."

We both laugh and he kisses my cheek. "All I'm saying is that if you know what you want, you can get it."

"You already said that."

Drew is a mythological creature—the head of a boy on the body of a man with the voice of a siren. He hands me hope like a plum, all-purpose, all-occasion hope, ready to serve. I hesitate, then decline. His feelings are hurt and he takes his arm from my shoulder and turns away. I apologize and he accepts the apology, but something has altered in the exchange. He wants me to see myself through his child-man eyes. I try. But when we use our critical judgment, we see nothing even remotely alike. Why can't he see the same way I do, so I can learn to see myself through his eyes? Because his critical faculties are impaired, I have no faith in him. He tries to persuade me that my standards are false. "There's no real difference between Stephen King and Henry James," he says. "They're both writers, aren't they? Haven't they both written lots of books?"

I want to believe what you say about me, Drew, but how can I believe you when you're capable of such puerile thoughts?

He won't give up. "Do you think Henry James could have written about a killer car any more easily than Stephen King could write about rich Americans hanging out in Europe?" When he notices that I'm not convinced (he may be shallow, but he's perceptive), he clarifies his point: "All I'm saying is that Stephen King writes great Stephen King books and Henry James writes great Henry James books."

"Yes. That is all you're saying."

Irony isn't his strong suit. Please grow up, Drew. Be smart for me. Be right for me. Don't clunk off your pedestal, don't trip onstage. Tell only the truth for me.

A heat wave hits the city. A brown-out is declared: excessive use of air conditioners is to be avoided. People stream out of town on weekends. Those with money escape to Fire Island, the Hamptons, the Jersey shore. Teenagers take early morning subways to buses to beaches to buses to subways. Everyone else lives in the parks. Riverside Park fills with sunbathers, dedicated and methodical as monks. I try to spend more time there, but Emma hates the heat. I should leave her home, where she is happier, but I feel unwelcome in the park without her. "Dogs make great companions," I tell her, attaching her leash. She thinks companionship has its limits.

I'm in search of shade when I notice Rover chasing a Doberman pinscher around a blanket, where Drew appears to be sleeping between a woman and a guitar. She's wearing a black, one-piece bathing suit; he's in shorts but no shirt. He rolls over on top of her.

Emma stops dead at the water fountain, waiting for me to lift her up to give her a drink. I'm holding her up to the spigot when Drew shows up beside me. The two big dogs stand on their hind legs and drink from opposite sides of the fountain. Emma is intimidated and wants to get down. I run the water for Rover and his new friend.

"This is Rita," Drew says, introducing the Doberman.

I give the dog a pat and start to walk away.

"No, wait . . ." He rests his hand on my hip and tells me how good I look. "I have a terrible crush on that young lady," he says, glancing over at his blanket. "I'd like you to meet her."

I refuse the invitation.

"I think you'd like her."

"I don't even like her dog."

Drew disappears. I lose my power to conjure him up. *Now*, I think. He'll be in the park *now*. But when I get there, he's not. I ask some of the park people if they've seen Rover's owner. Which dog? they ask. Which one is Rover? I keep looking in Drew's window when I pass his apartment, but he's never home. There are signs that someone's been there—the bamboo shades go up and down, the bedroom windows open and close.

He reappears in the park, playing Frisbee with Rover. The dog has learned how to catch it on the fly, but now he won't bring it back. After each toss, Drew crosses the field to retrieve it from Rover's mouth.

He's been around, he says, agreeing that it's odd we haven't run into each other in a while. He's glad to see me because he has some news. He plucks a blade of grass and chomps down on one end.

"I'm in love."

"Congratulations." As usual, he doesn't hear the sarcasm in my voice. "Who is she?"

"Her name is Rebecca. I met her in the park. She has a Doberman pinscher named Rita. She's very sweet, but a little young and maybe even a little spoiled."

"Rebecca or Rita?"

"Let's walk." We follow our usual route near the river. "When Rebecca and I first started seeing each other, I was afraid of Rita. I never knew a Doberman before. But when I began to accept the relationship, she and I got along fine."

"You and Rita or you and Rebecca?"

"It's time I made a decision, that's all," he says, ignoring me.

"What kind of decision?"

"Whether I'm ready to make a commitment."

"Isn't that a little premature?"

"Is it? I'm very much in love with her. What else do I have to know? Besides, it's silly to think there's only one right woman— or man." He winks at me. "It's a question of commitment. I feel about marriage the same way I feel about Rover—he wasn't there until my brother gave him to me and then he was. Suddenly, I had a dog."

I laugh at him, at his reflections on marriage, and at me, for my infatuation.

"I'm glad you're not mad at me."

"I'm not mad."

"And you believe me when I say I want us to stay friends?"

"I believe you."

"I still want you to listen to my songs, if you want to." My assent seems obvious in the silence. "And I want you to meet Rebecca. She and Rita are moving in."

That, too, seems inevitable.

The big question in the park is whether this is the worst

August in five years or a decade. I can never remember weather from one year to the next. As the extreme heat and humidity continue, my dogwalks become shorter and shorter, until Emma refuses to walk the three blocks to the park. In the evening, packs of old women stroll through the neighborhood, shaking their heads, whispering, complaining, stepping off the curb, then right back up, then down, then up; others cajole tottering, ancient men. A few of them are solitary—out for a stroll with their canes. They all dress in Florida colors: goldenrod, hot pink, chartreuse. They wear wide, spongy sandals. They dye their hair brownish or blondish. I feel self-conscious about the color of my hair, my public grayness, my obvious youth.

When Emma balks in the heat, old women stop to watch. If I yell when she fails to heel, or yank her leash, they tell me, as if I hadn't noticed, that it's terribly hot, the hottest August in five or ten or twenty years. I'm learning not to yell at Emma on the street, not to attract attention or word-of-mouth bad press. Have you seen that young woman? A pointed finger and a sad shake of the head—so cruel to her sweet dog.

I tug gently on the leash and ask Emma politely, even deferentially, if she could please cooperate and not make me look like a shrew. When I reach for her, she rolls over onto her back, her paws fanning the air. I pick her up and the old ladies smile. They are as delighted as Emma. But I'm holding an overheated, hairy dog in my already sticky arms—I feel like I'm wearing a sweater—on the hottest day of the year. I stroke Emma and whisper in her ear (the ladies must think I'm whispering endearments), "If I had wanted a sweater, I would have brought one." When the ladies are out of sight, I stand Emma on the sidewalk and casually mention if she doesn't walk the two blocks home, I'll find a new dog who will. She walks by my side, panting hard. I slow my pace to hers.

Drew introduces me to the woman he loves and her dog. "Rita and I have already met, remember?" He doesn't remember. Rita and Rover are both leashed. Rebecca is walking Rover, who pulls toward me and tries to jump up to greet me, but Rebecca corrects him sharply, "No!" Rebecca is as striking as I imagined—pale, translucent skin, stick-straight light brown hair that hangs almost to her waist, one bright blue eye and one dark brown. I used to know a malamute with the same color eyes.

We're all on our way to the park. "That's pretty," Drew says, touching my skirt. "Is it new?" I shake my head no. "I've missed seeing you and Emma around."

"We've been around," I say.

"I haven't been doing afternoon walks on the weekends because Rebecca has been taking them out earlier."

"You're a lucky boy."

We join the group of dogwalkers already gathered. Drew and Rebecca are planning to go to a puppet show, and they invite everyone to come along.

"What about you?" Drew asks.

"No, thanks."

"Do you have plans?"

"Just me and my laundry."

"Then come with us. We'll have fun."

"Thanks, anyway."

He grabs my elbow and pulls me a few yards away from the other dogwalkers. "You're acting like an eight-year-old."

"Bullshit."

"You are. You're acting like a little girl. I want you to come."

"I don't give a damn what you want. You're going with Rebecca. Why the hell do you need an entourage? Isn't one fan enough?"

I try to walk away, but he tightens his grip on my arm. "I

don't think you'd have a bad time, that's all. I really don't think you would."

"Take my word for it."

He shakes his head and whispers, "Jealousy is a stupid waste of time."

Jealousy, my mother always says, is the green-eyed monster who mocks the meat that it feeds upon. When we rejoin the others, Rebecca is teaching them how to make a honking noise by blowing through a blade of grass. You're cutting off your nose to spite your face, I think—another of my mother's expressions. Because I'm not going to a puppet show with him? No, because I didn't sleep with him.

All the other dogs are much bigger than Emma, and although she would play with them individually, the group overwhelms her and she stays right with me. A woman appears with an affenpinscher, an Emma-sized dog with a black, wiry coat and a distinctive, densely whiskered face. I recognize the breed from pictures in dog books, but this is the first one I've ever met. Emma is attracted and keeps jumping up against him, trying to get him to play, but he is staring up at his owner with a worried expression. Something about the shape of his legs reminds me of a black widow spider. He is without a doubt the homeliest small dog I have ever seen.

"What a cutie pie you have there," the woman says to me.

"Thanks. Yours is an affenpinscher, isn't it?" I ask, showing off. This woman is probably asked the breed of her dog more often than I am. "He's the first one I've ever met."

"They're not very common. Is yours a Maltese?"

"A bichon."

"I thought bichons were much larger."

"She's on the small side."

"Well, she's adorable." When the woman reaches down to pet Emma, her dog successfully bodychecks mine. "I hardly ever see dogs as cute as mine," his owner says, petting him instead.

Beauty is in the eye of the beholder, I do not say. I do not ask her if she has impaired vision. I do not ask her if she has forgotten her corrective lenses. I say nothing at all— not until I'm well out of earshot, on my way home, when I reassure Emma that she is the cutest dog in Riverside Park. I wish I could tell her about the transforming power of love.

I call Drew. Luckily, Rebecca doesn't answer the phone. Drew says everyone is meeting at the bus stop on 72nd Street and Broadway. He's glad I decided to stop being a stick-in-the-mud.

I sit beside Rebecca on the uptown bus. We are the only women in our little expedition. Drew is across the aisle between Rosy's owner, a wealthy stockbroker who chain-smokes and is afraid of very small dogs "because they're so easy to step on," and Grindel's owner, who is still in high school. I ask Rebecca how she and Drew met. Rita stole Rover's Frisbee. Rita— *unlike Rover,* she tells me—can catch a Frisbee on the fly *and* bring it back. At first, Rebecca had no idea who he was. When she found out he was Drew Gold—the heartthrob of thousands of English adolescents (she had spent a year studying zoology at Oxford), she was embarrassed. She should have recognized him right away, but she never associated that Drew Gold with this guy named Drew who played Frisbee with his dog in the park. For a while, she was afraid to tell her friends who he was. He wasn't exactly the kind of man she had envisioned herself with on those rare occasions when she even thought about a man. Her parents were divorced and she wasn't all that keen on men in general. Drew still thinks he's a kid, she says. He's got a lot of growing up to do. But she's glad he's a singer, because he'll be on tour for several months every year and, since they're living together, at least he won't always be underfoot.

I can't resist the puppet show, based on Flanders and Swann songs. In Act I, an armadillo falls in love with an armor-plated tank. The armadillo is ardent, but the tank isn't moved. Another unlikely pair, I think, glancing at Drew. In Act II, a lady warthog who has done everything in her power to disguise the fact that she is a warthog—makeup, perfume, pink bows in her hair, new blue satin gown, scarlet-tinted teeth—is shunned at the annual jungle ball. *"No one ever wants to court a warthog,"* she laments, *"though a warthog does her best."* Finally, an impeccably dressed gentleman warthog enters. He hates her dress, her makeup, her tinted teeth, but he asks her to dance anyway, singing, *"but won't you take the floor, because I'm absolutely sure, that you're a warthog, just a warthog, the sweetest little neatest little dearest and completest little warthog—underneath."*

We decide to get some ice cream and walk the twenty blocks home. Drew rests his hand on my shoulder while ordering his two-scoop cone with sprinkles. I wonder if Rebecca is absolutely certain of their relationship. I know I'm no threat. I don't know if she knows. Rebecca doesn't care for any ice cream. I order mine in a cup because, until I find a warthog of my own, I can't afford to drip chocolate down the front of my shirt.

Drew and Rebecca walk hand in hand. I dawdle, pretending to window-shop, then duck into the bookstore at 81st Street, open till midnight. When I emerge from the store, Drew and the others are nowhere in sight. On Broadway, everyone but me seems to be heading north. The heat that rises from the sidewalk, even at this hour, gets trapped in the heavy pedestrian traffic. I keep bumping into pockets of heat as if they were people. Excuse me, pardon me, I know I shouldn't be here. I turn on 79th Street and walk one block to West End Avenue. West End is quiet, as always. Doormen wearing old band uniforms are perched on stools outside their buildings. They fan themselves with the Chinese take-out menus that are constantly being delivered to every building on the Upper West

Side. I wish Emma were here. She would give me a reason to be out on the street.

The question is, by going out with Drew and Rebecca tonight, did I spite or not spite my face? I avoid the mirrors in the lobby of my building and the foyer of my apartment. In the privacy of my bedroom, I touch my face with my fingertips as if I were blind. I seem all right. Emma keeps jumping up against my knees. "What are you hopping for?" I ask, my variation on Drew's question to me: What are you hoping for? How the hell should I know?

"Why are you still hopping?" I lift her into my arms and laugh and hold her close.

I'm visiting my parents in the suburbs. I've brought along my black-and-tan Doberman, a thin, young dog, not quite perfect, its skull a bit too narrow, its muzzle a trifle long. I'm sleeping and they're taking care of the dog. I wake up exhausted because I've slept too little or too much, I can't tell which. I go out to the back stoop with the dog. Two men I've never met are trying to guess its age. I wonder why they don't simply ask me, but apparently they don't think I know. I try to interrupt to offer my help. "Listen to me! Why won't you listen to me?" Finally, one of them declares that the dog is definitely five years old. I think he's a fool—not for guessing incorrectly, but for not asking me. "You don't know what you're talking about," I scream. The dog won't be five until October. He's my dog. I'm just visiting here and when I leave, the dog goes with me. Understand? He's *my* dog.

I'm in my own bed. I know I don't own a Doberman, but I do own a dog. I can't remember what kind. A mutt? No, not a mutt. I picture all sorts of breeds, but none of them seems right. Suddenly I realize that the dogs in my mind are too big. No wonder I can't find mine. I must be looking right over its head. I focus my attention closer to the floor and

Emma appears. That's my dog. I concentrate and picture her clearly for the first time. There she is. She's still asleep. Now that I've learned how to find her, I let myself wake up. Emma is curled at the foot of my bed. I apologize for forgetting her, even in my dreams.

I think: She'll be five years old in October.

$\mathcal{M}$ALIN and I agree that the chaos in his office has become an object of widespread ridicule and someone should do something about it. I nominate him. He says a job this big requires a team. I tell him to hire the Yankees.

"We're talking teamwork," he says. "We're a goddamn department. We are *co*-editors of Introductory Materials."

"You're the Editor. I'm the *Associate* Editor."

"Then I'm your boss."

"You're also the one who destroys your office and my files. All you have to remember is to put things back where you found them. It's not my fault if you're untrainable."

He slumps in his chair as if I had shot him and hangs his head in mock shame. "If you think this place is a mess, you should see my apartment."

"It can't be worse than mine."

"Can you be bribed? I have more stories."

From the reservoir of Malin's memory, his childhood stories flow toward me. They quench a thirst I never knew I had. I worry that someday I will leave him empty, dry-mouthed, with no more stories to tell. But no matter how many he tells me, the water keeps rising to its former level. "You always have more stories."

"You know we'll have a good time."

"I also know I won't get paid."

"Neither will I, if that's any consolation."

"It isn't."

"You're a hard-hearted woman."

"At least I can file."

"How can you turn me down in my hour of need?"

"I'm rejecting the work, Malin, not you."

"What time did you say I should meet you back here? How about eight o'clock sharp?"

"What do you mean 'meet you back here'? What's wrong with five o'clock sharp?"

"*You* have to go home and walk Emma. And I . . . ," he mumbles, "I have to meet someone for a drink."

"Then why don't we do it tomorrow night?"

"Because tomorrow is Friday, and Norman and Jerry and I are going fishing this weekend."

Malin has told me about all of his friends, but since he and I don't socialize outside of the office, I've never met any of them. I would like to know Norman, but I'm not eager to meet Jerry, who ran off with Malin's girlfriend Ellen while Malin and Ellen were living together. Malin defends him on the grounds that he was the seduced and not the seducer, but I think he should have demonstrated more self-restraint. "The boys are going fishing?"

"Don't give me any grief about fishing, Ann. Don't tell me you feel sorry for the poor goddamn fish. We sit around in a boat drinking beer all day and we're damn lucky if we catch anything."

"And where are you going tonight?"

"This is serious: I'm having a drink at the Algonquin with a beautiful, blonde-haired woman who happens to be about a foot and a half taller than I am. Actually, she's my third or fourth cousin. Why don't you go home and get Emma and walk her back here instead of taking her to the park? I would enjoy meeting Emma."

Without having met her, Malin is as familiar with Emma as I am with Cat and Bad Boy, his childhood horse and dog, whom I've met again and again in the stories he tells. "Let me get this straight: I'm supposed to go all the way home and come all the way back just so you can take a beautiful woman out for a drink, meet my dog, and have me organize your office for you?"

"I'll make it up to you, Ann. I promise."

"How do you plan to do that?"

"It's a surprise."

We discuss whether relations between relations thrice removed constitutes incest. I tell him to go see if he's even interested. If he is, we'll do a little research and find out.

Malin shows up half an hour early. I'm sitting on the corner of my desk, surrounded by stacks of files, manuscripts, galleys, blues, unbound books. Emma charges the door, barking at the whoosh of the elevator doors and the click of the key in the lock. I recognize Malin's step, as always, without looking up. He greets Emma at the door. "Well, hello there."

"Emma this is Malin—Malin this is Emma," I say. I've given up asking Emma to say "how do" in public. "How did it go?"

He perches on a nearby desk, pulls off his sports jacket, folds it over the back of a chair, unbuttons his collar and cuffs, rolls up his shirtsleeves, takes off his tie and rolls it into a ball, securing the end with a piece of tape.

"Do you know how good it feels to be walking down the street knowing you're on your way to see someone you're totally comfortable with? Someone you love talking to?"

The questions are clearly rhetorical. "Why are you ending your sentences with prepositions?"

"Propositions?" He opens the desk drawer, takes out a ruler, and uses it to bat his tie over my head.

"Something tells me you're not talking about your cousin."

"I didn't want to see that bimbo. Halfway there, I knew I was only meeting her so I could get back here and tell you about it. I practically ran back. I suppose you think I'm weird."

"You know I do. Besides . . ."

"Besides what?"

"Sometimes I wish I could be the gorgeous bimbo who gets to go to the Algonquin."

"No, you don't. You want to be exactly who you are and still go to the Algonquin."

"Is that an invitation?"

"No. But when we finish up here, why don't we go out for a drink?"

I point at Emma. He kneels on the floor on one knee. Emma anticipates his touch by rolling over onto her back. While he strokes her belly, she keeps her eyes on me. I'm watching them both, although I can't see Malin's face. I almost reach out to pet him with exactly the same measure of affection he is demonstrating toward the dog I love.

"Then why don't you come over for a drink? You can experience genuine chaos at my place."

"Because by the time we finish up here, it will be too late to do anything except go to bed."

He grins at me. I throw an unbound book at him, which he catches.

"How was the fishing trip?"

"Norman canceled at the last minute. Jerry and I had a great time. It rained both days. We got up before dawn and spent the whole time out on some stupid lake trying to catch fish who were down there thinking we were the dumbest, wettest, most pathetic fishermen they had ever seen. After a while, I started heaving the beer cans overboard, hoping I might get lucky and hit one or two fish in the head."

"That's called pollution, Malin."

"You said it."

"Did you really have fun?"

"Not really."

Not at all would be my guess, from the altered tone of his voice.

"Do you remember the time? . . ."

He's trailing off again, the way he always does when he's about to tell me something he didn't know he would tell anyone. I close his office door. "Do I remember what?"

"Do you remember last winter, around Valentine's Day, I came in to work one Monday morning very late and very hung over? I didn't tell you, but the woman who showed up that weekend was Ellen. I never knew if she saw Jerry, too. When Norman canceled, I thought I might screw up my nerve and ask Jerry about it—if we both got drunk enough."

Malin has told me about all his former girlfriends. Ellen is the one he still misses, still longs for, although from the way he's described her to me, she was the least interesting, the most selfish. Love is blind, as my mother used to tell me. I never knew what she meant. Was she giving me carte blanche to love anyone at all, or was she advising me to open my eyes and see? When Malin and Ellen were living together, Ellen was twenty-two and Malin, who is exactly my age, was thirty. He was divorced and had convinced himself he would never remarry—until Ellen. She said she wasn't ready, but he was willing to give her as much time as she needed. He had no idea how unready she was until she packed up and left without leaving a note. Jerry was the one who called, from Disneyland, to say they were together and they were all right.

"I had no idea that was Ellen. No wonder you were so upset."

"She swore she wasn't planning to see either of us that weekend. Since I know she spent time with me, I have to assume she might have tried to see him. It's stupid, isn't it? Who cares after all this time?"

"You do, obviously."

"My grandad used to say that even a bulldog has to learn when to hold on to something, when to swallow it or spit it out."

"I don't think dogs can spit."

"Maybe that's the problem."

"Let her go, Malin."

"I can't."

"She's not worth it. Believe me, it's not often I think a man is worth more than a woman."

He laughs.

"You know what surprises me?" I'm about to tell him how shocked I am that he's maintained his friendship with Jerry, who cuckolded him, sort of, even though Malin and Ellen were married only in Malin's mind. The fact is, Malin and Jerry continue to be better friends than Malin and I. The fact is, Malin's friendships are none of my business.

"Are you going to tell me or keep me hanging in suspense?"

"I'm surprised you and Jerry didn't talk about this sooner. Why did you wait an entire year?"

"I'm philosophically opposed to confrontation."

"So did she call him?"

"Not as far as he knows. He thinks he was probably out. How do you like my office?"

I follow his lead and let him change the subject. "How long do you think it will take you to wreck it?"

"I appreciate the vote of confidence, Ann."

"When are you taking me out to dinner?"

"Who said I was taking you out to dinner?"

"To thank me for helping you clean up."

"I thought I mentioned a drink."

"You did, but not in connection with the office." I don't remind him that, as I recall, the offer of a drink was related to his desire to spend time talking to the person he realized he enjoyed talking to.

"Why don't you come over to my place and I'll cook us dinner."

"You never told me you can cook."

"I make great chili."

"I hate chili. How about hamburgers and french fries?"

"You've got a date. Is Thursday good for you?"

"Thursday's fine. Give me a time."

"Seven or eight?"

"Eight. What can I bring?"

"I would really enjoy it if you would bring Emma."

"As a guest or as the main course?"

My first observation upon walking into Malin's studio apartment: how disproportionately high the ceiling is for the size of the room. I can't tell if the pictures on the smooth, white walls (old family photographs, an aerial shot of the Grand Canyon, a map of the Roman Empire) are hung too low because of Malin's height, or if he's used to lower ceilings, one-story, rambling houses that complement the New Mexico desert where he grew up, space extending on a horizontal rather than a vertical plane.

"I'm glad you could come over. I've always thought it would be a good idea for us to see each other outside the office, for a change." He fetches me a Coke from his half-size refrigerator under the sink. "Sorry—no ice. Unless you want a hunk of frozen beer." He takes a beer from his tiny freezer. "Would you like a tour? This is my apartment," he says with a sweep of his arm. "It's the same size as a foaling stall. We had a broodmare at home, and she had about this much space."

"And she didn't need room for her stereo."

"What kind of music do you like? I don't have any Drew Gold."

"Anything except rock."

"Lilly just sent me some old cowboy music for my birthday, reissues of recordings that first appeared on 78s. You might like it."

While he sits on the floor, flipping through his records, Emma and I sniff around. She vacuums his carpet, searching for crumbs, while I notice his bookcase, where several pairs of child's cowboy boots, obviously well worn, have been placed in ascending order according to size directly under some dog-eared volumes of Marcus Aurelius. I pick up a tiny red boot and smile down at him, knowing it has to be his.

"They were all mine. Mother saved them. She saved everything."

I set it back on the shelf with its mate. "Why Marcus Aurelius?"

"I'm a stoic at heart. Don't let this hedonistic exterior fool you."

The cowboy boots, in red, blue, and green leather, some of them with miniature spurs, are arranged so that I can see, as if in time-lapse photography, the little boy growing into man-sized boots. Now that he's a city boy, he wears inconspicuous shoes to the office (although snakeskin cowboy boots are all the rage), brown, tied things with thick crepe soles, and sneakers on the weekend.

There is a photographic portrait of a beautiful woman near the terrace door. That must be Lilly. How did she get to be so young, I wonder, younger than I am now? "Did you always call your mother by her first name?"

"I must have started calling her that when I was five or six.

That picture was taken the year before she and my dad were married. They had been childhood sweethearts."

"Do you have any more old pictures?"

Malin sits on the floor in front of the closet and drags out a cardboard box. I sit beside him. Emma crawls into his lap. The box is packed with all sorts of memorabilia: photographs, letters, report cards, drawings, more cowboy boots. "Look at all this junk," he says, but he handles the contents like the crown jewels. "This is a boomerang my grandad made for me. He claimed it would be more faithful than any woman and last longer than a dog."

"Has it?"

He laughs. "Do you see any dogs here? Any women?"

I see a dog and a woman, but if he doesn't, I'm not going to point them out.

"Which reminds me—how's your romance with your rock-star friend going? You haven't mentioned him in a while."

Malin knows as well as I do that there is no romance. "He's living with a woman. He's even talking marriage."

"I'm sorry. But you were never seriously interested in that guy, were you? He didn't sound like he was in your league."

I don't ask him what league I'm in, although I assume it must be for some solitary, rather than team, sport. Why do his compliments always sound like the opposite? "If they do get married, and if I'm invited to the wedding with a guest, would you be my date? I have the feeling I won't want to show up alone."

"I'd be happy to go with you."

"Thanks. Show me some pictures. I've seen Cat, but not Bad Boy."

I already know several Bad Boy stories—how once a year he used to chase the Goodyear blimp to the horizon. How he went to court with Malin's father, an attorney, and slept like a rock until the verdict was read. And my favorite: When Malin was three years old, and Bad Boy was a brand-new, nameless puppy, Malin wanted to walk around on all fours. Why should he have to drink milk from a cup when the puppy drank from a dish on the floor? He didn't throw a tantrum. He just became stolid, implacable as a cow. His mother acquiesced, caressed his hair, told him he would always be her favorite puppy. She put down saucers of milk for him to lap up, let him take graham crackers from her hand with his teeth. The puppy phase lasted exactly two weeks, right through two meetings of Lilly's afternoon bridge club. Everyone pretended not to notice. Sometimes, between bids, he would bark. When he first told me this story, I wondered if he still barks sometimes, if he ever barks at passing dogs, but I didn't interrupt him to ask. Lilly reached down to pet him as he crawled by, kept asking him what on earth happened to his tail. When he chose to walk again, she showed him how to hold the puppy in his arms, taught him the correct way to play with it, said he should never let a puppy nip at his fingers, but above all he should always be gentle. "Bad boy," Malin scolded, whenever the puppy tried to chew his hand. No one could think of a better name.

"As it turned out," Malin says, "the name was ironic. Every once in a while he messed up—my dad hated it when he chased the Goodyear blimp—but most of the time he was too good to be true. My dad said Bad Boy had more integrity than most men he knew. I should be ashamed to admit this, but I kept trying to get him in trouble. I used him as a scapegoat for everything from leaving my toys in the parlor to eating cookies on my grandmother's davenport. Cookie crumbs between the cushions used to drive my grandmother over the edge."

We spend an hour playing show-and-tell with Malin's pictures. Then he moves to his bed (the room's too small for a couch) and, apologizing for the lack of furniture, offers me the rocking chair, the only other comfortable place to sit. He tells me stories about Cat and Bad Boy and his cousin Louise (he called her "Weasel"), who spent summers with him when they were kids, and who died of a drug overdose in college. But mostly he talks about Lilly: stories from her childhood and stories from his, all of them told and retold by her father. Finally, Emma, who has noticed that it's way past dinnertime, interrupts him by pacing back and forth near the stove, which smells like food. She stands on her hind legs, sniffing the air like a groundhog. Malin takes the hint.

"You must be starving."

"Starving."

"Why didn't you tell me to shut up? I could keep drinking beer and telling you these stupid stories forever."

All this time, he's been keeping the hamburgers warm in the oven. He takes them out and slides in an aluminum-foil pie plate full of frozen french fries. "Dinner will be ready in . . ."—he's reading the package—"fifteen to twenty minutes or as soon as they turn golden brown."

He forgets to turn up the heat in the oven and doesn't notice me do it for him. "Do you ever use your terrace?"

"Sure. I stand on it. Sometimes I sit on it. But you can't eat on it, because with all that traffic the food ends up tasting like exhaust. We could have an aperitif on the terrace, except you don't drink and I forgot to pick up more Coke."

"I've been practicing drinking Kahlua and cream so I'll have something to drink on auspicious occasions. It's the closest thing to chocolate milk I could find."

"Why don't I go get some? You can do me a favor and keep an eye on the french fries—if you wouldn't mind, that is. Should I put on a different record?"

"Put on the same one again. I wasn't really listening to it when you were telling me stories. But I'd prefer if you'd get me a Coke."

Now that I'm alone, I snoop around, Emma at my heel. His one kitchen cabinet is mostly empty, except for a few glasses, a mismatched smattering of dishes, and one dented can of okra. His bed is neatly covered with a hand-knitted, many-colored afghan. Did his mother make that for him? His grandmother? In the office one day, some of the editorial department entertained themselves on a coffee break by guessing which editors make their beds before going to work in the morning and which do not. Malin and I both fell, unquestionably, on the unmade side.

Ersatz cowboys are singing about cloudy skies and lost sweethearts. *Get along little dogie*, they sing. I repeat the line for Emma, emphasizing the long *o*. "That's *dōg-ie*," I say, "not *doggie*. They're singing about motherless calves, not bichons frises."

Malin's desk is as messy as his office desk, although it does reflect a halfhearted effort to arrange the papers into piles. On top of one stack is a postcard, which I try not to read, even though I consider postcards to be more or less public property. "All my love, Lilly," it's signed. I'm sure Malin wouldn't mind. "Dear Malin," she writes, "I've just come across poor old Lightning's saddle and thought you might want it. It would make quite a conversation piece, wouldn't it? Should I send it? Otherwise, of course, I'll just keep it for you. All my love, Lilly."

Being alone in a man friend's apartment—especially a man who seems like he might be more than a friend—makes me want to violate it. I want to claim territory to which I have no claim, to lie down on his bed under the blankets, to rest my head on his pillow where I don't belong. I want to take a shower and dry off with his towel.

Instead, I go outside on the terrace. "Malin," I say, and hear him answer with the same lack of inflection he uses on the phone, only this time I imagine his face close to mine: Ann.

By the time he comes back, the potatoes are golden brown and as cold as the hamburgers. "I was beginning to feel abandoned."

"I'm sorry," he says, touching my shoulder. His usual deli was closed and he had to go to the other one and then he ran into someone who used to live in his building.

A woman? I wonder.

Emma keeps barking at Malin and paces back and forth, sniffing the hamburgers on top of the stove. "That's enough!" I shout.

"You're going to think I was raised in a barn. Should we eat this stuff or order in some Chinese food?"

"Let's give it a try."

Malin reheats dinner for the second time, clears off the papers on his desk, and sets it for a romantic dinner for two, his typewriter as the centerpiece, a roll of paper towels for napkins. He indicates that I should take the desk chair and drags the only other chair in the room, the rocking chair, over to the table for himself. But when he sits down in it, I laugh; he's not tall enough to reach the table comfortably. He rests his feet on the rockers and rocks. I suggest we move to the floor, picnic-style.

All the time he was growing up, he tells me, handing me the ketchup, his parents and grandparents kept telling him that one of these days he was going to sprout, just like a soybean, and grow as tall as his father and grandfathers, all of them a perfectly respectable size, right around five-feet-eight or -nine. He believed them until he turned sixteen, and then he gave them one more year, just in case, and finally he gave up hope. "That's when I decided I might as well keep acting like a child."

But his voice betrayed him, I think. It deepened and matured, turned full-blown—the imperious voice of a judge or minister. Although he kept trying to play the fool, it belied his seriousness. During his freshman year in college, he had driven his sports car into a pond on a dare, just for a lark. By the time he entered graduate school, he gave in to the tenor of his voice and studied the mathematical foundations of epistemology.

"I want you to know that I come by my character flaws naturally. I remember the time my grandad thought he'd play a little joke on Mother by hooking the back loop of my blue jeans on a nail on the side of the barn. I couldn't have been more than three years old; I couldn't have weighed much of anything at all. I have no idea how long I was out there. Mother says she found me banging my heels against the barn— not mad or anything, just to pass the time."

The rescue is easy to imagine: "Oh, honey," she says, unhooking his pants. Malin half smiles as she lifts him away from the barn and holds him close for a moment, then touches the back of his head before standing him upright on the ground. He clasps her legs in a tight embrace.

"Your grandad was quite a guy, wasn't he?"

Whenever company came out to the ranch, Warren would entertain them by performing tricks with his bullwhip. "Malin," he'd say, "Son, why don't you come on over here?" They had all seen the act before and knew what would be coming next. Malin approached warily. Warren asked for the loan of a cigarette from one of the guests. "It's a Lucky Strike," he announced, placing the cigarette between Malin's teeth. "Hold on to it, don't *bite* it, now." They all laughed. The brand name was a good omen. Warren instructed Malin not to move, as if he didn't know that on his own, and walked to the far end of the patio, where he uncurled the whip with a flick of his wrist and, with a snap that seemed to crack Malin's teeth and watered his eyes, divided the cigarette in two.

To me, these stories are not funny, although Malin relates them with good humor, as if they are. Malin senses correctly that I am less interested in the antics of the grandfather—the hero of Malin's stories—than I am in the stranded, eager-to-please little boy, the hero in the version I hear. In the darkness of Malin's apartment, across our half-eaten dinner, neither of us makes a move toward the other, although for a moment I imagine myself holding him, enfolding him, keeping him safe.

Lilly should have protected you, I think. I would have. But Lilly lived with her father, husband, and son, and they all needed her protection. I protect Emma. I take care of a dog.

"I got a postcard from Lilly today. She found my grandad's old saddle and thought I might like to have it."

I don't confess to having read the card. "Does it come with a horse?"

"I wish it did."

When Lilly was growing up, the prize horse, kept in one of the two broodmare stalls at the back of the barn, was Warren's Arab stallion, the only ungelded horse on the farm, the only gray. He was strictly off-limits to everyone—the family, the hands. Warren's horse was his personal property, as personal as property could get.

But one day he had this feeling at the back of his neck, like a change in the direction of the breeze, that he had just spotted Lightning in the distance. The feeling, like the horse, was there and then it was gone. He went to check the stall, just to make sure. No horse. He grabbed his shotgun, got into his truck, and took off after the thief. He would teach him a lesson, scare him so he'd never go near that horse again.

That was the plan. It seemed foolproof until he saw Lightning, true to his name, streaking toward him, Lilly riding bareback with only a bridle, her straight hair streaming back as if she were moving through water, her white blouse and her sun-bleached blonde hair darkening the horse under her, except for his mane and tail, still silver in the midafternoon sun.

Malin's retelling of this story transforms it from purebred

truth to something of a mutt: part truth, part fairy tale, part parable. He says the first time he heard it must have been before he could walk or talk. His grandfather told it so many times that everyone older was sick of it. That must be why Malin says he doesn't tell these stories much. Cat was only an Appaloosa gelding, but long after Lightning was gone he was horse enough to spur Warren to storytelling. Malin has no child or horse of his own. Is that why he passes the stories on to me?

"What will you do with the saddle?" Usually, Malin doesn't need a prompt, but the story of Lilly and Lightning seems to have stranded him too far from his apartment. "Where will you keep it?" I ask, leading him back.

He glances around. "Any ideas?"

"A sawhorse might be a nice touch."

"And easy to feed. I always hated taking care of horses."

"Even Cat?"

"Especially Cat. Feeding Cat before and after school was my job. The first few months were easy because it was warm outside and Cat was spending most of his time out in the run-in shed. But as winter came on and the days shortened, I dreaded going over to the barn in the dark. Sometimes Warren would take pity on me and help. I would put off feeding the horse as long as I could, then if Warren didn't show, I ran like hell from the house to the barn."

Malin raced through darkness wet as fog against his face, no match for the demons at his heels. He stepped onto a curled lead rope and almost threw up. He lunged for the light switch and turned it on, trying to ignore the shadows the dim light cast along the walls. He struggled to scoop the grain, sticky with molasses, out of a burlap sack. He held onto the coffee can with his left hand and tried to open the two latches on Cat's stall door, a bolt and a hook-and-eye, with his right hand. Finally, he had to put down the scoop to work at the latches with both hands. He swung the door open and pushed against Cat's shoulder to back him up and bent down to pick up the can, but Cat knocked it right out of his hands. Damn horse, he thought, trying to sound to himself more man than boy. Cat nosed through the straw bedding looking for grain. Malin scrambled out of the stall, away from the cobwebs that stuck to his fingers and the spikes of yellow straw that pricked at his clothes. He managed to fasten the latches and wheeled around to run and ran smack into Warren. "Where's the fire?" his grandfather said. Warren checked Cat's feeder. Malin knew Warren could tell what had happened and, without being told, went to fetch more grain. "It's not fair to penalize an animal for a human mistake," Warren said. He checked the water bucket and saw that it was three-quarters full, but dirty. "What do you expect him to do when he's thirsty, go over to the house for a beer?" Malin dumped the bucket, splashing brown water onto his jeans and sneakers, and refilled it from the hose. Warren climbed up to the hayloft and threw down a bale of timothy and a bale of straw. Then he told Malin to pick up the lead rope and tie it on the stall where it belonged. He turned off the barn light and the two of them stared out the barn window, covered with flyspecks and cobwebs, at the porch light across the road, where their supper was waiting. Warren stood with one foot propped up against an open bale of dusty timothy that Malin had promised him he'd already cleaned up. Malin shoved his fists into his pockets to get them warm, shifted his weight from foot to foot, and tried to kick the barn cat, who pressed against his legs.

"Your mother was quite a horsewoman when she wasn't much older than you," Warren began.

Not now, Malin wanted to say. I'm too cold. From the stall behind him, a sudden rush of running water as if a bathtub faucet had been opened, followed by the sharp ammonia smell of urine. Malin tried to listen to the story about his mother, but he was hungry and his concentration gave out. He nudged the hay with his foot, snagged a piece of it with his fingers to shove between his teeth, man-style. He thought but did not say aloud (he was just practicing, he told himself): That Lilly could stick to any horse like glue.

"Why don't we try the terrace for a while—if the fumes don't kill us."

Malin's terrace overlooks a parking garage on the other side of the street. "Nice view," I say.

"Can I get you another Coke?"

"Thanks."

"You sure you don't want me to put something in that for you? How about a little rum?"

"Quite sure."

It starts to rain. Malin and I stand outside in it for a minute before we let it chase us indoors. I reach for the paper towels.

"They forecast rain," he says.

Finally: a man who can recognize rain. "I wish I had thought to bring my umbrella. I don't mind summer rain at all, but Emma hates it."

"Maybe you better spend the night . . ."

A lapse, now, on my part—a missed beat—like someone pulled the plug. Did I hear what he said? I heard what he said. Was that a throwaway line or an invitation?

". . . I have a sleeping bag . . . ," he says, smiling. "Did you see that lightning?"

"Obviously," I answer, referring to the sleeping bag on the floor, although he probably thinks I'm talking about the lightning. "I love thunderstorms in New York." Storms that must seem dramatic outside of the city seem merely theatrical, melodramatic, here. Did he mean one of us would take the floor? Invite me to stay, Malin. Invite me to spend the night. Give me another chance. But there is no direct invitation from him, no acceptance from me, only this momentary lapse in the conversation, a cavern as wide as the Grand Canyon on his wall.

"You don't know how much I appreciate your listening to my stories, in the office and here, tonight. I hope I haven't been boring you to death. It's getting to the point that I know you've heard a lot of them before, but I don't know which ones."

"Did I seem bored?"

"No," he admits, embarrassed.

"Don't be embarrassed. I don't know why I love listening to them, either." Why am I seduced by a man I'm not especially attracted to simply because he tells me tales? This has happened before. Stories affect me like proverbial etchings. *Come on up to my place and I'll show you my stories.* I keep jumping to the conclusion that the storytelling hour will be a precursor to bed: tell me a bedtime story. But so far I have been mistaken. During story after story the men who tell them seem energized, but when the last one is over they seem spent. They always assume I am as fully satisfied as they are. Once upon a time they would have been right. But I'm no longer so easy to please. Who are you, Malin? Are you my little prince? Or are you the kingdom's court jester? Do I want you or the stories you tell?

The rain changes direction and slaps against the closed terrace door. "Poor Emma, you hate getting wet, don't you?"

"I have an extra umbrella that you're welcome to borrow," Malin says.

At the office, I'm working on the "Women in Literature" series, volume I, England, with novels by Austen, both Brontës, Eliot, Woolf. Malin is working on the "Novels of the Sea" series: Conrad, Melville, Stevenson. We are both happy with our work, temporarily engrossed, free to ignore each other. I suggested that we should swap: since I'm afraid of fish and I can't swim, the sea series would be educational for me; God knows, I said, you could stand to learn a little more about women.

Malin uses the telephone to call me from his office, although all he needs to do is shout. "Ann. Can you take a short break? We've been working too hard lately. People are beginning to talk."

I go into his office and close the door behind me. Behind Malin's desk, the photograph of Malin, his fifteen-year-old girlfriend, and Cat is tacked to the bulletin board under a chart of emperors taken from our new edition of *The Decline and Fall of the Roman Empire,* one of his favorite books.

"You never told me who the girl is," I say, pointing past him at the snapshot.

"Caroline Henderson. We went to junior high together until she moved away."

Malin had been watching Caroline for a month before he ran into her in the hallway between the boys' and girls' gyms. He watched her snap her gum and cavort with her friends, whirling around to make a point he couldn't hear. Her friends noticed him and discreetly disappeared, eyeing him, yelling at her, "See you at lunch." It was now or never. He approached her quietly, the same way he had learned to approach Cat. To go up to a horse, Warren had taught him, you talk softly if you need to talk, if you have something you want to say. You can talk to him or touch him, but you better find a way to let him know you're there. "Go ahead, boy. Go tell Cat you're here."

It wasn't until after he had said hi and asked her about the Thoreau assignment for English and inquired, finally, if she would like to go to the movies on Saturday afternoon that he noticed she must have swallowed her gum. He was fifteen, ignorant of the ways of women and the world. He could not have known then that she deliberately had swallowed the gum for him.

"How long did it take you to figure that out?"

"Figure what out?"

"That she liked you. That she'd do something stupid like swallow her gum just to impress you."

"I suspect I've always been dense about things like that. How about you?"

"I don't think a boy would ever have swallowed his gum for me."

"I wouldn't be so sure. . . . Sometimes when we're talking together like this, Ann—the other night at my apartment, or here in the office—and I start telling you stories . . ."

"Except maybe Billy. In fourth grade. He brought a little Steiff bear to school. I admired it and he gave it to me. I thought of Billy last week, for the first time in something like twenty years, when I was looking at the Steiff animals in a toystore and it occurred to me that maybe he brought the bear to school to give it to me, that he intended it as a gift all along." Whether planned or spontaneous, Billy's gift appears from my current perspective to be an act of unparalleled generosity.

"I'm sorry, Malin. I interrupted you." He can no longer remember what he wanted to say. I do: "Sometimes, when we're talking together like this . . . ," but I don't tell him. Maybe he really can't recall his thought. Maybe he's changed his mind. Why did I cut him off again? We smile at each other, both of us shy, acknowledging another opportunity missed.

"Do you still have the bear?"

"I lost it. It had only one arm. I used to take it with me wherever I went. I remember dressing it up in turquoise felt— I even remember cutting out the felt with my mother's pinking shears. But I don't remember losing it or missing it. Then one day I noticed it was gone."

Seven

*I*T'S my wedding day and I'm getting married, finally, just in the nick of time, right under the wire, before I get too old. I'm wearing an antique white satin gown trimmed with lace. When I look across the crowded room, the dress seems splendid, perfect in every detail, the gown of my dreams. But when I turn away from the guests and examine it more carefully, I notice for the first time that the lace is beginning to fray and curl up where it should lie flat, and there are yellowish stains where whole strips of it have fallen free. Just above my waist, the fabric is marred by a row of catches obvious to me now, although I never noticed them before. I keep rubbing the tiny raised threads with my fingertips, as if I could smooth them down. There are pearl buttons down the bodice and at my wrists, but the one on my right cuff is missing, leaving the sleeve agape.

I know the dress looks terrible, but my mother reassures me that it's fine. I wanted to wear her dress, didn't I? It's a very old dress, after all, and no one would expect it to be perfect.

The wedding is about to begin, but no groom has arrived. I am marrying a man named Edgar. I try to picture him, but I can't. No exact picture, not even a vague one, no memory of a man ever met, or imagined, named Edgar. I whisper in my mother's ear that perhaps I should call the whole thing

off. If I loved a man, I tell her, I would be able to picture
him. My mother insists that every bride feels this way on her
wedding day. I don't think she's right, but I acquiesce. How
can I marry a man I've never met?

We haven't rehearsed the ceremony and I don't know what
I'm supposed to do. Something will be expected of me. My
mother leads me toward a dingy stairway that looks as if it
belongs in a tenement and instructs me to wait at the top.
Several guests have been assigned the task of guarding me from
the bottom of the stairs until it's time for the wedding to begin.
When I ask her why, she says it's traditional. But I think she
just made that up; they're going to make sure I don't run away.
As I slowly climb the rickety stairs, I keep staring at the bands
of yellow-brown stains like old glue across the front of my
dress. I find a full-length mirror. The stains are so obvious
they look like stripes. My hair is a mess. If I'm getting married
today, why didn't I comb my hair?

I wake up long before dawn, thinking of Edgar, trying to
assemble a face that doesn't belong to someone I know. But
my imagination fails me; I see only familiar faces. Glass wind-
chimes from a nearby terrace do better: they engage in a random, improvised tune. I lie awake, listening, watching. I am
trying to locate a shape among the tinkling glass that will
resemble the outline of my fiancé's face.

Now I remember: Drew's getting married today. No wonder
I had that dream. I glance at my alarm clock—just after five
A.M. If I'm up by six, I'll have plenty of time to throw on some
clothes, take Emma to the park, undress, shower, dress, and
get to the wedding by nine. Beside me, Emma sleeps. I ask
her if my plan seems all right to her. She opens one eye to
see if I'm saying anything worth her attention, then closes it.

I'm still in bed, listening to the chimes, thinking about
Edgar, my wedding dress, and the red dress I bought especially

to wear to the wedding, when Drew comes toward me. Why didn't I notice him before? "Long time, no see." He says he's missed running into me in the park. I say I've missed him, too.

"Just remember that our not sleeping together was *your* idea, not mine," he says.

"You mean it was my fault?"

"I really wanted you. That's all I know. You still can't tell when someone wants you."

But I'm willing to learn. Can you teach an old dog new tricks? I begin my first lesson by slowly unbuttoning his shirt. I have to practice counting aloud: one button, two buttons, three buttons, four. I watch his expression for some sign that I should continue or stop. *You can do what you want.* I open his shirt and pull down his jeans and underwear in one quick motion. Too fast, I think. Don't go so fast. I kneel by his side and give myself all the time in the world. Even though my knees scuff the ground, I am comfortable and secure, my center of gravity lowered, my weight evenly distributed as if I had four paws. Drew is less steady, standing erect on two feet only, the earth far below him, spinning. He lifts his arms out to his sides like a tightrope walker. *You can get what you want.* But sometimes you need a little help. I reach up with open palms and hold on to him and keep him in perfect balance so he won't teeter and fall.

Have I ever told you, Drew, how my father used to tie a string between the andirons on the fireplace, then thread a green and gold gyroscope and set it spinning? It spun on his fingertip, it spun all the way across the string, it spun when he made it spin in my hand.

I lean back to see his face. His eyes are closed, his head slightly tipped back, his lips parted. Have I ever told you, Drew? My hands do what they will. He stands upright and does not fall. I hear a gyroscope whirring.

Shopping, again. I have nothing to wear to Drew's wedding. Why do I always end up having to do last-minute shopping? Why can't I do anything on time? I slam the car door and walk into a suburban five-and-dime. Although it's midday and sunny outdoors, in here it's as dim as dusk, as quiet as a library. Small oriental carpets protect dark hardwood floors. The salespeople glance up when I walk in, then go back to their paperwork. Where are the dresses? I am on my own. A patchwork of mahogany and glass display cases (they remind me of the ones in museums that are filled with artifacts of ancient civilizations) stretches out in all directions as far as I can see. Where are the dresses? I look inside one of the cases. It contains replicas of animals. I look inside the next one. More animals. What good luck! I can kill two birds with one stone by finding the perfect wedding present for Drew, the perfect dress for me.

A saleswoman informs me that a purchase is completely out of the question. This place has been set up for catalogue sales. Nothing may be moved; no object may be sold. She is the guardian of the animals. I explain that I need only one for a special gift, but she is adamant. She leaves her post and goes into the back room. I can tell she is still keeping watch. I must obey the rules, although they make no sense. One small animal will never be missed.

The cases are filled to capacity. Some of them appear to be organized according to species or habitat, while others aren't organized at all. Often the animals seem preposterous because of their relative size: an ibex larger than a rhino, a polar bear smaller than a chimp. A giraffe feeds on a miniature tree; a zebra looms over them both. I walk past crystal snails and swans, pewter pigs, stained-glass peacocks, porcelain rabbits, brass foxes, spotted, ceramic frogs. I find a case holding birds made of real feathers, white owls and chartreuse parrots. Another holds jade turtles, gold and turquoise seahorses, silver fish with amethyst gills and amber eyes.

I catch my own reflection in the glass case containing the fish and try to fix my unkempt hair with my fingers.

Where are the mirrors? If there are no dressing rooms, how am I supposed to try on clothes? I can't find any windows, either. The only glass in this store is the glass that separates the animals from me. I know this is called "a climate-controlled environment." Is the guardian of the animals the one in control? On the opposite side of the room, there are ponderous oak doors as high as the ceiling, with heavy brass rings.

"What are those rings?"

"You use them to knock."

"Why would you knock?"

"To get in or out."

"Here? To get in here?"

The saleswoman stalks me, keeping her distance. I'm looking for a stairway. The dresses must be upstairs or downstairs. In a corner of the room, on top of a mahogany breakfront, I see a life-size, yellow-eyed, gray fur-covered cat. It must be stuffed. Nothing here is real, nothing may be purchased, nothing carried home. But the cat looks real, as if it's playing possum. When it blinks, I believe it is real. At last, an animal that can be moved.

"Is this cat for sale?"

"Which cat?"

There is a long-haired calico dozing on top of one of the cabinets, where cylinders of fluorescent light keep her warm. A pair of black kittens, snuggled together like yin and yang, sleep on the windowless window ledge. A tabby is on a shelf nearby, curled up but awake, watching me. I whisper hello, but I don't reach out to pet it until it yawns and stands and stretches, its taut haunches rising against my palm.

"What on earth do you think you're doing?" the woman yells. "Where is your mother?"

My mother, where is my mother? Where is she? Is she here?
I don't know, I say—*I don't remember*—with the dresses, I
think. I think she's with the dresses.

The pulsing of my alarm clock signals to me that I am only
dreaming and, like a beacon of light piercing the darkness
offshore, it reveals a path and draws me along it home to my
safe bed. My body is cramped in on itself; my face is hot and
wet with tears. I wipe my face with a dry corner of my pil-
lowcase. Slowly, I roll onto my back, straighten out my body,
and stretch. Reaching out with my right foot, I run my toes
along the right edge of the mattress, then use my left foot to
find the far edge. I touch the top edge along the headboard
with my fingers, then scrunch down under the blanket to scan
the opposite end corner to corner with the arch of my right
foot—defining the boundaries of my world. I'm reminded of
a drawing in one of my elementary school social studies books:
"The World Before Christopher Columbus." When everyone
still assumed that the earth was flat, they thought if you traveled
too far in any one direction, you would reach the edge. If you
stepped off land, you would plunge into the sea, where fanged
and clawed sea-monsters swam along with the fish. But if you
accidentally stepped off the earth, you would plummet into
the sky.

Where is my mother? I know where she is. She's at home,
asleep, where a mother should be. She wouldn't mind if I
called and woke her up, but my father would. My father would
say, "Don't you have any brains?" I tiptoe toward their bedroom door and knock on it too softly for anyone to hear and
slowly nudge it open. She sleeps on the side of the bed near
the door. I stare at her, wishing her awake. "Mom," I think.
Finally, she senses my presence and awakens.

"What's wrong, sweetheart?" she asks.

"I had this bad dream," I whisper aloud.

Emma, as usual, ignores me. I have to get up, although I

want to stay in bed and be held by my mother; I want to hold my dog. But Emma isn't interested. She thinks it's time her lazy owner got going. I dress quickly and take her outside. No park today. I explain to her that Drew and Rebecca are getting married this morning and I don't want to go to the park. Downstairs, I turn left, heading east, but Emma pulls me west. "Habits die hard," I tell her. I consider going to the park by a different route so I won't walk by his window. But I suspect I would give in. I know I would. I know I would stand outside his bedroom window and stare.

I walk Emma once around the block and back home, give her breakfast, and reassure her that we'll go out for a real run later on. She seems satisfied with the promise and jumps back on my bed while I shower and get dressed again, this time in my brand-new, bright red dress that's easy to spot. Today I don't want to get lost in the crowd. I wish Malin had been willing to be my date for the wedding; he said he wished he didn't have to back out, because it would have been fun, but there was this last-minute weekend fishing trip that he felt in good conscience he couldn't pass up. In my new dress I look as good as I can make myself look at the moment. If I examine myself in the mirror too closely, I will lose the courage to go.

It's a short walk to the Museum of Natural History, but I hail a cab heading up Broadway anyway, since I'm not comfortable in high heels. Of all the places in New York City where Drew and Rebecca could be married—the synagogues, churches, restaurants, private clubs, even the parks—they had to choose this museum. Rebecca's father, a geology professor and a curator at the museum, had suggested the dinosaur room, tongue in cheek, to his zoologist daughter. She convinced her mother and Drew's that it would be the ideal place.

I pay the cabbie too much money for the fare and start up the first set of shallow steps to the plaza, where I pause before beginning the second set of stairs. Animals with serpentine horns or tusks are engraved on either side of the plaza, along with the names of venerable professions: scholar, scientist, soldier, statesman. There are no rock stars here.

That was the easy part, I think. Slowly, carefully, so I don't trip, I begin climbing the second set of stairs. Above the main entrance, the words *Truth, Understanding, Vision* are carved in the granite facade among four ionic columns. The letters are roman capitals, formal and elegant; they contrast sharply with the graffiti I notice to the right of the doorway: "Love and Trust." A peace sign, an artifact from my college days, fills the misshapen *o* in the word *love*.

There are three revolving doors. A uniformed guard appears in the center one. I show him my invitation. He stands aside and pushes the door for me, motioning to the right. I step inside the door but stay there for one full rotation so that I pop right out. I know I must look comical to him and try to fake a smile. I attempt some sort of gesture to indicate that I'll be right back, then run down the stairs as fast as my high heels will let me. I stand at the foot of the steps, hidden from the guard's view by a massive statue of Teddy Roosevelt on horseback at the center of the plaza. I could take a cab home. I could walk home. I could try to go back inside. I could stand here forever, like a statue. Maybe Teddy could give me a lift home on his horse.

Make a decision, Ann. One way or the other. Stay or go. I know if I stall too long I'll be late for the wedding, and I certainly won't have the nerve to walk in. Up the stairs again, staring at my feet. The guard says, "Welcome back." I ask him for the time, even though I'm wearing my watch.

"Eight forty-five."

"Thanks." I start down the stairs again, then—worried that one of my park friends might see me leave—stop on the plaza. There are two concrete benches. If I smoked, I could sit down and take out a cigarette. I could wait for someone I know to show up. But the other park people may already be inside. Why didn't I ask one of them to meet me here? I'll never make it all the way to the dinosaur room alone.

OK, everyone, can I have your attention, please? Please? Good. Today, as you all know, we're going to the museum. The bus is parked right outside. Let's all walk, not run, and not make too much noise so we don't disturb the other classes, and go right outside to the bus.

There's a hole in the bottom of the sea
There's a hole in the bottom of the sea
There's a hole, there's a hole
There's a hole in the bottom of the sea . . .

Quiet down, everyone. Could you stop singing and let me hear a little silence? Thank you. We're almost there. Here are the rules: Everyone is to stay together in a group. Museums are for looking, not for touching. If you have any questions, you must raise your hand and wait your turn. Try to speak as quietly as you can. Try to whisper, like this: Does anyone have any questions?

There's a wart on a frog on a bump on a log in a hole
  in the bottom of the sea
There's a wart on a frog on a bump on a log in a hole
  in the bottom of the sea
There's a wart, there's a wart
There's a wart on a frog on a bump on a log in a hole
  in the bottom of the sea

The bus turns into a long, maple-lined driveway marked "The Astor Museum—Open Wednesday Through Sunday, 11:00 A.M. to 5:00 P.M.," and follows it to the parking lot adjacent to the museum. It's an enormous white building with three fluted columns and massive wooden doors with golden rings.

Here we are. Do you remember the rules? Please line up with your buddy in a straight double file. We don't want any strays. And let's button our mouths as soon as we're inside. That means everybody—no exceptions—that means *you* and *you* and *you.*

People are passing me on the museum steps. They are dressed for a wedding. How long have I been sitting here? I check my watch. For a minute or two, that's all. I go back upstairs to the guard.

"Anything wrong?" he asks.

I shake my head no but I'm stuck at the entrance. "Are there any exhibits in the hallways?" He doesn't understand the question, so I repeat it, keeping my voice as steady as I can.

"No." I don't believe him. He pushes the door again, but this time I don't step inside.

"I'm afraid of natural history museums. I know it's stupid." I'm casual—a fraudulent half-smile and an awkward shrug of the shoulders are meant to communicate that I'm just being silly.

But if you could read my mind, I think, you would tell me this: why would anyone want to see a case filled with deep-freeze Eskimos, their lifelike dogs harnessed and hitched up to sleds that are permanently parked and permanently ready to go? Tell me: when visitors look at all those taxidermic marvels and animal remains, at pelts and skulls and skeletons, exactly what do they see?

A group of young people stroll up the stairs, flash their invitations, and walk right past me.

"Why don't you just stick close to them," the guard whispers to me.

I thank him with another smile and jump into the revolving

door, allowing their momentum and his (he's in the slot behind me) to get me inside without having to push the door myself. I follow the foursome, my high heels clanging against the marble floors, slowing me down. Wait for me! I want to cry out, to complain: No one ever waits for me! At last I reach the dinosaur room. "Groom's side or bride's?" the usher wants to know. I look past him at the particles of dusty light filtering through the tall, skinny windows near the ceiling. I'm relieved to see that there are windows. Thank God, I think. From the quizzical expression on the usher's face, I'm afraid I may have spoken aloud. Three dinosaurs occupy the center of the room. The windows are out of reach. They let in light, not air. I will never make it inside. I should never have come alone.

"Bride's side or groom's?"

"It doesn't matter." He's smiling at me, but I can tell he's impatient to hear a better answer. Behind him, light and dust sweep like snowflakes downward. I'm stalling to see if the dust will settle before I walk in. I already know it won't. It will continue forever. I imagine myself standing on the groom's side among a dozen of Drew's former girlfriends, all of us gathering dust as we watch the winner take all.

"Bride's," I say. I take one last gulp of wholesome air and follow his gesture to the left. I don't know any of Rebecca's friends or family, and end up standing off to one side, alone.

Inside the main entrance to the Astor Museum, we have ten minutes to hang up our sweaters and jackets, browse through the museum literature—brochures and floorplans—and return to our double file. We know without being told that we will not move forward until we are all as quiet as churchmice. I am among the first of the girls to be quiet; the boys, as usual, take longer. Although I won't break the rules and talk, I pray that they will keep talking forever.

Finally, the line proceeds from the brightly lit lobby into

the museum itself, pitch-black and hollow, silent, reeking of formaldehyde and old-lady perfume. I trip in the darkness and stumble. My buddy steadies me and whispers, "Are you OK?" Gradually, my eyes are beginning to adjust—this room isn't pitch-black at all. Only the center of the room is empty. Around its perimeter, fish are suspended in glass cases that are meant to look like fish tanks. Now that I can see clearly, the perfume no longer fools me. The tanks contain no water. All the fish are dead, their stony eyes glimmering in the greenish lights like puries or cats'-eyes, their sharp mouths open and their fins flapping in air like birds' wings.

The wedding is running fifteen minutes late. I'm not exactly surprised, given Drew's disregard for time. Maybe he's gotten cold feet. Maybe Rebecca has yellow-brown stains down the front of her dress. Maybe she can't remember who she is supposed to marry.

Meanwhile, I can't stay here. I spot a sign with an arrow pointing the way to the mammal collection. I follow it to another sign: "The Evolution of the Horse." Horses are pets. Small signs with explanatory notes accompany each phase of the exhibit. Have they been written out by hand, or is that only a typeface meant to imitate calligraphy? I try to read about the development of Cat's ancestors from the four-toed eohippus to the Pleistocene's solid-hoofed equus, but I'm reading just the headings; I'm looking at the text only in order to analyze the letter shapes. Nevertheless, I know I look like an average visitor to the museum. I know I look like I understand what I'm reading.

Where the hell are the bride and groom? Don't they know I have to get out of here? To my left is a free-standing glass case containing the skeletal remains of a baby mammoth. *Baby mammoth*—a contradiction in terms. Is a mammoth the same creature as a mastodon? The assemblage of bones gives me no clue. Go find out, I tell myself. When hell freezes over, I answer.

I escape back to the wedding, to the bride's side. Around me, the other guests are chatting noisily; apparently, they're in no hurry for the ceremony to begin. I turn away from the dinosaurs, as if I intended to talk to someone in the row behind me. When I turn around again, Drew will pledge his eternal love to Rebecca, who will receive it and pledge him hers. A rabbi will bless their vows. Which dinosaur will be their witness? I muster my courage and prepare to turn around, holding my breath, beginning my turn, still turning, as slowly as I can, then more slowly.

Am I still turning now?

My class is herded into a room with a slippery turquoise floor—peacock blue, I call it—that's the color of the ink I've been using in school to copy out our list of new vocabulary words (I have the neatest handwriting), which my teacher posts on the bulletin board. Imbedded in the center of the floor is a kind of clock that you can walk on if you want to. Instead of telling time, it tells the story of evolution, its brass arrows pointing to pictures of various animals. In place of the number one is the earliest form of animal life, which looks and behaves exactly like a plant. Moving clockwise, I can follow the transformation of sea creatures into amphibians, then reptiles, finally the earliest mammals. Number twelve is supposed to be Man. I stand at the rim of the clock, close to the picture labeled "Eohippus—Horse." It looks more like a goat than a real horse. I decide to stay right here, the safest place in the room.

My teacher invites me to rejoin the rest of the class. They're studying a mastodon in a glass case that almost reaches the ceiling. I know the mastodon is there because I accidentally glanced up and saw it. I recognized its woolly hair and the curved tusks that remind me of snakes. I pretend I don't hear her as she calls me again, and when she calls my name louder, I shake my head and concentrate on the picture of the runt horse, not much bigger than Lucky. To get from here over to her, I'd have to cross too much of the slick blue floor that shines like ink or water. My evolutionary clock is an island. I can't leave it because I don't know how to swim. Downstairs, right under my feet, only the sea creatures are free; all the other animals are wrapped and packed away in watertight crates that have to be anchored with chains.

My teacher doesn't scold me or come to fetch me, because I'm always so good. I can do what I want. I can even go outside by myself, where the sun is shining, and where rolling green lawns end at the lighthouse, the beach, the bay. Outside, it doesn't smell like formaldehyde and feathers. Outside, it smells like sea air and cut grass. The walks are lined with mountain pink; there are wild white dogwoods—my mother's favorite— in bloom on the other side of the lawn.

Rebecca enters the dinosaur room holding her father's arm and wearing a sprig of lily-of-the-valley above her right ear, her long hair braided and wound at the nape of her neck. Her bouquet of white rosebuds and baby's breath bobs down the aisle between the two groups of guests. When she reaches Drew, he extends his hand and plucks her like a flower. Accepting his hand, she relaxes and almost smiles.

When the rabbi begins to speak, I examine the dinosaurs for the first time. The tyrannosaurus looms above them all. The brontosaurus' head tilts at a contemplative angle, as if he were listening to the prayers. "Behold you are sanctified to me in accordance with the laws of Moses and Israel." Drew's brother Frank hands the rabbi the rings. The rabbi gives one to Rebecca and one to Drew. Drew repeats the vow and slips the ring onto Rebecca's finger; then Rebecca does the same.

I can't figure out what kind of dinosaur the third one is. I peer through the spaces between its bones as if they were venetian blinds.

The rabbi pours a glass of wine: "Blessed art Thou, O Eternal Our God, King of the Universe, Who has created the fruit of the vine." He repeats the prayer in Hebrew. I'm distracted by the dusty white light that sifts past the dinosaurs into the glass of ritual wine. I imagine the dinosaurs blinking out the light like kittens basking in the sun. The rabbi offers the glass to Drew, then Rebecca. They each take a sip. She returns it to the rabbi, who drains the glass, then wraps it in a white napkin and places it on the floor directly in front of Drew. When he steps on it, a chorus of *mazel tov* bursts from the crowd as they gather around, obscuring my line of vision, so that I miss Drew's first married kiss.

Eight

*E*MMA is eight years old.

In Riverside Park, time is measured by the passing seasons and the changing configuration of owners and dogs. Some of the dogs have died from disease or old age: Allie, Sweet Pea, Nana, Rosy. Or from a freak accident: Jason ate fly bait, Molly swallowed an apricot pit. A few have simply disappeared—from the park, from the street (where their owners were careless or naive enough to tie them outside a store), from a kennel where they were being boarded. Usually, I hear about these events secondhand. Bulletin: Stanley the dachshund (one of a pair, Stanley and Stella) was killed by a car when he chased a squirrel across Riverside Drive. Occasionally, and I don't know why, the bulletins don't reach me, most likely because everyone assumes that I've already been told. But since even a fifteen-minute change in schedule can mean that a dogwalker runs into an entirely different group of park regulars, I try not to worry if I don't see a particular dog for a while. Sooner or later, most of them reappear. Where have you been? their owners ask me, as if Emma had been missing.

I know it's time to worry about an absent dog when its owner appears with a new one. I've noticed that the purebreed owners tend to replace their dogs with the same breed, while the mixed-breed owners are more likely to take in stray mutts or shop for puppies at the ASPCA. What will I do? Will I "replace" Emma with another bichon frise? Will I get another dog? How about a cat? Who knows? Perhaps Emma will be immortal.

Every once in a while, a missing owner who isn't ready to get a new dog will reappear without any dog at all. "You have to admit that walking a dog three times every day, day in and day out, in good weather and bad, is an incredible pain in the ass," these former owners say. They are right; I admit it. But I also agree with the other camp of former owners, the ones who lie in bed in the morning, waiting for a dog who isn't there to lick them awake and fetch its leash and gallop to the door. Both groups are afflicted with an excess of memories, provoking either guilt or sorrow. They congregate in the park to dispel them by swapping dog stories with those of us who still have dogs. Even the owners who are grateful for their newfound freedom confess that they miss the park. They take every opportunity to throw a stick or ball or Frisbee for someone else's pet. I wonder if they're thinking about getting another dog. I recognize the question to be one I never want to answer myself, and yet I can't help asking it of strangers: "Are you considering getting a new one?"

Those of us who started coming to the park at the same time with puppies or young dogs now own middle-aged dogs, dogs in their prime. Because small dogs generally live much longer than large ones, I may be lucky enough to have Emma for another eight years. "I will keep you forever," I tell her, only, not wanting to lie, I say, "I will keep you forever in my heart." Emma jumps off my lap in search of crumbs from my dinner, sits down for a quick scratch, then wanders off to find the coolest spot on my living room floor. Grandiose declarations of affection mean nothing to her. She is as confident of my love as I am of my breath. "I love you, honey," I say, needing to tell her, although she doesn't need to hear.

When Emma is gone, I will not go back to the park. I make this promise to myself knowing full well that eventually I will break it.

I call Dorothy, ostensibly to give her an update on Emma and thank her again (we haven't spoken to each other in three years), and at least partly because I want to keep in touch with her just in case—I hate to admit this—just in case anything happens to Emma.

"I will never understand how you knew that Emma would turn out to be exactly the dog I wanted."

"Experience. After fifteen years in this business, you get a pretty good sense of people by talking to them for a while on the phone. I think of myself as a matchmaker. I *am* pretty good at it, if I do say so myself."

"*Very* good at it. Maybe you should try human matchmaking. I'll be your first client. Do you think you could find me a man who suits me as well as Emma?"

She laughs. "You've never met my husband, have you, or you wouldn't ask me that. We would all be better off if I stuck with dogs."

"I can't thank you enough," I tell her. I know that sounds trite. I know she must hear that all the time. I want to articulate with particularity and intensity how happy she has made me. But I can think of only foolish, true things to say: "I thank you from the bottom of my heart."

I was sitting on the couch watching television—my whole family was there in the living room—with Lucky fast asleep beside me, his head resting against my leg. I remember that clearly: he was sleeping, and his head was buttressed by my leg. I don't remember petting him at that moment, although I imagine I must have been, since I couldn't resist petting him whenever he was within arm's reach.

He woke up as if startled and slid to the floor in a heap, then struggled to his feet. His shoulders heaved, he snorted, then vomited, and I thought he would fall. "Get him outside," my mother yelled. Then he did fall, and I ran out of the room, and then my father must have fallen, because the next time I saw him he had slumped over and my mother was holding him in her arms to keep him from collapsing into a heap and he was dragging her down, too, so that I was afraid they would both fall, and I was thinking I have to help, I have to be strong and do something to support them all, when there was this sound, this animal noise unlike anything I had ever heard before, the bellow of a prehistoric beast—where is Lucky? I thought, where is the dog?—only the wailing wasn't coming from Lucky, but from my father, erupting from him as if from the center of the earth, and I ran away again as fast as I could but no one could tell because I pretended to stand still, to hold my ground. "Don't!" my mother said, harshly, and I didn't know if she was yelling at him or consoling him. "*Don't*— he's only a dog." No one believed her, so she said the same thing over and over again: "Remember, he's only a dog."

Lucky's death was a kind of primitive music lesson: What is sound? Where does it come from? It comes, like monsters, from the center of the earth. What is the difference between sound and silence? We came home from school or shopping, put the key in the back door, unlocked the lock, pushed the door open. No thump as the dog jumped off the bed. No scrabble of paws against linoleum. Where does music come from? Music comes from the sea, from the rising and falling tides. What is the difference between sound and music? What is noise? Noise is random: television, dishwasher, the clattering of pots or dishes, the slamming of drawers, human voices, conversations, stories told and ignored. What happened to the rhythm of the tides? It vanished in the act of opening the door: *You* go first, no *you*—I did it last time, no *you*, no. . . . None of us could get used to opening the door.

My father's rampages about the dog continued, even when Lucky wasn't there. We were lazy, we just didn't think, he would say. If a job is worth doing, it's worth doing well. It was a good thing we didn't get another dog. We wouldn't remember to give him water, either. He would be the one to feed him, to give him a drink. He would have to do everything.

"The thing you have to keep in mind about your father—and you're old enough you should know this by now," my mother said, "is that his bark is worse than his bite."

"Get another dog," my sister tells me. She means: Do something about your attachment to Emma. Get a puppy now before Emma gets old and dies. When her dog died, a year after I bought Emma, and grief knocked her down and wouldn't let her up, a man appeared, helped her to her feet like a gentleman, gradually became as devoted to her as her missing dog.

I'll be all right, I think. More of a wish than a belief. The promise I made to myself when I first thought of buying a dog: I'll get a dog and when it dies I'll survive.

The man was magic, she says. Too good to be true. Perhaps I better not hope for a man. "Get another dog," she says.

On my way to the park, I meet a woman walking her gray poodle. Emma likes him and stands with the tip of her nose against his, her tail wagging furiously. He takes one step backward, then another. The woman explains that her dog's girlfriend—her other poodle—died just last week. She was white, like mine. This one just turned fourteen; the other was one year older. "He's grieving," she tells me. "He doesn't understand where she is so he keeps looking for her. It's so pathetic. How can I explain it to him?"

Emma is very attracted to this dog and jumps up against

him in the bichon frise version of a bear hug, her front legs around his neck. He begins to wag his tail, but only intermittently, while Emma is squeaking with pleasure. "Mine's not a poodle," I say. I'm still a sitting duck, an easy mark for every sad old lady on the Upper West Side. I'm tired of tragic stories; I've had it with dogs in mourning who aren't ready to get involved.

"Your dog doesn't need a home, does she?" the woman asks, tentatively, without a trace of humor. She reminds me of her dog.

"Pardon me?" My words are polite, but the tone of my voice reveals my real question: What the fuck are you talking about?

Like her dog, she takes a step backward.

Do you see me standing here? Do you know who I am? I am this dog's owner. I am the one who loves her, who takes care of her, who has helped make her into the cheerful wench she is at this moment, trying to seduce your miserable, inconsolable dog. Who the hell do you think you are? Do you think you can just walk away with my dog? Do you think I can be replaced? Emma won't leave me. This is called devotion, in case you haven't heard the word. Deal with your dog's death however you can. Emma is mine.

I am her home.

Rebecca is in her usual place in the park—the grassy triangle separated from the rest of the park by the temporarily closed entrance ramp leading to the southbound West Side Highway. She and Drew have been walking the dogs there to keep Rover isolated; in the past few years, he's become increasingly aggressive around other males.

Rover and Rita charge me, barking; I can see why some of the park people don't like Drew and Rebecca—their dogs can be pretty intimidating. As usual, the dogs seem happier to see me than Rebecca does. "Hi, guys," I say. Rebecca and I have been spending more time together in the park since she has become, unofficially, the principal dogwalker in their marriage. I comment that I haven't run into Drew in ages. These days, he's only doing the late night walk, she says, and the only reason he's doing that is because he doesn't like her to be alone in the park late at night. She says I should come over sometime. Drew would love to play me the new songs he's been working on. Besides, I wouldn't recognize the place. She has painted, put up shelves, hung paintings and photographs. The bedroom is now the living room and the living room is the bedroom. Do I remember his horrible ripped-up orange couch? She threw it out. They have houseplants and a fish tank and bird cages. There are finches and parakeets in the cages and dwarf seahorses in the fish tanks. She's going to try to breed the seahorses. The thing that's fascinating about them, besides the way they look, is their reproduction. The males have the babies. She thinks that's not a bad idea. On my way to the park sometime, I should stop by.

Sure. I remember Drew's invitation to me when we first met: to stop by sometime and listen to his albums.

Sure.

Buck calls, after not having called in more than a year, to say he thinks he might be coming east for a visit, after all.

"How far east?"

"Pretty far."

"The Orient?"

"What are your plans for Halloween?"

"Let me check my calendar."

"When did you get a calendar?"

"Everyone in New York has one. They need a place to pencil people in. Should I pencil you in?"

"I think so."

"Should I ink you in?"

"That sounds more risky."

"I figured."

"What's new?"

"Not much. How about you?"

"I'm thinking about selling my house and buying another one a few blocks from here."

"Does this mean you're definitely not coming back to New York?"

"I'm still thinking about it. I might even check out Madison Avenue while I'm in town."

Buck is in advertising. I have no idea what he does, but I love his title: Creative Director. The last promotion he ran was for lawn seed.

"Will you be staying with me?"

"If I'm welcome."

"You're always welcome. Are you still seeing the woman you started seeing after Tracy whose name I suddenly don't remember?"

"Stacy."

We both laugh. "How could I have forgotten that? Is she coming with you?" I should have asked him before I invited him to stay.

"Not this trip."

"Your decision or hers?"

"Ours."

"I'm glad," I say. "I apologize, Buck. That was tacky. But I would rather see you alone."

"You may be disappointed."

"Are you still tall?"

"Pretty tall."

"Then I won't be disappointed."

"If my plans change again, I'll call—I promise. If I send you the flight information, will you meet me at the airport?"

"Not a chance. I won't believe you're really here until I

find you at my apartment door. Will you take me out to dinner?"

"Only if you meet me at the airport."

"It's still fun talking to you, Buck."

"I've missed talking to you."

I've begun talking to myself—not really speaking in sentences—just saying a few words and phrases aloud. "No one wants me . . . ," "I'm not pretty . . . ," "I'm lonely. . . ." I don't know why they're coming to the surface, why I should hear them now for the first time. They are hardly news to me. Who am I talking to? Apparently, Emma doesn't notice that I'm talking out loud and that I'm not talking to her. Maybe she assumes that I am. *Since Ann and I are alone, she must be talking to me.* But she doesn't stir. Words of no consequence—words that have nothing to do with food—do not disturb her sleep. I experiment by using the same tone of voice and saying, "No one feeds me . . . ," "I'm not thirsty . . . ," "I'm hungry. . . ." Emma wakes up and is on red alert, making me laugh.

Whenever I notice I'm talking aloud, I tell myself to stop, but in the early morning, or late at night, most often in the dark, I become vaguely aware of words spoken, as if by someone else. In the darkness, I speak to myself, expressing the thoughts that in daylight I'm not willing to hear, all of them fragments only, beginning in the negative mode: "No one . . . ," "I'm not . . . ," "I never. . . ." Who am I talking to? Is anyone listening? Am I hoping that someone will overhear? That someone will prove me wrong?

I've taken up the study of calligraphy with Geoffrey Maxwell, a British calligrapher now living in Toronto, who has come to New York to study illumination during the day and teach calligraphy and bookbinding at night. I heard about him from the art director at the Odyssey Press, who knew I had a closet interest in calligraphy. The workshop is part of a book-lovers' series sponsored by The New York Public Library.

At first, we'll be learning the italic alphabet, beginning with the lowercase letters, Mr. Maxwell tells us. For the first few weeks, that means we will be writing like e e cummings. We will all be poets. After all, he says, a poem is no big deal, is it?—the difficult part is remembering not to use any capital letters. He says in case he didn't mention if off the bat, he would appreciate it if we would call him Geoffrey. The only Mr. Maxwell he knows is married to his mother.

He begins by teaching us how to hold our fountain pens. The nib must form a forty-five degree angle with the paper. Does everyone recall what a forty-five degree angle is? He draws a right angle on the blackboard and divides it in half, just to make sure. He wants us to fool around for a bit—to make some doodles or squiggles, lines, circles, whatever—just to get acquainted with the feel of the pen against the paper. Mean-while, he'll be walking around the room to take a look at everybody's hand position. As we all know, he says, it's much easier to form good habits than to break bad ones. Are we beginning to see how holding the pen at this angle causes the downward and upward strokes to vary in thickness from very thick to very thin without turning the pen? He walks by my drafting table and pauses to look over my shoulder.

"That's fine. You are . . . ?"

"Ann."

"Try to relax, Ann." He touches my right hand. "I think you'll find that it's not necessary to hold on for dear life."

We are starting with the letter *i*. "Do you all know the difference between serif and sans serif letters? I'm sure you do, but you may not be familiar with the terms. I'll draw them on the board." He writes the letter *i* with and without a serif. "As you complete the downstroke on your *i*, I would like you to notice that by simply lifting your pen from the paper in a nice, smooth completion of your stroke, you will be creating a serif at the base of the letter." I practice that motion for the remainder of the class—the bold stroke down, the lifting of the pen from the paper, which leaves a serif in its wake like the mark left by the receding tide on sand.

Rebecca, Drew, and I are in the greenroom of the Frog Prince, a vegetarian restaurant during the day that turns into a club on weekend nights after ten. A knock at the door. When I open it, a woman bounds past me and grabs Drew, kisses him on the mouth, wishes him good luck, then bounds out.

"A friend of yours?" I ask Drew.

He explains that she's a groupie who's been following him around for years, going to all his local gigs, writing him love letters, calling him up at all hours of the night until he changed his phone to an unlisted number. She even showed up in England one time.

"I never knew she followed you to England," Rebecca says.

"That was before your time," he says.

"You don't mind?" I ask Rebecca.

She shakes her head. "She's just a weird chick. I feel sorry for her. As long as she can't call us anymore. Her phone calls used to drive me crazy."

"Does she know who you are?"

"Of course she knows who I am. She sent us a wedding present. She thinks we're best friends. All three of us. I don't care if she writes him letters. I don't pay any attention to the fan mail."

"I keep forgetting you get fan mail," I tell him.

"Didn't he ever show any of it to you? He's got a devoted adolescent following, especially in England. I guess it is a little hard to believe."

Not for me, I think. Not at all—speaking, for the moment,

as an adolescent. But I pretend to agree. "It is very hard to believe."

Drew on stage, welcoming the crowd, getting himself in the mood. The groupie sits right up front, at a table close enough to the stage to be rimmed in light. Rebecca and I sit toward the back, her choice. She wants to talk. While Drew sings, she tells me about their financial problems, the intricacies and intrigues of the music business, the incompetence of Drew's record company—a bunch of shoe salesmen who can't tell the difference between a hit song and a pair of white patent leather shoes. Money is tight. They had to sell Drew's baby grand to help pay off some of the debt he accumulated in producing his last album, or else the recording studio wouldn't let him do the new one. In America, unfortunately, Drew Gold is still hardly a household name.

"He sold the piano?" Rebecca doesn't seem to notice the nostalgia in my voice, my sentimental affection for the piano where once upon a time I would sit and watch her husband sing.

"The thing about marriage that's most surprising," Rebecca says, "is that you think you're getting married to a man, but you're marrying a whole family. People think that's not true anymore like it was in the old days, when extended families still lived together, but it is. Faith is already putting pressure on us to have children. She doesn't mean to; she probably isn't even aware of it. But I can tell from the way she dotes on me that she's thinking about it all the time. I think she wants a granddaughter, since she wanted to have a girl herself. Faith is crazy about kids, which is pretty ironic, considering the kind of mother she was. In and out of hospitals with her nervous breakdowns. No wonder Drew and his brother Frank are a little strange. Do you know Frank? I always assume you know everybody. I don't think Faith was really crazy. I think she wanted to be a serious opera singer and she gave it up for marriage and family and then her marriage fell apart and then she did. I bet her shrink was a *man* who was so stupid he believed her when she said she was crazy."

Rebecca talks straight through Drew's first set. At first I am shocked by her rudeness; although I know she's heard the songs countless times before, she probably hasn't heard them as often as the groupie, who is mesmerized. After a while, I realize Rebecca is nervous, scared for Drew and herself, uncertain of her attachment to a man who leaps on and off stages with a guitar. Even though she is chattering right through his songs, she is talking only about him, about their life together. I will tell him that later. Don't worry, Drew. She is talking only about you.

The groupie applauds him wildly, stands, cheers, calls out the names of her favorite Drew Gold songs. He barely notices. He is too preoccupied with Rebecca, who isn't paying any attention.

"Did Drew ever tell you about the time their mother went off to Italy and left Frank behind?"

I shake my head no and try to listen to Drew, who is finishing up his encore. The applause interrupts her. When Drew heads back to the greenroom for his break, she does not go with him.

"How old was Frank?"

"Fifteen. Faith packed up and went to Italy for the summer, to study voice. She was such an opera freak. She even named Frank after some tenor named Franco Corelli. Frank's real name is Franco—do you believe that? That's some name for a nice Jewish boy. Anyway, I have to give him credit—the kid had a lot of chutzpah. He decided to stay home by himself. Everybody thought he was somewhere else. Drew assumed he was staying with The Enemy. Their parents assumed he was staying with Drew."

"Who's the enemy?"

"Their father. That's what Drew always called him. He and

Faith split up when Drew was fourteen; Drew never forgave him for it. The Enemy *said* he wanted Frank for the summer, but Frank didn't believe him. Finally, he and Faith gave in and said Frank could stay with Drew. They decided Drew and Frank might be good for each other. Frank might keep Drew in line—fat chance—and Drew might help Frank loosen up. The Enemy assumed Faith, or more likely her boyfriend, had made the financial arrangements—but as usual, he didn't bother to check.

"Anyway, Frank did fine on his own. I think it was the summer before tenth grade. When the first month's gas and electric and telephone bills came, he ignored them—that's the same system Drew uses now. When turn-off notices came, he sold the encyclopedias, a set of bookshelves, and Drew's old bed and dresser. He paid the bills in cash at the bank, where his mother used to pay them. When the mortgage payment came due, he put up signs for a garage sale and sold off all sorts of stuff—the drier, the lawn mower, I think he might have even sold the refrigerator. He said his mother had to go out of town at the last minute and left him in charge.

"When Drew found out what Frank was doing, he couldn't believe it. He thought this time his kid brother might have gone off the deep end. He said the basement was amazing: Frank was drying his laundry on lines he had strung around the room like a giant set-up for cat's cradle. But Frank seemed OK, so Drew saw no reason to tell on him. He gave him some money and made him promise not to sell anything else.

"Drew told me most of this story, but there's one part that Frank told me when Drew wasn't around. I don't know if Drew knows. One night, Drew's girlfriend Terry showed up (You know Terry, don't you? She's such a twit) and scared him half to death because no one ever visited except Drew, and he always used his key. She said she wanted to spend the night with him. He assumed she was probably getting even with

Drew—maybe she found out that Drew was fooling around with someone else, which Frank knew—but he let her seduce him anyway, because he didn't want to be a virgin anymore. They slept in Faith's room because of the double bed. He told me that after Terry fell asleep, he stayed awake as long as he could, pretending he was the one she really wanted, not Drew. I felt bad for him."

Rebecca interrupts her story long enough to order herself a beer. I glance over at the table where the groupie was sitting. She's not there.

"Do you know Terry?" Rebecca asks me.

"I met her once, not long after I first met Drew. She was taking care of Rover while he was in England."

"Drew was an ass to leave Rover with her."

I agree with her but don't tell her so, since I think it's inappropriate for me to call Drew an ass. "She seemed excessively territorial to me, especially since he didn't seem all that interested."

"She's a twit. I can't stand her. She thinks she's hot shit."

Where is the groupie? I wonder. Is she at the bar? In the ladies room? In the greenroom with Drew?

A moment or two later, I don't care. I'm too caught up with the story of Frank the whiz kid, living on his own. He took to math and science, according to his mother, "like a duck takes to water, like Drew and I take to music." Faith used to say, "Frank's at home in school. Drew's more of a free spirit—undisciplined, like his mother." But she was wrong, at least about Frank. He didn't need school. He needed a place to tinker, take things apart, see how they worked, *if* they worked, understand all the ways they could break down and be fixed, improved, healed. He had become enthralled by the endless possibilities of adjustment, how the most minute increments in tightening or loosening wires, screws, and springs could have such salutary or catastrophic effects

Now that he had the whole house to himself, he started with the small appliances—the toaster, blender, vacuum cleaner. Then an old reel-to-reel tape recorder. Finally, his own stereo system (his inheritance from Drew)—amplifier, turntable, speakers. He began picking up discarded, broken equipment for spare parts. At first, he worked in his bedroom. Then Drew's old room. He needed more space. He rolled up the carpet in the living room, spread out his tools, his junkyard of audio equipment. Then he broke his promise to Drew and sold the rug to buy more tools.

All he cared about was how things sounded. He didn't seem to care about music, only about the subtleties of sound. He had perfect pitch. He hung out in audio stores and asked the salespeople as many questions as he could about enhancement capabilities and compatibilities. The more he learned, the harder he worked, the more he fought with Drew, the more he fantasized about sleeping with Terry again and building the best stereo system anyone had ever heard. He called Terry only once, but she and Drew were back together again. She told Frank to drop dead.

Faith came back from Italy and proceeded to rebuild the household, piece by piece, the same way Frank had taken it apart. She bought a new stove, couch, carpet. The books weren't hers and she didn't care if they were gone. Her collection of opera recordings was completely intact. She cleaned the house for two weeks and cooked meals but said very little. When the house was back in reasonably good shape, she called her doctor and went back into the hospital for three weeks—"a week of penance," Drew observed, "for every month away." When she came home, except that her medication had produced a few unpleasant side effects, she seemed all right, better than she had been in a long time. But Frank knew he could get along without her and wouldn't let himself be mothered, at least not by his crazy mother. He kept thinking about Terry.

She wasn't exactly the maternal type. Nevertheless, he thought
Faith wouldn't be a hard act to follow. He was wrong.

"Have you ever met Faith?" Rebecca asks me.

"No."

"I really like her. Faith has class. Besides, she always did
her best. Sometimes she didn't do such a hot job, but she
always tried."

"Who used to take care of the dog?"

"Poochie mostly took care of herself. She was like those cats
that wander off for months at a time and adopt a new family
for a while and then come back. That summer when Frank
was home alone, Poochie stayed with him, as if she knew it
was her job to take care of him. Faith had had her spayed, so
at least if she did take off, she wouldn't get herself knocked
up. That may be one of the most responsible things Faith ever
did. And Poochie always came back. Until the last time, of
course, when she didn't."

"I miss you at work," Malin says. "Karen is doing fine—
but she's not the editor you are. She doesn't catch my mistakes
for me. Besides, she isn't nearly as much fun. Do you ever
miss working together?"

Yes, I do, but I won't admit that to him. "We work together
all the time." Now that I've become one of Malin's free-lance
writers, I work at home and keep my own hours. I like it that
no one, not even Malin, is looking over my shoulder—something he couldn't have done anyway unless I were sitting down,
given his height. I almost admit that I would enjoy seeing him
more often like this—in his apartment rather than his office—
but I don't want to scare him away.

"Lilly was here for the weekend. She asked about you."

"How does she know who I am?"

"I talk about you. More than you'd probably think."

"Why did she ask about me?"

"She always asks about you—ever since I told her about the birthday present you gave me last year."

I would love to meet Lilly, but apparently the notion has never crossed Malin's mind. My birthday gift to him: I sneaked into his office (even though I no longer worked full-time at the Odyssey Press, I kept my key) and set up a display of miniature toys that traced his life story along a "road" from Arkansas to New Mexico to New York. Three of the toys were animals: an inch-high Cat, a slightly taller Bad Boy, and an inch-long alligator, representing the mother alligator that chased eight-year-old Malin away from her nesting place, up an embankment, and half a mile down a deserted road. When Malin got home, terrified and out of breath, protesting that he didn't mean to bother the alligator, Warren, as usual, had a moral: "Good intentions are no guarantee against undesirable consequences." It was a stock response. Malin, unjustly persecuted by the alligator, looked to his mother for comfort and vindication. Lilly explained that maternal instinct is a powerful force. "But I wasn't doing anything wrong!" he complained. She said he better let his grandad take him fishing, because the alligator was protecting her young and there wasn't anything anybody could do about that.

There were other toys—a red sports car (like the one he sank when he was in college), beer cans (always appropriate), and a tiny plastic tree, representing the job he had the summer before he started the Ph.D. program in philosophy at Columbia. He was a newlywed, temporarily living in Tulsa, his wife's hometown. At Flowerland, Malin was crew supervisor for a group of high school kids, all of them taller and stronger than he was. They planted and tended several varieties of artificial trees for treeless homeowners. During the summer they installed the trees, and the following winter, when Malin would be exploring the question, "If you cut a tree down and turn it into a lectern and then burn the lectern, what has happened to the essence of the tree?" they would remove the leaves, which detached like pop-beads from the branches. In the springtime, when Malin would be getting ready to sever his marriage vows, the crew would reattach all the leaves.

I knew I had to work fast to get out of the office before Malin showed up, but for the first time in his life he was on time. He thanked me with a kiss on the cheek and invited me to join him later for drinks with Norman and his wife. But a few hours later he called to uninvite me; apparently, they were already a foursome: Norman had invited his wife's sister along. Malin called again, after midnight, and apologized twice—for waking me up, for breaking our date. He was overwhelmed by my gift and at a loss to express his gratitude—how did I know him so well when he felt like he barely knew me at all? He left everything on his desk as long as he could, and then unfortunately he had to clear it off and get down to work.

"The car's on my bookcase," he said. "I put the alligator in my philodendron. When I'm working at my desk I can see its beady little eyes peering at me between the leaves."

"What about Cat?"

"I brought him home. Maybe I'll ride him around the apartment."

"You should wait until you inherit Lightning's saddle. It's not safe to ride bareback."

"First I have to find an apartment big enough to hold the saddle."

"Malin, I don't suppose you would . . . Never mind."

"No, tell me. What were you going to say?"

"You wouldn't like to get together now, would you?"

"Now?" he whispered. "I would love to, Ann, you know I would . . ." and I realized he wasn't alone. Why can't I learn to keep my mouth shut? Why did I decide to give him that stupid present in the first place? I take them both back, Malin, my question and my gift. I closed my eyes and tried to reconstruct the road map and the toys exactly as I originally had placed them so that I could reclaim them all. But they were no more accessible to me than the animals I tried to buy for Drew on his wedding day. Malin said that the alligator was in his philodendron at work and that Cat was at his apartment, but I knew where they really were—locked away in glass cases. I wanted to shatter the glass and steal them. Even though the guardian of the animals was nowhere around, I still remembered her rules: Nothing may be touched, nothing carried home.

"Hasn't it ever occurred to you that I would like to meet your mother?" I ask him.

"Would you? Let's plan on it the next time she comes to town. She would enjoy that."

"How is she?"

"Lilly's doing fine. She's been seeing some bank president or something. I think she's thinking about getting married."

"How long has it been since your father died?"

"A long time."

Malin and his mother were on their way to Rainbow to visit his father's parents when Lilly told him to turn off the highway at Texarkana and guided him to a motel. Lilly called her in-laws to report they had been delayed by car trouble. Then the two of them ate dinner and went out dancing until after midnight. Upstairs in their motel room, they sat talking on the balcony overlooking the pool, almost whispering, looking straight ahead and not at each other, Lilly holding a club soda with lime, while Malin downed one six-pack of beer and began working on a second. The darkness was perforated by pinpricks of light around the pool and by the glowing tips of Malin's cigarettes.

"You smoke too much, honey."

"I thought you would tell me I drink too much."

"That, too."

He agreed with her, speaking in an accent that was becoming more like hers the longer they spent time together, and less like the hybrid it had become in New York, where he had been living for more than ten years. Lilly told him that night for the first time—he had to search back through his memory for clues he should have seen before—that she and his father had been talking about a separation the night before he died. Malin had known they were having trouble of course, but he had assumed they would work things out. That wasn't quite the case, she said. She had gone off to her sister's house to think, and that's why he had been alone at the ranch (Malin was off at college) the night the house burned to the ground.

"You do smoke too much," I tell Malin.

He fumbles for his lighter. "I know."

"You didn't suspect your parents might be breaking up?"

"I guess I wasn't paying attention. Then—as now," he adds, "my self-involvement gave me the excuse not to see what I didn't want to see. I knew my father couldn't stop working and Mother . . . I knew Lilly couldn't stop partying."

"Where are the cats?" Roy and Dale, the two cats he's been babysitting for a friend, have disappeared. I notice that the door to the terrace is ajar.

You did it again, didn't you, Malin? Just like last week, the story you told: Roy and Dale, out on your balcony, sniffing hot, summer-city, exhaust-filled air not fit for a cat. "Their existential moment," you called it, ignoring your own. The cats mirror your tentativeness—should they stay or flee, and if they run, where to? Can they find their way home? Will you tell your friend you lost his cats? You call them back to you, you cajole, beg, bribe, but they don't listen. You swear you will keep them safe. You promise vigilance, but turn your back, leaving the door ajar. You allow them to escape to the terrace, to the ledge high above the street—should we go? should we stay?—then pluck them from the precipice and toss them inside onto your bed. They know. They suffer your petting but remain aloof.

"Did I ever tell you I had a cat when I was little? One of the barn cats, really, only I sort of adopted him. When he was still a kitten I snuck him into the house at night under my jacket and he slept with me in my bed. The day we moved away from Rainbow I ran over to the barn to get him. I had finally convinced my folks that Cricket was my pet and not just one of the barn cats, but I couldn't find him. Lilly helped me hunt around, but we had to leave and Cricket got left behind. My grandad said cats were resourceful and Cricket would do fine on his own; he'd probably find himself another boy my age to sucker before we drove out of the county. I cried like a fool."

Malin is sitting in his hanging chair. He folds his legs and tucks his feet under him, allowing the momentum of the swing to run its course.

"I still love this chair."

"I'm glad."

We had been wandering through a crafts fair outside the Museum of Natural History when I led him toward a display of macramé hammocks and hanging chairs, the hand-twisted and knotted ropes simultaneously as sturdy as riggings on a boat and as delicately complicated as a web. "This is what I wanted to show you."

He bought a hanging chair with arms of lacquered birch, too much money, but perfect—too perfect to pass up. How did I know he'd have to have it? We walked side by side, carrying the chair. He kept sneaking glances at me to figure out how I knew. "You are so easily mystified," I said. "Or you pretend to be."

The chair swings toward the center of his apartment, swivels if you try to stop it and, released again, keeps up its swing until it gradually slows down and begins to sway and eventually comes to a stop. It has become something of a pet—"How's the chair?" I ask him—something between us, *our chair.* He shows it off to his friends, most of whom I've still never met.

"My friend Ann found it for me."

"Who's Ann? Are you seeing someone named Ann?"

"You remember her. We used to work together."

"Oh," they say, disappointed. Nothing exciting here. No sexual monkeying around on the spectacular swinging chair: *They fly through the air with the greatest of ease. . . .*

Safety net, I think. That's what it is. My safety net suspended in Malin's apartment. I suspect it will one day become a relic of our friendship, a piece of memorabilia, like his childhood boots. His houseguests, the cats, can climb on it when I'm not there.

"In the spring in the part of New Mexico where we lived, when the weather conditions were exactly right and the wind seemed to sweep the last bit of clouds and haze from the air, you could look out in the distance and see Mogollón, a snow-capped mountain ninety miles to the north. Mother made the mountain into a game—who would see it first? Sometimes I would have this feeling, something about the briskness of the wind, the clarity of the air—the conditions seemed right—and I would keep watch for it. When it appeared, I ran like hell to find Mother. She pretended not to see it. She said I was just teasing her. She said things like, 'Honey, why are you pulling my leg?' Mother liked to win. She'd be staring right at it and she'd say, 'I wonder when it will appear.' "

The chair has stopped swinging. "You want a ride?" he asks.

"Sure." I take the chair and Malin stretches out on his bed. "Getting tired?"

"No."

He looks exhausted to me. "It's getting late. I should go home."

"Are you tired? I've probably worn you out with all my stories. I'm amazed by the way you listen."

"It's not much of a talent, Malin."

"I don't understand why you always get so insulted whenever I tell you you're easy to talk to."

"I don't see why it's much of a compliment. Men always feel comfortable talking to me."

"Then why do you get offended?"

"I'm just saying that being easy to talk to isn't necessarily an asset."

"Because it's easy for you?"

"Because it's just plain easy."

He shakes his head. "Ann, I've been married once, I've lived with three women, and not one of them knows half the stories about my childhood that you know."

"You know how much I love hearing them . . ."

"That's not the point. You still think you have nothing to do with them, but you're wrong. The stories happen *between* us. You engage them. Without you, they disappear. That's what I mean when I say you're easy to talk to. I consider it a very high compliment, one about which I'm totally sincere. I don't have any idea how you do it. Somehow, when I'm talking to you, I remember stories I didn't even know I knew. You make me tell you the truth."

The way I'm truthful with Emma, I think.

Malin gets himself a beer from the refrigerator and offers me a drink. Roy follows him like a dog. He suggests a Kahlua and cream, the only drink I like, waving the unopened bottle of Kahlua he claims he bought especially for me. He takes a sip from my glass—"I don't know how you can drink this stuff"—to prove again that he bought it for me. I give him back the swinging chair and sit on the edge of his bed.

"I guess the stories aren't enough," I say.

"Do we really need to talk about this?"

"*I* need to talk about it. I can't speak for you."

"All right."

I tell him that I want us to be either clear-cut friends or more than friends, and that I think I would prefer the latter—given the choice. He returns my smile. "But I'll settle for just friends. I need things to be clarified one way or another. Even if we're going to stay friends, good friends, I feel like you have to do more to keep up your half of the friendship."

"I still don't want to close any doors, Ann."

"But you don't want to walk through any, either."

"I can't. Not yet." Malin says there hasn't been a day since I left the Odyssey Press that he hasn't missed me. He says that maybe he shouldn't be telling me this, but when we worked together he used to fantasize about what it would be like if he could grab me and pull me down on the floor behind his desk. Nevertheless, he can't sleep with me because, according to him, "in the hush following sex, a promise gets made." What promise? A promise not to leave your terrace door ajar? He knows only this: he can make no promises at all. At least not now, not yet. The only vow he has made is to himself: he will not hurt me, or any other woman, again.

"You can't make a promise like that."

"Yes, I can."

"Not unless you become a monk. Or a seer. Why can't we just start at the beginning? Start with not knowing?"

"Because I do know."

"Then why do you want the door left open?"

"Why do you have to have it closed?"

He only *thinks* he wants it open. He tells me that he knows he doesn't want to marry me. Therefore, he doesn't love me.

Therefore, he shouldn't go to bed with me. Therefore, he will not kiss me.

Kiss me, Malin. Where did you get your logic? Is that what you learned in graduate school? I've never studied logic. Kiss me, Malin. If we ever end up in bed, I'll find a way to tell you stories.

"I'm sorry." A door bangs closed in my face. "Ann." His telephone greeting travels from the hanging chair to the bed as if it were a long-distance call, traveling across a wide expanse. "You are right about our friendship. I haven't been much of a friend to you. You've always been the one to keep it going." He gets up and comes to sit beside me. The chair keeps swinging. "Look at me, Ann." He turns my face toward him. "Are you crying?"

No. I'm trying to swim, although I don't know how. Trying not to drown. Trying to survive, my hair streaming backward, like his mother's.

"You are crying." He touches my wet cheek and gets up— at first I think he might be running away from home—and fetches me the roll of paper towels. He tries to wipe my face, but I won't let him. He closes the palms of his hands as if in prayer and holds them between us, then opens them slowly, like a child revealing something precious, a seashell or a stone. "Ann." For the moment, only my name, naming me. "Are you willing to put our friendship here?" We're both staring at his small hands, too small, I think, to hold our friendship. "You've taken care of it so far. Now it's my turn, if you'll let me."

He's waiting for my answer. "Yes," I say, thinking: Let him be the guardian of our friendship.

Dale and Emma are sleeping at the foot of Malin's bed, while Roy is pacing like a prisoner near the closed terrace door. "Try not to lose the cats, Malin," I say on my way out.

"Let me come down and get you a cab."

"I won't have any trouble getting one this time of night." I reach for Emma. Dale reminds me of a caterpillar as she uncurls without awakening, then curls back up. I gently pick up Emma and carry her to the door.

"Let sleeping dogs lie," I tell her.

Nine

*I*T'S the kind of day you stumble upon and kick aside like a broken toy. Nothing to be done. You just know you can't fix it—a tin chick that won't peck, its spring wound too far for too long.

It's seemed like four o'clock since I got up at nine. Still raining. The first chilly fall rain. I melt caramels to make myself one caramel apple for lunch. Then I remember Drew. I remember him as if I were recalling a childhood pet, a memory lost and reclaimed, like a dream. Drew. I place his album on my turntable and the moment I hear his voice fill my bedroom I am healed. The first words he sings: *Autumn leaves are falling like rain. . . .*

"Where's Drew?" I ask Emma. "Or, speaking in your terms, where's Rover? Let's go find them."

I carry her under my umbrella to the park. Since Drew hardly ever walks the dogs, I have no reason to expect to see him; nevertheless, I'm disappointed when he's not there. Apparently, I've lost the power to conjure him up. Poor Emma, I think. I've dragged her along on a wild goose chase. Fortunately, the rain lets up just long enough for her to scout around and do some serious squirrel hunting; when it starts raining again, she quits. I get to carry a muddy, wet dog.

I'm not paying much attention to where I'm going—I can travel the streets between my apartment and the park on automatic pilot—when Rover and Rita materialize just ahead of me, right outside Drew's building. Drew looks, not surprisingly, since it's only a little past one, like he just woke up.

"Good morning," I say. We kiss each other on the cheek. I'm glad he's in a bearded phase. "How did you get stuck with dogwalking this time of day?"

"Rebecca's out of town. Rover, wait up!" As usual, Rover hates for Drew to stop on their way to the park. I notice that Drew doesn't have the dogs leashed. Apparently, he uses the leashes only when Rebecca is around.

"So you're a single parent again. It's not easy raising the kids alone, is it?"

He laughs. "I think I can handle it for a week."

"I've missed seeing you around."

"Rebecca likes walking the dogs. She thinks she's better at it than I am. Rover, come!"

"She is." I don't tell him that the only reason I'm out in the rain is because I was looking for him. "I had a feeling I might run into you today."

We exchange our usual round of park pleasantries. The intensity of Drew's delivery is always incongruous with the questions themselves: "How are you? How's Emma? What's been going on? Anything new?" In the old days, before he and Rebecca got married, he paid more attention to my answers. But recently he doesn't bother to wait for the inevitable "fine," "fine," "nothing," "not much," before he nods and smiles, acknowledging that all goes well.

A sudden downpour cuts our conversation short. "Would you like to come over and visit this afternoon?" I ask him. "We could catch up." Catch up on what? I wonder.

"Sure. Why don't you wait for me in my building—at least you can get out of the rain. I just have to get these two out for five minutes. I would invite you inside, but the apartment's a mess—I guess since Rebecca's been away I've reverted to my untamed ways."

We're sitting on either end of my couch facing each other with our legs stretched out toward the center. We took off our soaking-wet sneakers and socks and put them near the radiator to dry. My jeans are wet, too, but I don't bother to change. It's a perfect afternoon for a fire in a fireplace. On a day like today, Chuck and Emma Bovary, lucky stiffs, would dry off in front of a raging fire. But the radiator and the oven are my only sources of heat. I suppose that Drew and I could go into the kitchen, pull up a couple of chairs, set the oven to a moderate temperature, and relax by the open oven door. I remember the last time he was here, when we stood in front of the stove together (was it really three years ago?), and I was waiting for the kettle to boil, and he crept up behind me.

At the moment, Drew and I aren't talking because I've decided to let him ask all the questions. After a few exchanges—"How have you been?"/"Fine"; "What have you been up to?"/"Not much"; "You look good"/"Not really"—neither of us has anything to say. I know I could rekindle our conversation by asking him more questions. Get the ball rolling again, as it were. But conversation is no longer what I have in mind. I remember the subway T-shirt he was wearing that day we traveled from the stove to my bed, when I was afraid I would end up in Coney Island, and he was still an unmarried man.

"I think you look good. Do you want to know *how* good?" He reaches forward and begins to slide his hands along the inside seams of my blue jeans from my ankles upward. "*This* good."

"I was listening to your autumn rain song this morning. I can't remember the title."

"Good enough to eat," he says, matter-of-factly, with his I-didn't-just-say-what-you-thought-I-said, altar-boy smile.

"Was that an offer?" I'm playing at being equally outrageous, making him laugh.

He begins to sing—not his song, but "Autumn Leaves." In elementary school, we had to sing it in the early fall, before we got to the Halloween songs. "*Falling leaves drift by my window, those autumn leaves of red and gold. . . .*" I close my eyes to listen. His fingers have a light, spidery touch. They remind me of an even earlier childhood song, about a spider. I hear myself sing it, although I'm not singing out loud: *The itsy bitsy spider walked up the water spout. . . .* It was the kind of song I hated as a little girl because we had to act it out:

Down came the rain (Wiggle your fingers and feel the
   rain coming down)
And washed the spider out,
Out came the sun (Make those suns big, as big and round
   as you can make them)
And dried up all the rain,
And the itsy bitsy spider
Walked up the spout again (Where are your spouts? Let's
   see those spiders climb!)

Was it "itsy bitsy" or "teensie weensie"? I can't remember. Who cares? Concentrate, Ann. Where is your mind? That's the question I always ask my teensie weensie dog when she's not paying attention to me. Where is your mind? Where is Drew's? In the gutter, I think—lucky for me.

Drew is using his hands now, his whole hands, not just his fingers. Slowly, they are moving higher. He's hamming it up: "*I miss you most of all, my darling, when autumn leaves begin to fall.*" Sing it again, Drew! Take it from the top! I'm concentrating on the song and his hands, the song, his hands, on his two hands, which have moved up in the world as far as they can. *He's got the whole world in his hands, he's got the whole world in his hands, he's got the whole world in his hands, he's got the whole world in his hands,* I hear, another elementary school golden oldie. I hear it so loud and clear I want to swing my hips, clap my hands, and tap my foot. If I could sing, Drew, honey, I would sing to you. If I could sing out loud, someday we could even try a duet. But after a few more minutes, there are no more songs—no more love songs, no more kids' songs, no more spirituals—the only music I can hear now is pure rhythm, the rhythm his hands are working on me. I hum along. Don't stop now! Encore! How I wish that I could sing.

"Maybe we better go to bed."

"Have I ever told you if I could have one wish, I would wish for a voice?"

"You have a voice."

"A voice good enough to sing."

"Let's go to bed."

I'm listening to him sing again, wordless melodies this time—are they songs I don't know or improvised?—but after a while, I can't hear him. I press my hands against his shoulders and gently push him in the direction I want him to go. Go on down, honey. You know how. You just let yourself fall and keep on falling straight through the bed to the bottom of the deep blue sea.

Drew, with arms outstretched, clings to my breasts. Even though he's the one in the water, I take hold of his hair like a horse's mane so I don't drown. I can't swim. Have I told you that before? He slides his hands under my hips. He's doing the dead man's float, his hair streaming out in a halo around his head. *Angel puppy,* I think. Malin lapped milk from a saucer on the floor. But Drew can sing: *There's a hole in the bottom of the sea, there's a hole in the bottom of the sea, there's*

a hole, there's a hole, there's a hole in the bottom of the sea.
Water fills his mouth. He gasps for air. I rescue him by tugging
on his arms. He raises his torso and lets me carry him all the
way to dry land. He rests. Then he inhales. His lungs expand.
He regulates the rhythm of his breathing. When its rhythm is
restored, he kisses me.

"My turn," he says.

"Your turn."

He lies beside me on his side. I'm facing him. He shimmies
up a little, and I shimmy down. He holds my face between
his hands and touches it like a blind man getting to know me.
My eyes are closed. With his fingertips, he touches my chin
and my mouth, guiding me. The blind leading the blind, I
think. What song, now? Will you still sing to me? How soon
will you be ready to get back in the water? If the tide rises even
higher, and we are swept out to sea, will you promise to save
me the way I saved you?

The ocean is at high tide before I know it.

I wake up and find the two of us beached on my bed in late
afternoon. Drew awakens and yawns, his bearded cheek between my breasts, his breath warm against my skin. Rain is
blowing in my open windows; my bedroom smells like rain.

"You could sing, you know, if you wanted to."

"Bullshit."

"My mother could teach you to sing."

"Your mother the opera singer?"

He lifts his head to look at me. "I only have one mother.
She teaches voice—sight-singing, interpretation . . . she has
a few students like you—people who have always been afraid
to sing. You should give her a call. She could help you, she
really could."

Drew and I lie together until we both sense it is time to
stop. I intend to walk him home on my way back to the park
for a second dogwalk, since Emma's first walk was curtailed

by rain. But she is daunted by the wet streets and refuses to budge off the top step outside my building. "It's not raining," I tell her. "Do you see rain?" But she *suspects* rain.

"When is Rebecca due back?"

"The end of the week."

We both know without having to say it that this afternoon will not be repeated. A piece of unfinished business—like a piece from a jigsaw puzzle you sweep out from under the bed long after you've thrown out the whole puzzle—connected to the past, perhaps, but irrelevant to the present or the future.

"Will you call my mother?"

"Sure. I'll tell her you're a hotshot in bed."

He laughs. "I keep wondering how long you'll put off getting what you want."

"So do I."

After two months of calligraphy classes, I know the whole lowercase italic alphabet. My favorite letters have ascenders or descenders—the portion of a letter that falls above or below the line. I especially like writing the word *dog*; I've even been trying to figure out connecting strokes so I can write it in the cursive style. Practice absorbs much of my spare time. Somehow, listening to Baroque keyboard music while I work helps me maintain the regularity required to get the shape of twenty-six letters to become second-nature to me, which Geoffrey predicts will one day happen. I practice on a slanted board in order to see all the letters exactly the same way, without distortion, from the top to the bottom of the page. I form each letter ten times, rest my hand and listen to the music, then form another, until I complete the entire alphabet. Then I practice them the way Geoffrey has recommended—in family groups: *bdh, gyq,* etc.

Geoffrey says my work is very good, indeed, that I have quite a good eye, but I need to relax because the spacing between my letters is a bit cramped. I'm not allowing the letters to breathe. He suggests I use a broad steel brush and begin practicing very large letters, working with a relaxed, free hand. Some students lack discipline, he says. It's obvious in their work right from the beginning. I, on the other hand, have a surfeit. Rhythm is as important to calligraphy as shape. First, I must learn how a letter should look, then I must teach it to my hand, and then I must give my hand free rein to execute it. "*Hold* your pen," he says, "don't strangle it." He's flipping through my practice sheets. "By the way," he adds, "I see you've been trying to work with connecting strokes. There are some letters in italics that form natural connections: the *i*, *t*, and the *e*, for example." He takes my pen from my hand and shows me the strokes. "Why don't you try practicing those? Unfortunately, *dog* doesn't have any connecting letters. Is there a reason that you chose that particular word?"

I tell him that I'm fond of ascenders and descenders. I don't mention dogs.

"Then I wonder why you didn't write *god* instead?" I can tell that he's teasing me. He says as soon as I get my steel brush, I should begin from the beginning, with the letter *i*. Meanwhile, for the duration of the class, he'll lend me his. He recommends that I work as fast as I can, to offset my tendency to be overly meticulous.

"You mean I'm uptight," I say.

"I mean you're overly meticulous."

"But my letters are inconsistent."

"Variations aren't necessarily imperfections, although they can be, of course. If you require absolute consistency, that's *type*, done by a machine, not *calligraphy*, done by an aspiring human hand."

I like the feel of the flexible, broad steel brush against the rough sheets of cheap newsprint. But I'm too old to play. At least I think I am. Geoffrey would disagree. I try to be less

serious, to be someone else. There's no use trying to be someone else. Did Drew say that? Or did I? I try to follow Geoffrey's
advice to work as quickly as I can. This is easy. Page after
page, the pen glides down the paper, leaving bold, black *i*'s—
rows of them, columns of them, randomly scattered *i*'s, patterns of *i*'s, Rorschach tests of *i*'s—they remind me of fish
scales and birds' feathers.

"Is this what you wanted me to do?"

"Exactly. Do you see the movement you've created here?"
He flips back through my pad to my earlier work. "You obviously have a fine natural ability to form correct letter shapes.
But I would call this *penmanship*. On the contrary," he says,
pointing to the steel brush work, "this is the beginning of
calligraphy." He thinks I'm progressing very nicely, but I should
keep working with the steel brush every day, in addition to the
regular classwork. And I should remember I don't always have
to work in black. There are some wonderful colors available,
especially when I'm using the steel brush instead of the fountain pen. As always, I must pay less attention to the letter
shapes, which I have already begun to master, and more attention to the relationships between the letters. We are working
on the letters based on the *i*: the *f*, *j*, *l*, and *t*. I am to write
fjlt as if it were a word. But it isn't a word, I think. I'm an
editor at heart. I practice the word *jilt* instead.

Drew calls me for the first time ever, to tell me that his
mother is expecting to hear from me.

"Excuse me?"

He laughs. "So you should give her a call."

"What did you tell her?"

"Exactly what you told me."

"I'm not calling her, Drew."

"Do you have a pen? Never mind—you don't need a pen.
She has a studio in the Ansonia. Her phone number starts off

the same as yours—777, and ends with 1492. You can remember that, can't you? Just remember the Niña, the Pinta,
and the Santa Maria. With a name like Faith, how can you
go wrong?"

"I'm not calling her."

"Call her."

"Why should I?"

"Because it's about time you got what you want."

Next week is my birthday. I was thinking if Malin got around
to calling by then, I might ask him to go out to dinner to
celebrate my birthday with me. But I'm not holding my breath.
I haven't heard from him in two months—not since he took
charge of our friendship. So much for social skills. Sit, Malin.
Say "how do." So much for friendship.

Instead, I muster all my earthly courage and call Drew's
mother (dialing a telephone never killed anyone, I tell myself) and explain that I'm a friend of Drew's and he suggested
she might be able to teach me to sing.

"Yes," she says. "Drew mentioned you. He believes you
can sing but you're afraid."

"Drew thinks turkeys can fly."

She laughs. "Do you know what it means to be tone
deaf?"

"Yes."

"Are you?"

"No."

We meet at her studio in the Ansonia, one of the most
famous landmark buildings on the Upper West Side. A grand
piano fills most of the room. There is a desk covered with
music, and a daybed where Faith says she sleeps the nights
she stays in the city. She spends half the week here, half
of it at home in New Jersey. I notice a tiny kitchen and
bathroom off the foyer near the door. She offers me a cup of

tea. "My next lesson isn't for two hours, so we'll have plenty of time to get acquainted," she says. "Tell me about you and singing."

Let's all stand up and push in our chairs and stand directly behind our desks with two feet flat on the floor, our hands at our sides and nowhere else. No slouching, please. And no slumping. There are no humpbacked camels here. By now we should all know the words to today's song by heart, so we won't need our books. I want to hear big voices, not mousy little voices. But I don't want to hear any bellowing. There are no cows in this classroom.

> *Oh, Shenandoah, I long to hear you*
> *Haul away, you rolling river*
> *Oh, Shenandoah, I long to hear you*
> *Away, I'm bound away . . .*

Stop, stop, everyone! You're all doing very well, but please try not to raise or lower your heads when you reach for very high or low notes. Does everyone understand? Let's begin again, at the beginning.

I understand. I'm trying to do the best job I can. It isn't so hard if no one notices that you're using a mousy little voice. Only a few minutes more and—if I live—singing will be over until tomorrow, and then after tomorrow there's only one more day, and then no more singing until next Wednesday, one whole week from today.

> *I'm pushing on when dawn's a-breaking*
> *Going cross the wide Missouri*
> *My true love she stands a-waiting*
> *Away, we're bound away*
> *Across . . .*

Ann! Would you *please* try to remember not to lift up your head.

Faith smiles Drew's smile. "I was wondering," she begins, then pauses and starts again. "Do you recall your mother singing to you?"

I don't remember her singing, her not singing. I remember my father's songs because they were so silly: *Old Grogan's goat was feeling fine, stole all the clothes right off the line* . . . but I don't tell Faith. "I'm not sure."

"You have a pretty accurate memory when it comes to school."

"How do you know it's accurate?"

"Because the way you describe school reflects your feelings about it. Sometimes memories are interesting if they simply recount the facts, like a reporter. Sometimes you can get an interesting perspective that way. But usually the memory is more complex; it likes to combine facts with your feelings about them. Memory gives you your own truth, a valuable commodity, whether it corresponds to so-called reality or not. In fact, it would be fascinating if, years from now, I could overhear your recollection of our first meeting today." She invites me to sit beside her at the piano. Again, she reminds me of Drew.

"I just want to find out a little more about your voice." She hits middle C on the piano, sings the note, and asks me to sing it with her. She's not looking at me, for which I'm grateful. She plays the note again, sings, waits in vain for me. "Try it a little louder." I manage to make the softest audible sound anyone can make—my "mousy" voice, I think. She travels up the scale slowly, one note at a time, saying "wonderful" or "terrific" after each step, through an octave and a half.

She says she thinks she can help me. She is willing to be my teacher; I have only to let her know if I am willing to be her student. She hands me a questionnaire she gives to all her students in order to familiarize herself with their musical backgrounds—how much they know about music, what kind of music they like, whether they've studied voice or any instrument, done any songwriting or composition, etc. "One more thing," she says. "If you decide to study with me, we'll need a concrete goal. In your case, I would think your goal might be two or three songs you would like to learn. Or perhaps one song and a performance—I shouldn't use the word *performance*, I mean more that you could learn to sing along with your friends. Think about what you want to accomplish. If you want to choose the songs yourself, be careful to choose songs that are important to you but also easy enough that they won't discourage you. All right? That means you shouldn't plan on anything from *Aïda*." We both laugh. She rests her hand on my shoulder.

I wait a few hours, then call her.

"Do you have a plan?"

"I'd just like to learn one or two songs. By myself. That will be accomplishment enough. I'll never do it."

"I have an idea for the first one. If you don't come up with anything by the time we meet next week, we'll see what you think. Ann . . ." she says, as I'm about to hang up, "I meant to ask you something when we were talking, but I don't want you to feel obligated to answer. I was wondering what made you decide to call me."

I wonder if Drew repeated to her what I told him: that I wouldn't call her in a million years. "You're my birthday present. From me to me."

"What a generous present."

My dreams still have the same themes: dogs, safety, will I be able to swim or will I drown, or will I not be able to swim and live anyway, since drowning is too severe a punishment for a failing as minor as the inability to swim.

One of my park friends flees the park with her dog, a large brown and white pinto mutt also named Emma, and her new baby girl. I notice that three garbage cans near Riverside Drive are smoldering. My friend leaves the park because of the possibility of danger, not its presence, since the fires are contained. She has a child to protect. I stay behind, brave and childless, with Emma, and when the fire department arrives, torrents of frothy water flow from behind me, flooding the park, creating a lake. The water rises to my knees, past my waist, and up to my neck. I tip back my head and raise my chin to keep it out of the water. I hold Emma up as high as I can, her tiny face level with mine, her cat-sized paws, under water, pressed against my throat. "I can't swim," I say out loud, a pure admission, a confession of failure, which no one else hears. I could free Emma and let her swim on her own—all dogs can swim, I think. But I do not have the courage to let her go. I manage to grab hold of a fence with one hand, then lose my grasp and half float to a tree and grab one of its branches, its pine needles shedding in my hand, the soaking branch much too slight to support me, yet somehow it does and I stay afloat, the branch in my right hand and Emma in my left, until the fires are out, and the water stops rising.

The pine tree. I awaken and remember the pine tree. That was my clue. There are no evergreens in my section of Riverside Park. Pay attention, Ann: *this is only a dream.*

Faith would like to teach me a lullaby—"All Through the Night." If I agree, that will be our initial goal. Later on, perhaps, we could establish new ones.

She senses without my having to respond that I've agreed.

"Regarding our lessons, I expect my students to be punctual, which means not too early as well as not too late. I prefer that lessons be as private as I can make them, and that includes no accidental listening outside the door. My students fall across a wide spectrum of goals and abilities and I don't want them discouraged by inappropriate comparisons. I allow ten minutes between lessons to minimize the possibility of overlap, and to give me a chance to relax. Do you remember your dreams?"

"Yes."

"If any of them seem relevant to your study here, feel free to tell me about them. We both know," she says, patting my arm, "that singing isn't always about singing."

She digs through the music on her desk and unburies a photocopy of the sheet music. "Organization isn't my strong point," she says. During the next week, she would like me to spend some time with the song lyrics—reading them to myself, reading them out loud if I want to—but under no circumstances am I to try to sing them, not even hum them, out loud. I can sing them "in my mind's eye," if I must, although she doesn't especially encourage even that. Meanwhile, I can keep on singing with Drew's records, but she'd prefer if I sang along with a woman, too.

I take home the lullaby and copy it in italics, using the uppercase letters that I've finally learned. I write it out using different size nibs, then several more times using my steel brush and different color inks. I bring them to class. Geoffrey thinks I'm moving right along and offers to teach me my first flourish—the real word for it is *swash*—one that flows from the crossbar of the letter *t* in the word *night*. It's an extended horizontal stroke that rises naturally at its completion from the lifting of the pen off the paper. It is not—and this gives away the untrained calligraphic hand—a wavy, upward stroke. The distinction between the two is obvious to me. Geoffrey thinks I'm really catching on now, and if I keep progressing at this rate, I'll be ready to learn the rudiments of calligraphic design.

I show Faith a copy of "All Through the Night" written out in italics using peacock-blue ink on gray paper.

"That's exactly what I wanted you to do. Besides learning the words, you found a way to make the song completely your own."

I examine the lyrics over her shoulder. As usual with my own work, I can see only the mistakes. "The capital A is wrong. It leans."

She leans to the right, holds the paper up close to her nose and peers at it. "Seems perfect to me." She laughs and begins to play a richly ornamented version of "All Through the Night"— just so I can hear it. She knows I'm not ready to learn to sing. My capital A leans.

Today, we'll be learning a brand-new song: "Froggie Went A-Courting." This is a special song, so we're going to sing it a special way. Who knows what a verse is? Can I see hands? Right—a verse is a group of words that go with the melody of a song. Today's song has twenty verses. Since there are so many verses, this is what we're going to do: we're all going to learn the first one, and then we'll go right around the room and each of you will sing a verse of your own. Who knows what you call it when one person sings alone? A *solo*. That's very good. Ready? No, I won't answer any more questions now. You want to go to the bathroom? Of course you may. When you get back, we'll start learning the new song. But before you go, perhaps you can tell us what *courting* means, because I bet some of us don't know.

"It's like dating," I say.

I'll stay in the bathroom forever. They'll find me here when it's time to go home. I'll say I have a stomachache. I'll say I have a sore throat. I'll say anything they want if I can just please go home.

> *Froggie went a-courtin' and he did ride, m-hm*
> *Froggie went a-courtin' and he did ride, m-hm*
> *Froggie went a-courtin' and he did ride*
> *Sword and pistol by his side, m-hm.*

OK, everybody, that was very, very good. Now, we're going to go around the room so that I can assign each of you a number. I'll be number one. Pay attention. Does everyone know what his or her number is? I'm passing out sheets with all the verses, and I would like you to place a checkmark next to the verse with your number so you don't forget it. Let's all read number one out loud together, and then each of you can read your own verse.

I'm number nineteen, next to the last. I read quickly through all twenty verses. Mine is the only one that doesn't rhyme: *Mister Frog went hopping over the brook, a lily-white duck came and swallowed him up, m-hm.* How did I get stuck with the only one that doesn't rhyme?

Very, very good. Now I think we're all ready to sing. I'll begin with the first verse, then we'll all sing the same verse together, then we'll go around the room and each of you will sing your solo, and then we'll finish with everyone singing the first verse again together—that's called a *reprise.*

I try to sing the first verse, but if I'm singing, I can't hear my voice. The verses go by quickly. They're getting closer: number twelve, number thirteen. One more verse till number fifteen. I have to go to the bathroom. I have to go home. Number sixteen. My verse doesn't rhyme and I can't sing. Number seventeen. I don't know how to do a solo. Lorraine is number eighteen: *"Next to come in was an old gray cat, she swallowed the mouse and ate up the rat, m-hm."*

You mother-fucking sonsofbitches, didn't you tell me I can't sing?

Ten

*G*EOFFREY Maxwell is leaning against my bedroom doorjamb. In the darkness, and without my glasses, I can't make out his face at all; his body, silhouetted by the kitchen light, is a letter shape I don't recognize, one-twenty-sixth of a calligraphic alphabet I haven't yet learned. I have rented him my spare bedroom the two nights he stays in New York. On Wednesday evenings, he teaches my calligraphy class, for beginners. On Thursdays, he teaches the advanced class. Usually, he comes home very late (although both classes end at nine), after I'm in bed. I've explained the situation to Emma a dozen times, but every week she charges the door, barking, as if he were an intruder. "It's just Geoffrey," I tell her, but she never takes my word.

"Are you awake?"

He knows I'm awake because I just yelled at Emma to stop barking. Nevertheless, he's whispering.

"I wanted to tell you once again how much I've enjoyed staying here with you the past few months."

"In that case I'll raise your rent. Why are you whispering?"

"I feel comfortable with you." He has regained his normal speaking voice. "As if I have known you for much longer."

"Like an old shoe."

"You might try simply saying thank you, you know."

"Thank you."

"You *can* say it. I am overwhelmed. Bowled over."

"You can be pretty sarcastic for an out-of-towner."

"And you, like so many New Yorkers, are a chauvinist."

"Thank you."

"Who also happens to be a very attractive woman."

"Only in this light."

"You are. And sexy."

"What's wrong with you tonight?"

"I'm only telling you what I see when I look at you, how I feel when I'm around you. I'm very attracted to you, Ann. I thought you knew that. In fact . . ."

Did I know that?

"May I come closer?"

"How much closer?"

"This much." He approaches the bed. Emma growls. "Was that you or the dog?"

"Quiet down, Emma."

"Are you quite certain that wasn't you?"

He sits down beside me and caresses my face, finds my hand under the blanket and kisses it, places my palm against his cheek. Emma growls again.

"What are you so worried about?" he asks her, his voice soft and reassuring.

"Are you talking to me or the dog?"

He reaches for Emma, who leaps away from him and off the bed. He is left stranded between her and me, and for a moment seems off-balance, unsure if either of us wants him.

"Geoffrey." He flings himself toward me and lands heavily in my arms. "For a minute there, I thought you might leave."

"I thought you might prefer me to go."

"Not exactly."

"Not exactly?"

206

"Not at all . . ."

Geoffrey is the expert calligrapher and I am the novice, but for the moment, at least, we are surprisingly well matched: we both know how to use his pen to form a perfect flourish.

"You are very talented, Ann. The italic alphabet is already in your hand."

"What does that mean?"

"When you have mastered an alphabet, calligraphers say it is *in your hand*.

"How many alphabets do you know?"

"Several."

"Will you show them to me?"

"That depends."

"On what?"

"On when you stop asking questions.' He is practicing roundhand. He starts off with the letter o, the basis of the alphabet, the equivalent of the *a* in italics. It's a two-stroke letter, one semicircle at a time, starting near, but never at, the top. Roundhand, he says, has always been a favorite of his. Virtually all the letters depend on the same, full-bodied shape. "Should I tell you my secret? Do you know how sometimes at night when you see the new moon, you see not only the slender crescent that is illuminated by the sun, you also see—or imagine you see—the rest of the sphere, the full moon? When I begin the letter o, I visualize the full moon, although it is still in darkness, and if I relax and find my rhythm, the same way I've taught you to find yours, my hand illuminates what I already see."

He wants me to watch him work. "Keep thinking about the perfection of the circle," he whispers. "It is such a mysterious shape. It has no beginning and no end. You can fall through it, like a hole, or emerge from it, like a cave. Think about the roundness of things: the pupil of the eye, the moon, the mouth. Each time I form the letter o, think about the movement within the shape, the ceaseless rising and falling, and the movement outside, the circle rolling like a ball, spinning like a wheel, how it keeps on going as if it will go on forever, how it does go on forever, rotating and revolving, like the earth."

The trick, I think, is to let yourself be bolder than you are. To make the first stroke rounder, fuller, more plump than you think it should be. To work with confidence and allow your hand the freedom to do what it knows how to do on its own. The second stroke, which is shorter, completes the fullness of the first. Once I'm holding the pen, I can't help showing off. Geoffrey no longer guides me. I am his star pupil. I choose my own letters, my own alphabet. At first, I accelerate only to find the perfect rhythm, not too fast, not too slow.

"Perfect," he says.

The trick is to let yourself be bolder than you are. I pick up speed. I am doing fine, he says, splendid, in fact, the best damn calligraphy job anyone has ever done for him so far, impeccable letters, perfectly splendid forms—the outside shapes, the inside—the flow of the ink, and, best of all, the perfect rhythm, the pen a part of me now, like both alphabets, already there in my hand.

Near dawn, Geoffrey says he thinks I better call him Max. All his friends call him Max. Only his parents and his students call him Geoffrey.

On Wednesdays, Geoffrey is still my teacher. On Thursdays, Max comes into my bedroom late at night and disappears into his own room before sunrise. Sometimes, in the morning, I stand outside his partially open bedroom door and watch him sleep on his side, his pillow wrapped in his arms like a woman. On Fridays, both men fly home to Toronto, to Margaret, the woman they plan to marry in the spring.

Max turns over in his sleep, gripping the pillow. I stand very still so I don't disturb him. This is better than standing on the street outside Drew's in the dead of winter, I think. At least I'm home.

"Well, howdy."

Buck's fake Texas accent. "I can't believe it."

"Well, howdy."

"I still can't believe it."

"I told you I'd call."

"You always tell me you'll call."

"You're not that easy to reach."

"That's what I keep hearing from all the people who don't ever call me."

"I've been trying to get you for a week."

"Don't tell me: you're planning another trip east."

"All right, I won't tell you."

"You're coming east?"

"Not until May. May thirtieth, to be exact."

"You're actually coming to visit after all this time?"

"Eight years, I think. But that's only part of my news. That's why I called. I have something to tell you and the phone is second-best to telling you in person."

"That you're getting married."

"Goddamn it, Ann, how do you do that?"

"It's a miracle."

"How could it be a miracle? You do it all the time."

"I'm not talking about my having guessed right. I'm talking about you—I can't believe you're finally settling down."

"Neither can I."

"Congratulations, Buck."

"Thank you."

"Just give me a second to get used to the idea." I hold the phone at arm's length and stare at it, but it's inscrutable, unlike Buck's face, which is simply too far away to see. Buck gives me a little privacy, then comes back to me As he approaches, I can see that he's grinning.

"Who's the lucky girl?"

209

"Promise me you won't laugh?"

"I never laugh."

"It's Tracy. We're back together again."

I laugh louder than I should.

"So much for promises."

"That wasn't a laugh. It was a chuckle."

"More like a bray," he says.

"And the two of you will be honeymooning in New York."

"How do you know these things? Will you tell me that?"

"Any fool would know them, Buck. Do you have any idea how long you'll be staying?"

"Until my money runs out—probably a weekend. Unless I can find some way to combine it with a business trip. I'm hoping to finagle it so that the agency will pick up part of the tab. Do you think you'll be in town?"

"As far as I know." For that moment only, I let myself speak one truthful, unembellished line.

"I really do want to see you, Ann—if you're still talking to me. I want Tracy to meet you. I told her you're my best Jewish friend. I told her every Wasp man needs a Jewish woman in his life, just to keep him in line."

"So I guess this means we're not marrying each other when we both hit fifty."

"Unless I'm divorced by then."

"I'm not sure I would be willing to marry a divorcé."

"I don't want our friendship to end, Ann."

"Neither do I." It shouldn't, I think, given that it hasn't so far. I manage not to say, although I can't help but think: God knows I've had plenty of practice. "When is the wedding?"

"Memorial Day weekend, we hope. In either Chicago, near my family, or San Francisco, where most of Tracy's family is. I know you probably can't come, but I'll send you an invitation."

"Thanks. Are you scared?"

"About getting married?"

"Yes."

"Only when I'm awake."

"Afraid of getting bored—as usual?"

"Among other things."

"Take up a hobby, Buck."

"Hobbies have gotten me into trouble before."

"That's because you picked the wrong hobby."

Gradually, Buck and I run out of steam. This time, I'm more reluctant than usual to hang up. But I know it's my turn. He will feel too guilty about his marriage to hang up first.

"I better get going, Buck. I was just on my way out with the dog."

"How is Emma?"

"She's great. Small, but great."

"I'm looking forward to meeting her."

"I'm sure she feels the same way about you. How's your job?"

"I just got another promotion."

"That's great. And your new house?"

"Small, but we like it. We've been fixing it up. How's life in the big city? You never tell me what's going on with you."

"That's because nothing much is going on. I'm not getting married. I'm not fixing up my apartment. I guess I've been in a self-improvement mode lately. I'm taking all sorts of lessons."

"Like what?"

The singing lessons are private; the only person who knows about them is Drew. "Like calligraphy. When I get a little better at it I could address your wedding invitations for you."

"They've already been printed, I think. They're Tracy's job."

Having made such a dishonest offer, there is no telling what I will say next. "I'll call you soon, Buck, all right? I have to get going. Emma is staring at me. But let's keep in touch."

"I want to."

"I know you do. And congratulations to you and Tracy. Tell her I'm looking forward to meeting her." I wonder where Emma is. She's probably asleep on the couch. Hang up, Ann. Go find Emma. Hang up before you tell him another lie. Hang up before you accidentally tell him the truth.

Faith is teaching me intervals. I learn by matching notes. She wants me to hear the difference between one, two, and three full steps. We'll get to larger skips and half-steps later. We need a song for the day. She glances at my hair, smiles, and sings:

> *The old gray mare*
> *She ain't what she used to be*
> *Ain't what she used to be*
> *Ain't what she used to be*
> *The old gray mare*
> *She ain't what she used to be*
> *Many long years ago.*

"Sing with me," she says.

> *The old gray mare*
> *She ain't what she used to be* . . .

"I can't hear you," she says. She begins the song a third time, admonishing me that this time she'd rather not sing it alone.

Rebecca telephones to invite me to a Chanukah party. She's asked several of the park people I know—or the former park people, she supposes she could call them, since their dogs are long gone. Drew's away in England, but he definitely included me on the list of people he wanted her to invite. I'll be getting an invitation.

Why did she bother to call, I wonder, if she's sending out invitations? I remember her calling only once before, to ask me the name of my vet.

"While I have you on the phone, there's something I've been meaning to ask you. Do you mind? If I called at a bad time, or something, you could always call me back."

"What did you want to ask?"

"If you ever slept with my husband."

In the four years that we've been chatting in the park, Rebecca has never before referred to Drew by anything but his name. The tone of her "my husband" links him with property—not with mere possessions—but with land owned, worked, and trespassed upon. The tone of her voice links her with generations of women, unlike me, who have chosen to exchange vows of fidelity with men who may betray them.

Did Drew tell her?

"The winter before you two met, we came close a couple of times, but I chickened out. I didn't think I could handle it. He was such a compulsive flirt."

"No shit."

Now I know I'm getting old. Formerly, when truth was white and lies were black, I wouldn't have lied to her. Formerly, of course, I wouldn't have slept with Drew and wouldn't have had any reason to lie. Innocence can't be regained by the act of telling the truth. The truth is that Drew and Rebecca love each other (at least I know that he loves her) and that he and I screwed around. If I were Catholic, I would confess to a priest, but I still wouldn't tell Rebecca. I will not endanger their marriage. If Drew tells her, that is his decision. Then Rebecca can call me a liar, which I am.

"To tell you the truth, the only other female I know he's sleeping with besides you is Rita," I say.

"But I get even by sleeping with Rover."

"*Ménage à quatre.* Sounds pretty kinky to me."

I'm being glib with you, Rebecca—my defense for an in-
defensible act, a reckless one, in fact. I borrowed your husband
without your permission for an entire afternoon. There are
times, I want to tell you, when I get so lonely. Because no
one wants me, I feel like such a freak. You say, What's the
big deal? You say, I remember there was this six months, once,
when I wasn't seeing a man. I say, You don't know what I'm
talking about. Unless you're past thirty, you don't know anything about time. I am thirty-seven years old. And I'm in-
dulging in self-pity, self-serving self-pity, but I can't stop. Until
Max showed up, sometimes I would lie in bed and literally
reach out my arms and imagine I felt a man's embrace. Sometimes, when I saw couples holding hands on the street, I could
feel how their fingers were entwined. Drew would hold hands
with me in the park. In private we were nothing to each other,
but in public we were involved. He made me feel wanted,
even though I knew he wanted me temporarily, until someone
like you came along. He gave me two chances, and I blew
them. He gave me a third, and I took it. It should not have
happened. It will not happen again. But tell me this: Imagine
you were his little girl instead of his wife, and I were one of
your playmates. If he were to pick me up in his arms and spin
me around and around the same way he spun you all the time,
would that be wrong?

But you are no child! you say.

I used to be one. Does that count? I apologize, Rebecca.
This is no laughing matter. You are right, of course. I'm no
longer a child. If I want to behave as a child, I have to forfeit
grown-up privileges—such as going to bed with a man. Don't
blame Drew. He and I could have slept together when we
were both single adults. It's my fault, not his, that we waited
until we were both profligate children. I remember a line from
the first song he ever played for me: *I sleep with a woman who
thinks I'm a child.*

"It's going to be a *latkes* party," Rebecca says. "Everyone is supposed to bring a potato or a grater or some applesauce. You should bring Emma."

"Thanks very much," I say. "I'll definitely try to make it." Another lie. With a little luck, my last one to her.

Billy, would you kindly put away your bear and pass out our songbooks? Would everyone please turn to page thirty?

I like page thirty. It has a picture of two gray donkeys and four white sheep and one bright yellow star. I know it's a nativity scene, and the animals aren't as important as the pink baby asleep on the hay in the manger, but since I'm Jewish, it's all right if I like the animals best. The song is called "Adeste Fidelis"—that's Latin. Why can't we learn how to sing the whole song in Latin?

Because in this classroom, we all speak English. If this were third-century Rome, we would all speak Latin. Because we are Americans, we all speak English.

But I can't sing.

Of course you can.

No, I can't.

Then why don't we start with an easier song? "Joy to the World" is practically a scale and scales are as easy as the stairs right outside our classroom. A *descending* scale sounds hard, but really it's just like walking downstairs. Sometimes there are leaps, but leaps are easy, too—you just jump a few steps at once. You know how to jump steps, don't you?

No, I don't. I'm afraid. I could fall flat on my face.

You have to try, Ann.

I don't look up. I won't take my eyes off the sheep.

Let's go back to "Adeste Fidelis," then, if you like that one better. No one is expected to be perfect, but everyone is expected to try.

I shouldn't have to try. I never know what to do about the

end: *O come let us adore Him, Christ the Lord.* When I sing
the word *Him,* I try to sing it without the capital *H.* It's only
capitalized because Christ is the Lord for some people. But
he's not my Lord. The last line is the worst part. I'm not
supposed to sing the last line at all. Or maybe I am, since it's
only a song. Why don't I ever think about this ahead of time?
What do I do now? Why can't you leave me alone? *"Da-a,
dum-m the Lord,"* I sing, my head down, my attention focused
on the donkeys and sheep, who seem to like me, even though
I'm Jewish and I can't sing.

Faith says she thought I might enjoy singing Christmas
carols this time of year, but we certainly don't have to. "Why
didn't you ask your teacher about singing carols? Or your
parents?"
"I thought it was a stupid question."
"Why?"
"There are lots of things like that—things I thought I already
should know. I still pretend I know more than I know."
"And you pretend less."
"Maybe."
"I have an idea." She leaves the piano, rummages through
her purse, the desk drawer, a cabinet in the kitchen, the closet
in the foyer, and returns with a brownie, a candle, and a book
of matches. She lights the candle and sticks it into the chocolate, tells me today's her birthday, plays a few introductory
chords to "Happy Birthday," and warns me the candle will
burn quickly and I'll have to hurry if I don't want the wax to
ruin my reward.
I begin singing not quite as softly as usual. "Louder," she
says, "match volume as well as pitch." She plays and sings
with me, then asks me to sing even louder because she can't
hear me. "From the top," she says, beginning it again. I pick
up speed because the candle is dripping and this time I manage

to keep singing all the way through to the end.

Faith applauds, makes a wish, and blows out the candle, then splits the brownie between us.

"My lollipop."

She nods. "For a job well done. Would you like to know what I wished?"

"I think I can guess."

"Tell me."

"You wished for me—that I could sing."

"Almost. I wished you would believe that you already can."

As always, she ends my lesson with the piano version of "All Through the Night." She says I'm progressing wonderfully and I should be as proud of myself as she is of me.

"Listen," she says. She plays me a different "All Through the Night," this one transposed for my range.

Max arrives at my open bedroom door. Emma is doing her imitation of a watchdog. "Dirty little mongrel," he says, greeting her. Dirty is no exaggeration. She is in desperate need of grooming. Her fur is filthy, the same color gray as the slush on the streets.

"Isn't this still Wednesday?" I ask him.

"Yes, it is."

"I thought so. Then you must be Geoffrey. Class was fun tonight."

"May I come in?"

"Of course." He lies down beside me on his back and stares up at the ceiling. He's clasped his hands behind his head. In the darkness, I can't see his expression, but I sense that something is wrong. "What's wrong?" I ask.

"Nothing. Do you mind if I turn on the light?"

"No."

Now that I can see his face, I know that something's wrong. "What's going on? Are you moving out?"

"Not unless you want me to."

"Why do I have the feeling that our Thursday nights are over." More a statement than a question.

"Margaret and I will be spending Christmas week together. We'll be married in May. It wouldn't be right, would it, for you and I . . ."

"No, it wouldn't be right."

We lie together without speaking.

"What are you thinking?" he asks.

"Geoffrey is going to stay, but Max is moving out."

"Poor Max."

My friends are always saying "poor Emma" when she gets dirty and I have to bathe her, when she gets in the garbage and I have to clean it up, when she's fast asleep and I have to get dressed and walk her. "What do you mean, poor Emma?" I yell at them, fooling around. "What about poor Ann?"

He rolls over toward me, props himself up on his left elbow, and takes my right hand in his. "I want you to understand that this has nothing whatsoever to do with how much I like you, Ann, or how much I lust after you. Look at me." His expression says he wants me more than ever. "You are a very desirable woman. I think you may be the sexiest woman in the world." I laugh and push him away. "In the universe." He enfolds me in his arms and pulls me on top of him.

"So when does this new policy start?"

"Next week, I thought."

"So that's why you're here: to sneak in one extra night— just under the wire."

"I couldn't help myself."

"Should I call you Geoffrey or Max?" No answer, only the pressure of his body against mine. "I'm sorry, Max. I knew this couldn't go on much longer. More than anything, I'm going to miss the way you look at me."

"Who said anything about changing the way I look at you? I'm only human . . ."

We have tonight, tomorrow night—plenty of time, I think, all of tonight, all of tomorrow night. But in the middle of the night, as always, he slips out of bed and goes back to his own bedroom. On his way out of mine, he turns off the lamp. I try to take hold of the way he looked at me, to keep his expression before my eyes long enough to memorize it, but it fades quickly. I had hoped it would glow in the dark, like the Cheshire cat's smile. When I turn on the light, Max reappears, in the flesh.

"Would you like me to stay here with you tonight?"

"No, that's all right."

"That sounded more like a yes than a no."

"Go back to bed, Max. I'm fine."

"I thought I heard you crying."

"I was crying. I am crying. I'm feeling sorry for myself. Go back to bed."

"In a little while." He puts his arms around me and holds me. "I'm very sorry."

"Don't be. This doesn't have anything to do with you. I'm not . . . no one ever . . . no one . . ." Those fragments again, spoken to someone else, finally, not simply to myself.

He cradles me in his arms and rocks me and says he will never understand how I can be worrying about all the things I'm not when in his eyes I am the sexiest woman in the entire English-speaking world including America, Canada, Great Britain, and the whole of the former British Empire.

One of the production people at the Odyssey Press—this woman is a former friend of Malin's who never accepted his friendship with me—calls to ask if I've heard the latest.

"I heard that the new guy in the art department spilled coffee on original artwork three months after the artist died."

"That's the old news," she says. "Guess who's the newest in-house romance? Malin and Karen—your replacement."

"That's not news to me," I lie. "Malin told me he was going to ask her out."

"He must be grateful to you. If you hadn't left, the two of them would never have met."

So that's why Malin hasn't called me. He's trying to think of a tactful way to tell me what's going on. How could he be seeing Karen? She isn't exactly the blazing blonde beauty he's always yearning for. She's smart enough and nice enough—I genuinely like her—but why her? She's younger than I am. Is that why she seems a little lost, a little needy? Do you want to be needed, Malin? I need you. It's just that my loose ends aren't as obvious as hers. I've always suspected that she might unravel. Why her and not me?

On the other hand, this might make things easier, more clear-cut. Now that he's with Karen, maybe he and I will become better friends. He'll have to call me soon, whether he wants to or not. He'll be needing my latest assignment. I think I'll hold on to it until I hear from him. The little coward will probably ask his associate-editor girlfriend to call.

Instead of dealing with rejection the only effective way I know—shaking it off the way a wet dog shakes off excess water—I do what I always do: let it weigh me down until it evaporates of its own accord. Ordinarily, I'd call other men. I'd call the first one to prove the initial rejector wrong, and when my prospective savior also rejected me, I'd call another, and so on, until Buck—usually I end the cycle with Buck— told me for the thousandth time how much he values our friendship and misses New York and was just thinking about picking up the phone and calling me.

Only this time, Buck is getting married. That knowledge short-circuits the whole system of calls. I call no one. Instead, I take Emma to the park, where I'll dry off in the sun.

But it's late afternoon, almost dusk. The cloudy sky over the Hudson is inlaid with mother-of-pearl; the slate-gray river has no waves at all, except for an occasiona. swell. It reminds me of mercury, which I played with as a child. A shaft of sunlight penetrates the clouds and reflects off the metallic surface of the river, reminding me of slivers of mica, another childhood toy. For sporadic, brief moments the sun is brilliant and hot—I should dry off quickly, I think, positioning myself in its path—but it disappears almost instantly, and the wind by the river is cold. I have to keep walking. The concrete path around the perimeter of the chain-link fence surrounding the track has been plowed and tramped down, making it the perfect surface for Emma, who loves to play in the snow as long as she doesn't get wet. Neither of us likes to get wet.

On our way home, I see Rebecca headed for her usual place in the park. I wave to her; she waves back. I don't know what Drew told her or didn't tell her about our roll in the hay. But I'm afraid to talk to her again until I find out.

Now that I've learned two entire alphabets—italic and roundhand—calligraphy is about to officially end. For the last class, we are to choose one of the hands, or a combination, and work on a final project. If we want to, we can use any number of special materials—handmade paper, colored inks, even gold leaf.

But the art of calligraphy, Geoffrey reminds us, requires more than beautiful writing. The calligrapher's eye must find the perfect combination of materials and letter shapes in order to unite them with the most important component—the words themselves. Calligraphy is wasted on trite or stupid words. We must choose the heart of our projects with utmost care. The length is inconsequential—one word can be just as complicated as a paragraph or a whole page.

"I'm going to read you some words of advice written by a

Chinese calligrapher of the Han Dynasty," Geoffrey says. "Although he is talking about Chinese calligraphy, which is in many respects a very different art form, I think his advice is also meaningful for us:

> Your heart must be quiet and you must not try to work when upset. Do calligraphy when you feel well; no discomfort should come between your brush and your thinking and awareness. Take time with your work; if you are not at ease and comfortable, your characters will be clumsy. Make sure your hands feel relaxed, that your ink works well upon the paper; nothing will be gained by struggling with your tools. And last, do calligraphy only when it is the thing you must do, and when you have something to express which you must put down in this way."

The project takes me two full weeks of preparation. I try to follow the proper steps: I select and sharpen my nibs, practice mixing Chinese ink and water to the proper blackness and consistency, and find heavy, handmade, off-white paper of the perfect texture—just enough sheen to allow the pen to glide, and just enough roughness to keep it from careening out of control.

I wake up early, take Emma out for a quick walk and promise her a walk to the park later, eat breakfast, and get down to work. I have set aside the entire day. First, I draw guidelines on my paper, then plan the spacing using a tissue overlay. I warm up with a few pages of *a*'s and *i*'s. *Make sure your hands feel relaxed.* I am not at all relaxed; I need music; I reach for the Bach harpsichord music I usually listen to while doing calligraphy, and find myself holding a Drew Gold album in my hand. *Your heart must be quiet.* Drew is singing "Zoe" to me.

Emma and I go look for him. He appears at the front door of his building just as I pass by, the dogs charging out ahead of him. He kisses me on the cheek and yells, "Roverita, wait up," but they keep going. We round the corner and stop— both of us startled by a Christmas tree, a fifteen-foot Scotch pine, which has appeared at the entrance to the park. It's been stuck into the ground as if it had been planted and could grow, as if it were alive.

"I was here after midnight and this wasn't " he says. "Pretty amazing."

"What do you think it means?"

"Maybe Santa Claus is coming," he says, shrugging his shoulders. "What do I know about this stuff? I'm Jewish. What do you think it means?"

"I have no idea," I say, which is not what I'm thinking. I'm thinking: There are no evergreens in this section of Riverside Park. The three dogs are unimpressed. Rover and Rita try to urinate on it; I yell at them to get away. They're waiting for Drew to play fetch. Rita won't stop barking her head off until he throws the Frisbee he has in his pocket. Emma is waiting for us to continue our walk. But we can't all walk together by the river, where we used to, because Rover might run into other male dogs. "How's the rock-star business?" I ask him.

"Fine. I've been wrangling with the management of my record company. They own me but they won't promote me. We've sort of reached a stalemate. They won't meet my demands and I won't meet theirs. I've been trying to get them to release me from my contract. They think I'm going to roll over and play dead and I'm not rolling over."

"I have the same problem with Emma." He laughs. "Do you have a plan?"

"I'm thinking about walking away and declaring personal bankruptcy."

"That doesn't sound like things are fine "

Drew says it's no big deal. His debts would be wiped out, that's all. The only drawback is that he would lose the rights to the Drew Gold songs recorded so far—three albums. He gave away his rights the day he signed the contract. He'd never be able to record them again; technically, he wouldn't be able to perform them in public again, here or abroad.

"You couldn't sing your own songs?"

He shrugs his shoulders. "I'm not worried. First, they'd have to catch me. Besides—I could still sing them at home."

But could you sing them to me? It's been a long time, I want to tell him, but even now, every once in a while, you still sing to me.

"I do have one piece of news . . ." He throws the Frisbee for Rita to shut her up.

"You're pregnant."

"That's a pretty good guess," he says, laughing. "We're moving. We found a house up near Woodstock. It's on five acres, and there are woods right behind our property. The dogs can run around in the country all day."

"I went to Woodstock," I say.

"It's a nice artsy-fartsy town."

"No, I mean *the* Woodstock."

"You went to Woodstock? You *are* old. You really went to Woodstock? I thought you hated rock music."

I can see that I've gone up a notch or two in his estimation. I never knew that having gone to a sixties rock concert—even *the* sixties rock concert—would end up impressing any man, especially a man I like. "I don't want to talk about rock music— I want to talk about you. You're only teasing me, right? You're not really moving."

"You and Emma will have to come visit."

"But no one ever moves." I'm simply stating a fact, since the middle-income housing shortage in Manhattan makes it impossible for anyone with a reasonably priced apartment to find another. A move out of Manhattan is permanent.

"I'll come back again some day."

"When you're a rich little rock star."

"A rich little middle-aged rock star."

"When are you leaving?"

"By New Year's Eve. You should stop over and say goodbye to Rebecca."

"Speaking of Rebecca . . ." This is my first opportunity to ask Drew if he told her that we slept together. "Did you know that she called me—this was a while ago—while you were in England? She asked me if you and I . . ."

"I know. She told me."

"Did I say the right thing?"

"Absolutely."

"Did she believe me?"

"I'm sorry you got caught in the middle of that, Ann. It didn't really have anything to do with you. It got started because of something that happened in England—do you remember the woman you met that time at the Frog Prince?"

"The groupie?"

"She and I—never mind, she isn't important. Rebecca and I have worked everything out. We're even thinking about starting a family. That's one of the main reasons we're leaving. Neither of us wants to raise kids in New York."

"That's probably a good idea, especially for you, since you're still not convinced that a dog is safer if you train it or keep it on a leash."

"I still think you should have an affair with some young trombonist from Juilliard."

I laugh. That had been his suggestion a long time ago; I know why he chose Juilliard, since it's in the neighborhood, but he never said why he picked the trombone, one of the few instruments I dislike.

"If I do, you'll be the first one I'll call."

"I'll let you know when we get a phone. So, anyway, you should stop by sometime next week. I have a tape of my new album I could play for you."

"Does your mother have a copy?"

"I'll make one for her before I leave. Why?"

"In case I don't see you again, I could listen to hers."

"You'll see me again. How are the two of you getting along?"

"She's terrific."

"When will you be ready to sing for me?"

"When the swallows come back to Capistrano."

"Is that soon?"

"I think you'd better ask Faith."

He lies to me, telling me he's not going to say goodbye right now because we will be seeing each other before he leaves. I accept the lie like a gift and go home to complete my calligraphy project. I warm up again, practice a page of capital *B*'s, then begin to work. My first attempt is a failure because I'm still out in the park with Drew. Concentrate, Ann, or this will take all night. One day soon, I will find a moving van outside Drew's building. Either he will be moving out or some stranger will be moving in. His apartment will be emptied of dogs, finches, seahorses, guitars, synthesizers, husband and wife. A sign will appear in the window: "No rock stars here." I help. I sweep his apartment clean using the broom and dustpan he left in the middle of the living room the first time I was ever there. I sweep Drew out of his apartment and into my mind, just for the transition, a hotel for the night. *Your heart must be quiet.* I'm sorry, Drew, but you can't stay. I close down the hotel. He takes his wife and his pets and moves to the country and I begin my project again. My fourth try is not yet perfect. I want to do it again and again, to make it perfect, flawless, better than the best I can do. But I cannot. I throw the pens into the sink, wash them, then scrub my hands and dry them carefully. I hold my work up to the light: *Beauty is in the eye of the Beholder.*

I bring the assignment to class. Geoffrey, as usual, strolls around the room from desk to desk, holding up each work for all of us to see. This time, in addition to asking us how we selected certain materials, he asks why we chose the particular words. When he gets to me, he stares at my work a long time before he finally smiles and asks how I happened to choose a cliché.

"It's one of my mother's favorite expressions." That's all I intend to say, but I can tell that Geoffrey wants to hear more. "I always thought it was making the same point as her other favorite—'There is no accounting for taste.' But now I understand that what it's really talking about is the capacity to perceive beauty . . ."

Again, Geoffrey is unsatisfied. He's waiting for me to continue, but I'm too embarrassed, suddenly aware of everyone looking at me, at my work. Who cares about a cliché? "The distinction seems important to me, I guess because it shifts the burden from the object being looked at to the person doing the looking."

"And that's why you capitalized the *b* in *beholder*—to call attention to your understanding," Max whispers, speaking only to me.

"Show-off," I whisper back.

"Still, you mustn't entirely forget about the object being looked at." He moves a little closer and smiles a Thursday smile. "This is very beautiful work," he announces in full voice, for everyone to hear.

Although tonight is an official teacher-student night (for the past two weeks, we've managed to pretend that Thursdays are Wednesdays, too), Max knocks gently on my closed bedroom door and asks politely if he can come in just for a moment. He flings open the door and takes a flying leap toward my bed. Because this is our last week together until next semester, he thought perhaps I wouldn't mind a hug, for old-times' sake. Clichés, I wonder? We hold each other, but we're very careful with our hands. *Keep your hands at your sides and nowhere else.*

227

"This won't work, will it?" Max asks, sometime before dawn.

"No."

"I will have to find another place."

"I know."

"Will you still be in my advanced class?"

"Geoffrey's class," I correct him.

"Will you be there?"

"If he's sure I'm good enough."

"You're more than good enough."

"Doubtful."

"You still haven't learned how to say thank you."

"Let's try it again."

"All right. You're going to be a very fine calligrapher, Ann."

"Doubtful."

"And you're already an incorrigible pain in the ass."

"Thank you."

"You're welcome."

He kisses me. "This is more than a hug," I say.

"I can't keep my hands off you. I think you're beautiful."

"You must be blind."

"Only in your eyes."

Eleven

*B*UCK, Drew, Max, Malin—they have all moved from the heart of the city, where I live, to the outskirts, to the suburbs or the country or to other cities in different states, where I never visit, and no longer phone. They have all become relics, memories, except for Malin, who still looms in my mind like a dinosaur—extinct, but extant, at least in skeleton form: the remains of the last single man.

Malin's lack of love for me does not feel like what it is: nothing, an absence, a space. His lack of love for me is of massive proportions and weight, as weighty and dense as stone. I carry the absence of his love around my neck and it weighs me down and bows my head, pushing me deeper into silence. I spend most of my time alone. My friends call and I talk to them about their lovers and husbands, their careers, their dogs. They say I seem a little down and ask if I've heard from Malin yet. "Malin who?" I answer. They laugh. "The runt," I say.

They recommend I forget about him. Ditch him! He's dead weight. Not *much* weight, they tease, but dead weight nonetheless. Throw the guy overboard.

Ballast, I correct them. Since I can't swim, I have no intention of rocking the boat.

But they won't give up. They say there are plenty more

229

where he came from. There are lots more fish in the sea.

They know I hate going fishing. Especially the part where you have to bait the hook. If I could use a net, I might be tempted. Then if the fish turned out to be undersized, like Malin, I could release him with no harm done. At least I wouldn't have bloodied my inept fingers twice, the first time struggling to bait the hook, the second time struggling to remove it.

They say Drew was right. Apparently, I still don't know what I want.

This is what I want: to land a fish without piercing the lining of his storytelling mouth.

You want to catch butterflies or you want to go fishing?

I want to catch butterflies.

"Ann." Malin's unexpected, familiar voice on the phone, calling me after all these months to see if I will forgive him and let us become friends, again, the way we used to be. He misses me. He knows he let me down. How about dinner at his new apartment right across the Hudson in Riverbank, New Jersey, Tuesday, eight o'clock, or Thursday at the latest, if things blow up at work. Take-out Chinese this time—he's not willing to risk hamburgers again, even though he still owes me a decent home-cooked meal. He'll call Monday to confirm. Is Monday too late?

"Monday will be fine."

"Karen and I have broken up. I didn't know if you had heard."

"Personally or professionally?"

"Both, I guess. She hasn't been in all week."

"No, I didn't know." Gossip Central must have broken down, I think. "I haven't spoken to anyone at the office in a while. How are you feeling?"

"I'm doing fine."

"You want to talk about it?"

"Next week. I'm not ready yet. Actually, I'm still pretty shaky."

Monday comes and goes with no word from Malin, as does Tuesday and the rest of the week, predictably, I suppose, although I believed him this time. If I'm not more careful, I will end up like Drew, believing that turkeys can fly. On Friday afternoon, I call the picture researcher at the office ostensibly to discuss the captions I'm writing for my introduction to *Lassie, Come Home*, the first volume in the new Animal Classics series that includes *Black Beauty, Call of the Wild, The Yearling*, and eight others, all too sad to read. *Lassie, Come Home* is the only Odyssey Press book since Faraday's *Experimental Researches in Electricity* that I have been unable to read. I wrote both introductions relying entirely on secondary sources. I ask the picture researcher if there have been any changes in the schedule. Malin is away from his desk, she says, but as soon as he comes back, she'll go over the revised schedule with him. She'll call me back to confirm the dates. Or he will.

At least he's all right. For the moment I'm relieved to know he hasn't been murdered in the subways, that he's still healthy and fine and available to be murdered by me.

"Ann."

"Malin."

"The July first deadline hasn't changed. I can give you another week, if you need it."

"Thanks." Pause. I let the silence convey, more eloquently than I can, the silence I heard when my phone didn't ring. If I wait long enough, he will be able to overhear the phone call he promised and never made: *Ann. Hi, there. I'm just confirming dinner on Tuesday.*

"I know I owe you an apology."

"Good thinking."

"Should I hang up? Or try to explain?" When I don't answer, he chooses for me. "I've been in a very precarious state since Karen and I broke up. Actually, since she and I got together. For the last few months, I haven't been doing anything but going to work and coming back home. I haven't been seeing any of my friends."

"I'm not interested in how you treat your other friends."

"Will you let me explain? The day I called you was the first time in months I felt good enough to care about getting my life back to normal, whatever that is. The most normal thing I could think of doing was talking to you. Not to Norman, not to Jerry, but to you. I wanted to see you because sometimes being with you is as comfortable as being by myself—only I'm not alone. Do you know what I mean?"

He's talking about me the same way I talk about Emma, I think.

"I don't know how to explain it any better. I think sometimes that you're linked in my mind to the best part of me. For a while there, I wanted to be that part and just walk away from everything—and everyone—else. Then the mood passed and I was back where I was in the beginning—not wanting to see or talk to anyone, including you. Maybe especially you. But it's not your fault, Ann. It's never you. It's just me."

"How can you get us confused? I'm the one with the gray hair and you're the one with the receding hairline." I'm the woman, I think. You're the man.

"Ann, I haven't forgotten you. Sometimes I just act as if I have."

"What happens now?"

"I don't know."

"But you're putting our friendship back in my hands."

"I suppose I am. At least for a little while."

"And what if I drop it this time?"

"Then we'll find out if I can handle that as gracefully as you have."

"Practice makes perfect."

"I know I've been acting like a jerk and you have every right to make wisecracks, but I wish you wouldn't. You know I miss you. You know that even when I don't call you, I think about you, I'm concerned about you."

"And you know there's no way for me to read your mind."

"Actually, I've often thought you could."

"That's because you have a relatively simple mind." He laughs, almost, the closest thing to a laugh so far. "So what do we do now?"

"I need more time. Time to be alone."

"How's Karen?"

"She told me if we didn't continue being friends, even though she doesn't want us to be lovers, she would kill herself."

"Sounds like quite a romance. . . . I apologize, Malin. I shouldn't have said that. I guess I don't understand why some people score points for being desperate. I'm desperate, too, in my own way. No one seems to notice."

"Because everyone besides you is confident that you can take care of yourself."

"Sometimes I wouldn't mind a little break."

"I'm sorry, Ann. Truly."

The wedding song I try to sing to Emma

> *I love you truly, truly dear*
> *Life with its sorrows*
> *Life with its tears . . .*

"Malin, maybe you should take a little time off. Go visit your grandparents. Were you home for Christmas?"

"I went to Mexico with Lilly. I've used up all my vacation time."

"Take a few days with no pay. Even a long weekend."

"Karen's called in sick all week."

"Tell her you need her to fill in for you. Give her your team-spirit speech. Tell her you're a team, just like the Yankees, and you need her to pinch hit. If you have to, you can always take a manuscript along and work on it there. Go home, Malin. Let your grandmother feed you fried chicken and corn-bread."

"I'm already too fat."

"Don't be an ass, Malin. Go home."

I receive a postcard stamped "Rainbow, Arkansas" with a picture of a little boy eating watermelon:

Dear Ann,
    Please forgive the stupid postcard. You were right, typically. I can't tell you how much I appreciate your holding the fort for me at work. Wish you were here.
                                                            Love,
                                                            Malin
P.S. My grandad says I should marry a black-dirt girl.

I toss the card and the rest of my junk mail onto the kitchen table. But I'm still holding the little boy and his prizewinning, homegrown watermelon, practically as big as he is. I place them both on the ground, setting Malin down carefully on his two little feet like a toy soldier, standing behind him so he won't fall. You are too heavy to carry, I tell him. You're a big boy now. Let's take turns: this time, you try to pick *me* up. He wraps his arms around my legs but I am the size of his mother, much too large to lift.

These days, my arms seem emptier than usual. I have to resist the impulse to hold Emma and carry her everywhere, like the cautious old ladies I meet along West End Avenue with their overweight, under-exercised dogs, whose tiny paws apparently have never touched the ground. Emma trots, as always, at my heel. But I'm secretly pleased when I have to run an errand: the drugstore, the five-and-cime, the dry cleaners, the bookstore. No dogs are allowed. Can't I read signs? Unless they're carried, of course. I'm not permitted to put her down. I pick Emma up and carry her with impunity.

My friends are still advising me to forget about Malin. If he were going to call, he would have callec by now. The man will never change. A leopard can't change its spots.

What's that supposed to mean?

They apologize for using a feline axiom when a canine one would do: You can't teach an old dog new tricks.

But he will call me, I'm certain, if I give him enough time. He will call when he needs some part of me; he's no ordinary breast or leg man. He will call if he needs an ear to listen to his stories, a shoulder to cry on, a leg up to remount Cat when he gets bucked off. I've been boarding Cat. I had a box stall built for him in the bedroom where Max used to sleep. I call it the "Geoffrey Maxwell Memorial Barn," but Max isn't dead, he's just married. Coincidentally, Max and Buck got married the same weekend. I was invited to both weddings. Although neither one took place in a natural history museum, I declined them both.

Cat is an "easy keeper." That means he maintains his weight without eating much food. He's so easy to care for that no one, not even Emma, knows that he's there. As long as I'm taking good care of Cat, someday Malin will call me.

The old Russian lady, standing on the doorstep of Drew's former building, stops me on my way to the park with a gesture of her hand, something between my "stay" hand signal for Emma and a wave that belongs to a shy little girl. Is she beckoning to me? "Please . . ." is all she says. She doesn't seem to recognize either Emma or me. Where is her Maltese? Her other hand is on the doorknob. I can't tell if she's on her way in or out.

"You are fortunate . . . ," she says. "I am afraid . . ." She's twisting a purple handkerchief between her hands. Where did that come from? Was she holding it when she signaled to me? "My Sasha is dead." Her eyes well up with tears.

Home, I think. She's trying to get home. "Can I help?" She doesn't answer me, but I push the door open and guide her inside like an invalid. The doorman sees us coming and opens the inner lobby door. Emma balks; she always hated going to Drew's, where Rover, true to his breeding, would hound her until she cowered out of his reach under a table or chair. Drew doesn't even live here anymore, I think at her. I give her leash a sharp tug to communicate "heel!" I don't want to use the word because I don't want to call attention in any way to the fact that my small white dog is alive. With every painstaking step, I hope the woman will send me away, that she will say, I'm all right, I can make it from here, but she lets me ring for the elevator and accompany her upstairs, down the hallway (why are so many pre-war buildings painted this putrid shade of pea-green?), to her apartment door. She fumbles with the keys. I suspect she can't use them properly because if she does, she'll end up inside, alone. I wonder if her Maltese used to meet her at the door, like a normal dog, or if he waited for her on the bed, like my princess. "Let me try," I say, taking the keys out of her hands. Finally, I match each one with its lock and push the door open. I give her back her keys and step aside, but she's waiting for me to go in first. "I have to get going," I tell her. Her English is suddenly not that good; she fails to understand me. I stand at the threshold. I can already smell the old-lady perfume, the flowery funereal smell of this apartment that used to have a dog. I won't be able to breathe in there. I much prefer the rank, live-animal smells of a dog kennel or barn. She thanks me for coming as if I were a guest and says for my kindness I will be rewarded. I will be doubly blessed, in heaven and on earth. On the contrary, I think. I deserve no blessings at all for the cowardice in my heart. If you make me go inside, I will imitate Emma and cower under a chair. Tell me you're not inviting me in. Tell me you're not offering me a cold drink ("No, thank you"), a glass of wine ("No, thanks"), a cup of hot tea (I give up: "That would be nice . . .").

"What is your dog's name?"

"Emma." This woman and I don't know each other's names.

"Would she like a cookie?"

The dog answers for me by tap dancing at the woman's feet and following her into the kitchen. I can tell by the way Emma's nails click against the linoleum that they need to be trimmed. The linoleum, I notice, is identical to Drew's. Usually, I don't let strangers feed Emma junk food. But this time only, I will let her eat like the Maltese.

One moment the woman is sweet-talking Emma, feeding her treats, and I'm feeling ashamed of myself for not wanting to share a neighborly cup of tea, and the next she's doubled over, sobbing, too close to the stove, and the first thing I think is: burn yourself up if you want to, lady (the usual method is to leap on top of a funeral pyre), but I'm getting the hell out of here. I push her away from the flaming front burner. "Sasha," she howls, pressing her folded arms against her body and into her womb (womb, I think, where did I come up with that antiquated word?), "my Sasha . . ." I don't know what to do, so I do nothing. I know only what I will not do: tell her to stop. Cry as hard as you can. Cry your eyes out, I think. Can you swim? Then flood the apartment! Cry until your eyes wash out of their sockets and you can no longer see your missing dog. But please let me go home, please let me go home.

I know crying won't help; her memories will float to the surface and collect in perplexing cellular patterns, like lily pads.

Nevertheless, I'm crying, too, only she doesn't see me, silent tears overflowing as if someone were spilling cup after cup after cup of tea. I deny myself the comfort of touching Emma because this woman has no dog to comfort her. She cries and cries. But she can still see. I know she can. She doesn't need eyes to see the dog in the photograph she has already framed and trimmed in black and hung, like the centerpiece of a shrine, in the candlelit portion of her mind's eye.

He's only a dog, I want to say, but will not. These words do not belong to me. And yet if I speak at all, I know they will force their way out. I mouth them, but do not speak them aloud: Remember he's only a dog.

I pick up Emma and hand her to the woman, who wraps her arms tightly around her. Emma hates being held by strangers and stares at me, stricken. Do this for me, I think. I promise we'll go home soon. Do this for me because I can't do it on my own. You must do your part for other human beings, just as I sometimes take in strays to do my part for other dogs.

The woman begins speaking in Russian. I try to leave the kitchen to give her privacy (even though I can't understand a word), but Emma struggles to come with me, so I have to stay. The woman's tears slow and stop. She notices me and begins yelling, this time in English.

"The veterinarian says that the cancer was spreading and it would not be fair to the dog . . . to the *dog*, he says—but what about me? What does he know about me? What does anyone know about me?"

I call Malin. Karen answers the phone. His phone? Theirs? "Karen," I say, "Hi—it's Ann."

"Hi," she says, momentarily distracting me, so that I forget where I am—I just finished mucking out Cat's stall and I'm about to take him out for a stroll—when Cat wheels around and kicks me in the chest with his right hind leg and rockets past me. I lunge for his lead rope and hold on as hard as I can, but he escapes from my bedroom and drags me down the hallway. When I can't keep up, he tows me through the dirt. Why didn't I shut the barn door? He leaps the front gate, lands on the street, and hightails it off to Jersey with his halter and his lead rope, leaving me with a rope burn across my hands. I should have known better than to try to hold on. *Ingrate!* I yell. *Nag!* As if he could hear me. Will he take the Lincoln Tunnel or swim across the Hudson River?

"I'll go get Malin," she says.

In the background, a barking dog. I forgot about that: Karen owns an English setter. "Hush!" I hear Malin say, then "Ann." A longer pause than usual after my name. "I should have told you about this sooner. I'm sorry. Karen and I decided to try living together. I know I should have told you."

The pain in my chest flowers outward from the imprint of two hooves, no larger than Emma's paws. My hands are stinging; I can't hold the phone. I break out of my apartment like a cocoon and escape to Riverside Park, with its view of the river and expanse of sky, its public space, its shared breath. The park never closes. Emma has to gallop to keep up, but she thinks we're playing a game. "Faster," I coax, "as fast as you can." I'm almost running. No red lights slow me down. No old lady will catch me today.

I reach Riverside Drive in record time—not a single light or lady. There was something that almost stopped me, a shadow, I hope, although it might have been a dog. I saw it out of the corner of my eye when I was crossing West End. I'm about to cross into the park when the shadow reappears from nowhere directly in front of me, breaking my stride. I come perilously close to stepping on it. "Not now," I say aloud, "not today!" If I don't see a dog, it will not exist. Since Emma, I have picked up five strays and managed to find them all homes. I will never be lucky enough to find another. Let someone else save this one. I will not stop.

But the dog is freewheeling in the middle of the dangerous conflux of 72nd Street, Riverside Drive, and the entrances north and south to the West Side Highway. It looks like a shepherd-collie mix, old enough that its face is graying. I wonder how long it's been out on the streets. I have to stand still for just a moment to catch my breath. The stray mirrors me. It doesn't seem sick or hurt, but I don't want Emma anywhere near it. Someone else will rescue it, I think. Someone else. Someone who doesn't already have a dog. Why is the goddamn dog standing there like a statue? Why is it waiting for me?

I unclasp Emma's leash and command her to sit and stay. She takes a step to follow me. I repeat the command, using my hand signal for "stay." She listens. I wait for the light to change and the traffic to clear and move forward with one eye on Emma and the other on the stray. But Emma follows me off the curb. "Get out of the street!" She jumps back up on the sidewalk. This won't work. I stop and waver, the stray ahead, Emma behind. I will not risk Emma. I pick her up and carry her, even though she'll make it more difficult to collar the stray.

Now that I'm moving again, so is the dog. It follows the curved highway entrance ramp dividing the southernmost tip of the park. Go into the park, I think. In the park you'll be safe. The dog veers north and enters the park through the two-foot high, open-weave fence, which acts more like a decorative border than a real fence, and slowly makes its way back up the hill in my direction. But nothing about its movements makes me think it's aware of me. As soon as we're all safely in the park, I release Emma. "Free dog!" I say, as always. I slowly head toward the stray. I expect it to run off again, but it doesn't. "Good boy," I say, now that I'm close enough to see that it's a male. I toss him one of the dog treats I always carry in my pocket just in case I have to bribe Emma. He's waiting for more. I hold one in my right hand as I approach. "Good dog," I say. The dog accepts the treat and tricks me by letting me easily loop Emma's leash around his neck. Emma approaches but I yell at her to get away. That's the hardest thing for her to do. She doesn't necessarily come the moment I call, but her inclination is always to come to me rather than run away. I tell her to sit and stay. She thinks we're having a lesson and is watching me carefully, waiting for me to signal "come." The stray cooperates and walks with me as if he's used to a leash.

Dogwalkers gather. The next move is mine. According to an unspoken park rule, the person who first catches the stray must accept final responsibility. The others will contribute money or offer to help in any way they can, but only I can decide whether to take the dog home.

I hand Emma to one of my friends, who has offered to help by keeping her until I can figure out what to do with the dog. I continue to call it a stray, even though it's leaning against me with all its weight like a totally trusting pet. He obviously hasn't been out on the streets for long. My guess is that someone dumped him. Maybe his owner died. Or maybe his owner dumped him. My park friends are waiting for my decision. What will I do with this dog? Find it a home? Who would want a dog this old? For some reason, my attention is drawn away from the dog to a branch I recognize as a remnant from the Christmas tree that appeared from nowhere last winter. Although it's partially hidden in the unmowed grass, I can tell it has none of its needles. For some reason, it makes me think of a seagull's wing. I want to claim it and bring it home, like driftwood. "Are you going to bring it home?" one of the dog owners says, and I realize he's talking about the dog and not the branch. I could do that, I think. I could bring him to the vet's and have him checked out and then bring him home and keep him until I can find out if he's lost, and if he isn't, I could try to find him a real home. But who would want a dog this old? I could bring him to the vet's and have him put down—"put to sleep," as my parents used to say. At least he wouldn't starve, or be injured or killed on the streets. Is that what I should do? Not today, I think, I can't do that today. My friends are waiting patiently but I don't know what to do. When the dog turns away from me, distracted by another dog, I loosen the noose I've looped around his neck, pull it over his ears and off him without looking at his face, grab Emma, and bolt for home, tears streaming down my face. *Not today.* This is not a dream. I have abandoned a dog that reminded me of me. I take myself home.

I am the only stray.

"You asked me the first time we met if my mother used to sing to me."

"I remember," Faith says.

"She sang 'Rock-a-Bye-Baby.' She used to laugh at the end every time. I thought it was a funny song. How did I ever forget that?"

"You didn't forget it, Ann. Not really. Sometimes when we're not looking, memories sneak out the back door and run away from home. Usually, they come back."

"Poochie never came back."

For an instant, she looks as if she's trying to remember where she put something. "I'm sorry, Ann. I keep forgetting you know me in a different context. Poochie was hit by a car. I never told the kids. They think she ran away from home. To answer your question: Poochie never came back, but I did." She smiles.

"Did you ever see the tree someone put up in the park last Christmas?"

"No. But Drew told me about it."

"The tree disappeared—magically—the same way it appeared. I would have thought I had dreamt it" (in fact, I *did* dream it, I do not say), except that one of its boughs must have broken off and got left behind. I noticed it again yesterday . . ." I don't finish the sentence, which is *when I abandoned a stray.* "The branch reminded me of the song, and then I could hear my mother singing." I don't tell Faith that it was the same branch that saved me from drowning in my dream because it bent but didn't break. It's bare because all the needles shed in my hand.

Malin calls from the office to say he has a particularly challenging job to farm out and so naturally he thought of me.

"Thank you."

"Do you want to drop by next week and we'll talk about it?"

"Why don't you just stick it in the mail."

"I thought we might go out to lunch. Or would you like to come over for dinner? Lilly finally sent me Lightning's saddle. You're the only one who would appreciate it. Will you come? I'll bring the manuscript home."

"Why don't you just stick it in the mail."

Faith is sitting at the piano when I walk in the door. She smiles and begins to play "All Through the Night." "I'm sorry it's so hot in here," she says. "The air conditioner is on the blink."

"It's hot as hell today."

"I suppose it's a preview of what's to come—more dog days."

"The Arctic would be nice this time of year."

"Yes," she says. "I'd even settle for an air-conditioned movie."

I'm aware that our small talk is going on longer than usual, but I have the feeling I should try to keep it going as long as possible.

"Today is the day," she says.

I pretend not to understand. "The day for what?"

"But my guess is that you already knew that."

"The day for what?"

"Sink or swim," she says, smiling. She gets up and finds her cassette tape recorder among the rubble on her desk. "Listen to this." She's taped the piano part to "All Through the Night." "I wanted to have a free hand," she explains, taking mine. "I believe in giving people a hand." She laughs. "I believe in it quite literally." She rewinds the tape to the beginning and pats the piano bench to her right, inviting me to sit beside her. She opens the music. It's an easy song. I should remember that. It's an easier song than some of the songs we've already sung. She plays the right hand only, slowly, and instructs me to read along. "Did you notice it's marked *adagio*? I think you should try it very adagio." She laughs. "It's a lullaby, Ann. That's all you have to remember. After the hard work you've done here, I have total confidence in you. You worry too much. If you follow your intuition, this will be a piece of cake." She starts the tape. Together, we listen to the introduction, her hand holding mine. When the intro ends, she squeezes my hand, my cue to begin.

Singing is for daredevils—lunatics—I think. With nothing to support me but a series of stepping-stones composed of small, round notes, I'm supposed to get from here where I am to way over there, across silence perilous and deep as water. The stones all look alike. Will I choose the right one? And even if by some miracle I manage to pick the right one, I still won't be safe: the stones are all wet and slippery. I place my foot as carefully as I can, knowing that at any moment I might lose my footing and fall.

Something goes wrong with the tape. Faith unclasps my hand and turns off the machine and picks up in the middle of the song, losing only one measure. I reach out to grab her hand, but it's already busy on the keyboard. How can she just sit there playing the piano? "Keep going " she says, as if she could read my mind. Not today, I think, I can't go anywhere today. I'm stranded, unable to move in any direction. Keep going! Silence floods me, threatens to drown me. Keep going! Don't look down! Don't look at the water, slick, blue-black, deep as the river along Riverside Park.

"I can't," I say, "I can't."

"Ann." She stops playing the piano and asks me to switch seats with her, then takes my right hand in her left and begins to play the melody with her right hand only. "Think about the words, and the music will take care of itself. You know this song inside out. Sing it to me, Ann. Then we'll sing it again, together."

The words. The words that I wrote out in calligraphy using turquoise ink, *All Through the Night* in italics, the crossbar of the *t* in *Night* my first flourish, which Geoffrey taught me; I practiced it a hundred times before I once got it almost right. It skimmed to the right in a straight horizontal line, then as I lifted my pen from the paper it rose slightly upward, rising just high enough, if only I could cling to it now, to keep my head above water. *The words,* I think. Beside me, Faith begins again. So do I. This time, even if I slip, she is holding my hand.

Her hug envelops me like a life jacket. "We ll keep working on this for quite some time," she says. "But I promise that nothing else we do will be harder than today. You've earned a drink. You've earned champagne, but I'm afraid water will have to do." She fills two plastic tumblers with ice and cold water. I hold mine against my face before I begin to drink. "A toast," she says. "To you and your voice, which, in my professional opinion, is not half bad." We clink glasses.

Not half bad, I think.

"But next time, you're going to have to let me use both hands on the keyboard."

"What does 'not half bad' mean?"

"Almost as good as your hopes, and much, much better than your fears."

"What does that mean?"

"Do you always quiz your teachers?"

"Always."

"Your voice is inexperienced. Your musical instincts, however, are very good. With practice, you can learn to sing in tune. You came to me because you wanted to sing around the house, sing along with records, perhaps sing along with your friends, right?"

"Right."

"What I'm saying is that with work you can reach your goals because your goals are intelligent and reasonable. You would be surprised, I think, how often people set themselves impossible goals. Poochie had a better voice than one of my students who thinks he can sing like Caruso because he enjoys singing in the shower. Do you see what I mean?"

I laugh. Lucky for me, Emma can't sing.

Faith walks me to the door with her arm around my shoulders. When I open it, Drew's brother is sitting on the floor in the hall. What's he doing here? I wonder, forgetting for the moment that he is also Faith's son. How long has he been sitting here? Could he have heard me sing? He and I exchange hellos.

"I didn't know you two knew each other."

"Sure," Frank says, "we met in the park."

"I know everyone from the park. The whole world meets in the park."

Frank has grown a beard since the last time I saw him—probably the last time I saw Drew perform at the Yellow Rose. Because I haven't seen Drew in such a long time, the similarity between the brothers seems more obvious than it ever did before. Frank says he dropped by to see if he and Faith could negotiate a short-term, low-interest loan. If I feel like waiting for him in the lobby, he'll be right down and then he can walk me home on his way to the subway.

My apartment isn't on your way to the subway, I think, but there's no reason you should know that.

"I needed to borrow ten bucks," he says in the lobby, waving the bill at me before he jams it into his pocket. He holds the door for me on our way out of the building. "So you're studying with Drew's mother," he says.

"*Drew's* mother? I don't understand. I thought . . ."

"It's just a joke Drew and I have. When we're talking to each other, we say '*your* mother.' So how's it going?"

"Fine."

"What are you learning?"

"I'm learning to swim."

"Excuse me?"

I'm learning how to cross bodies of water "I said I'm learning to sing."

"That's what I thought you said. Since Drew's mother is a singing teacher, that doesn't come as a big surprise."

Maybe if I don't respond, he'll drop the subject.

"Is she a good teacher?"

"The best."

"I didn't realize you were a singer."

"Neither did I."

A pack of wild dogs is running down a highway—pet dogs let loose, not strays—sleek, immaculate, young dogs, galloping with their heads held high, like horses. They are traveling between the traffic and the sidewalk, filling the gutter, swift as a river. I can't tell if they're fleeing or heading toward something or someone I can't see. I watch them until they disappear and then reconsider and go after them. One is a boxer, young, beautiful, and studdy. Lucky, is that you? They are all wearing rhinestone collars, and silver leashes as long as reins. If I called them, maybe I could get them to stop. All I have to do is call them to me and pick up the ends of their leashes. I'll try. I call one and it stops running and comes to me. I pick up its leash. One. I have one. I clap my hands and another turns and comes toward me. Two. The boxer is an easy three. I'll never get the last two. They will gallop away. They will disappear across the horizon. But when I shout, they stop and stand and do not bolt. Why? If only I knew why. They let me catch them and I am so grateful I almost fall to my knees. They are mine. I stand in the highway and hold their shining, silver leashes, so long and luminescent they seem like the reins to Apollo's horses, each one reflecting the moon-light, the sunlight, the lamplight beside me, the headlights that speed down the highway, past me, past all my dogs.

I'm awakened in the middle of the night by the buzzer downstairs. Who would ring my bell this late at night? "Who's there?" I shout into the intercom, just in case it isn't a prank or a mistake, but someone who's looking for me.

"It's Frank."

I buzz him in, put on a robe, run a comb through my hair. At my apartment door, Frank apologizes for waking me. He thought I might still be up. He was just passing by.

My apartment isn't on a major thoroughfare. "Passing by on your way where—to the river?"

"I thought you might be in the mood for some company."

"You mean you want some company."

"I guess it was a bad idea."

He backs toward the door. "You want a cup of coffee?"

"No, thanks."

"You want to talk?"

When he doesn't answer, I take him into my bedroom, like an extra blanket. He wanders over to the window and stares outside without speaking until finally he says, "You have trees."

"I know." The three virtues of my apartment: the space inside, the trees outside, the cheap rent. "I like to wake up early in the morning and spend some time just listening to the birds."

"Sometimes I dread getting up alone in the morning."

I will wrap you in a blanket, I think, and carry you home to Faith.

"Do you ever feel like that?"

"No. But I have Emma. Every morning, I take her to the park. Would you like to come to bed?" He's fluttering by the window. "Come here, Frank." He lies down beside me.

"Did you ever sleep with Drew?" he asks.

Only once—when it was much too late, I think. Is he asking for himself, or is he Rebecca's emissary? "Why do you want to know?"

"I'm just curious."

"Does it matter to you if I did?"

"I don't know."

"I'm not going to tell you."

"Why not?"

"Because it's none of your business."

"But you wanted to sleep with him. You hung around him in the park."

"Lots of people hung around him in the park."

"Were you in love with him?"

"For a while."

"Then you must have slept with him. No one ever turned him down." I don't agree or disagree. "What are you studying with Drew's mother?"

I don't answer.

"Pop or rock or classical?"

I could lie and tell him I'm working on Aïda.

"Why won't you tell me what my mother is teaching you?"

"It's private. Why do I have the feeling that your whole family is in bed with us?"

"I'm sorry." He seems sullen and hurt; it's not his fault if his family follows him around, follows him everywhere, even to bed.

"She's teaching me a song."

"What song?"

I hesitate. A lullaby. Your mother who left you is teaching me to sing a lullaby. "I can't tell you that."

"Sing it for me."

"I can't."

"What do you need? A band? Back-up singers?"

"Not exactly."

"Just the beginning?"

"I'm sorry, Frank. I can't."

"Does Drew know what she's teaching you?"

"No one knows. It doesn't have to do with anyone but me."

"Maybe I should leave."

"You can if you want to." I stroke his hair to soothe him, as if he were a stray. "Can you sing?"

"Only in the shower. Drew got all the talent in the family. The talent and the looks. I got . . ."

"What did you get?"

"The brains."

"Are they useful?"

"I'd trade them for good looks."

"My mother always said that beauty is in the eye of the beholder." In my eyes, at least so far, Drew is much more attractive than Frank. I wonder if I should show him my calligraphy project. It's on a bookcase in the living room, hidden behind some books. Even though no one else can see it, I know it's there. I tried to give it to Max as a going-away present, but he refused the original and accepted only a photocopy, which he asked me to autograph. "Dear Max," I wrote. "For all the lessons . . . Thank you."

"Drew's mother always says that beauty is only skin deep."

"Well, there you have it—wisdom from two reliable sources."

"So did you ever sleep with Drew?"

I wonder if he's trying to get even with Drew for the Terry fiasco, ten years later. Let it go, I think, let it go. "If you ask me that question one more time, I'm going to throw you out."

"Do you miss Drew? I do. Not that we were always together, or even that we always got along. It's just that he was nearby: my security brother."

"Do I miss him?" Not at all, I think. "Yes," I lie, to empathize, although these days I rarely think of Drew at all, except as Faith's son. "What about your security mother?"

"Drew's mother." He turns away from me and half gets up to leave, then lies back down along the edge of the bed, winds my quilt tighter around his body, and stays. "Maybe I better go home."

"I probably shouldn't be telling you this, but Drew and Rebecca have both told me about your mother's breakdowns. She doesn't know I know any of this, so please don't tell her. You probably suffered from them more than Drew did, because you were younger. But Faith loves you as much as she loves him. My guess is that she didn't quite know what to make of you. She calls you 'my little wizard.' Don't give up on her."

Again, he gets up as if he might leave. "I don't know why I came here tonight. I shouldn't have barged in on you."

"I don't mind."

Frank is sitting on the edge of the bed, trying to decide whether to stay or leave, when Emma curls up on his leg and seduces him into petting her. When he stops, she nudges his hand.

"Do you like dogs?" I ask.

"No."

"You don't like dogs?"

He shrugs his shoulders. "When we were kids, we lived near

a busy street. I remember the first dog I got, a Scottie. It was supposed to be my dog and no one else's. He was hit by a car. After Scotty we got other dogs, but they all got killed. Drew and Mom act as if Poochie was our only dog, but she was just the last one. And the one we had the longest. All I knew was, I wasn't going to keep getting attached, not even to Poochie. I thought I was over it when I got Rover. I got him to keep, but then I couldn't deal with him so I gave him to Drew."

I had forgotten that. Drew told me a long time ago that his brother had given him the dog. I touch the center of Frank's back. "It's very late. Why don't you just go to sleep? You don't want to go anywhere. You don't want to do anything tonight but sleep." His body tenses as if he were going to defend himself, but only for an instant. "It's all right, Franco." Why did I call him that? "I'm glad you showed up tonight. You're right—I do want company."

He lies beside me and falls asleep suddenly, as if in a trance. Emma jumps from the bed to the floor in a pout. Don't leave me, I think. She has abandoned her post. Without her, I will not sleep. I try to call her without awakening Frank. I cluck and pat the side of the bed. But she thinks she has been displaced and cannot be consoled. After a while, I call her again. There is room for all of us, I tell her. In the darkness, my bed wide as the sea, solid as the earth. "Come back to me," I call, my voice urgent and hushed. I search for her in the territory beyond my bed. But without my glasses, I can see only what is close at hand. I fashion a long, lightweight, silver leash and collar, and guessing where she is, hurl the collar out into the darkness, and manage to lasso her like a horse. But the leash is elastic; no matter how much of it I reel in, I never take up the slack. Finally, after a very long time, when I have almost given up, Emma comes to me of her own accord and, since I am lying on my side, curls up in the fortress behind my knees, safe from the stranger beside me.

"My pet," I whisper, careful not to awaken him. But Frank hears me, and thinking I'm talking to him, shifts toward me an inch or two, his spine curved against my body, pressing against me like a cat. Like a cat, he contracts and rolls onto his back. Outside my window, a terrace light goes on. His expression, barely visible, reminds me more of Faith than Drew. My teacher, your mother, Drew's mother. I touch his dark, glossy hair, nothing like Emma's hair, white and wispy as spun wool. He sleeps. Our mother, our teacher, I think. Your mother who left you is teaching me to sing a lullaby. In his sleep, he stretches; the rumbling from the far side of the bed reminds Emma that we are not alone, but this time she merely repositions herself and does not leave. "Thank you," I whisper, as if in prayer. Now that I know Emma will stay with me for the rest of the night, I relinquish her leash. The terrace light goes out. Eventually, I should be able to sleep. I lie still, but awake. Wide awake, I practice singing to myself the song his mother is teaching me: *Sleep my child and peace attend thee, all through the night.* I sing to myself, trying to hear my own voice but hearing Faith's, then a new voice— *whose?* I wonder, not recognizing this offspring of hers and mine that sounds like a solo but is really our duet—until I am interrupted by Emma, who forgives me and creeps into my arms, and I stop listening long enough to tell her that I cherish her, which she already knows, and begin again; this time I pretend I'm singing to her, and the voice I hear is neither Faith's nor mine but my mother's, no longer singing, simply reciting: *I, my loved one, watch and keep thee, all through the night.*